THE BIG SMOKE

By

Nathan Srith

About the Writer

Nathan Srith is a husband and a father of two. He was born and raised in London. Coming from a mixed race – Sri Lankan/British background, Nathan grew up in a very diverse world. He was exposed to a variety of cultures and a wide array of cinema and TV, quite often viewing content he shouldn't have been. However, he attributes his early introduction to media to his vivid imagination and creative storytelling.

Nathan always had a fascination with compelling storytelling and a particular interest in how stories were put together, specifically how characters and subplots were interwoven within a story. Nathan would often write short stories and poems as a child, and later on, he wrote scripts throughout his TV and film university course. He currently works as a freelance script writer for an independent film company, a relationship counsellor, and for the NHS. Despite Nathan's occasional blunder with spelling and grammar, which he faults to a failing and inflexible school system, a dyslexic mother, and a father whose second language is broken English, he has always felt comfortable in putting stories together and coming up with unique ideas; the proof of this being in the number of awards he has won for his writing at secondary school and university.

Nathan's writing brings together his love of storytelling and the atrocious behaviour and treatment he has seen impact hard working people every day.

For Becki, Nishy, and Danny,
my absolute everything.

Acknowledgements

A special thank you and shout out to those who helped me on my creative journey in some capacity, be it through giving me your honest feedback, listening to my crazy ideas for hours on end, or simply being a source of support when I needed it. Thanks to:

Becki
Mum
Carl
Sid
Scaz
Kandi
Liad
Sherwood
Tina
Anna
Shonnie
Ollie
Pratheepa
Sue
Roya
Candy Denman

Thank you all!

*The Big Smoke is book one
of a three part series.*

Map of The Independent State of England

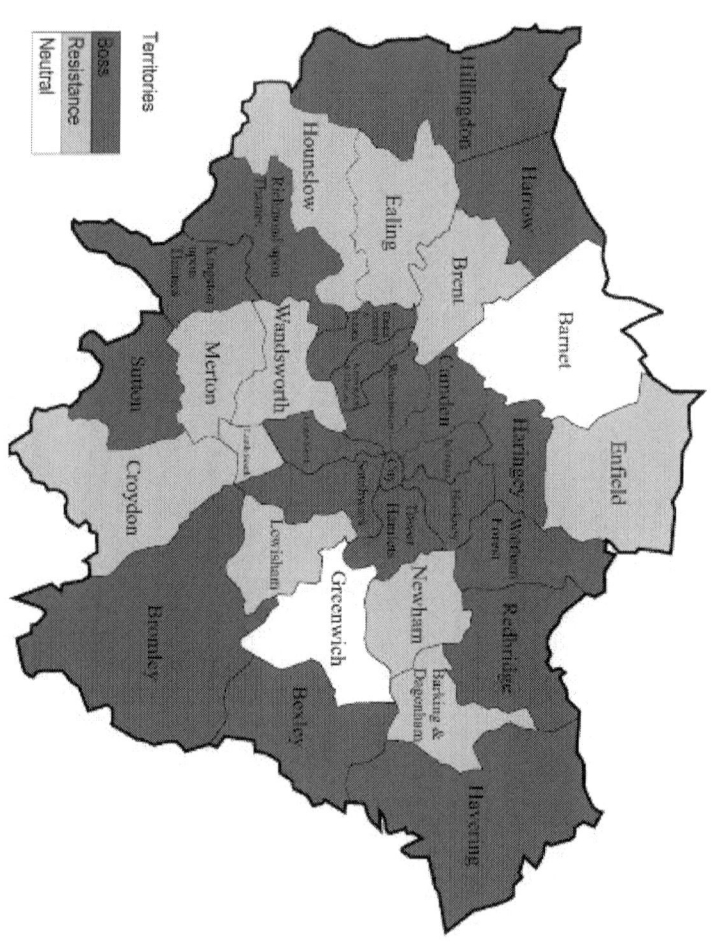

PROLOGUE

4ᵗʰ August 2011, 18:13
Forest Road, Haringey, London

The driver hated taking this route at rush hour. In theory, it shouldn't have bothered him – the longer the trip, the higher the fare – but the driver in him couldn't stand traffic. Granted, London traffic had nothing on the traffic back home in Pakistan, but it annoyed him, nonetheless. No matter what profession he had, he prided himself on doing his job well, and his job right now was to get his passenger from Leyton to Tottenham Hale.

He was still getting used to the diversity in London and was trying his hardest to keep any prejudice he had out of his mind, especially considering every fare he had would be vastly different from the last. His latest fare gave him that usual feeling of suspicion, but he had been getting better at pushing it out of his mind and treating his fares like they were his equal. The driver was not to blame for those initial feelings of discrimination; those prejudices were drilled into him from a young age by his parents when he was growing up in Karachi, Pakistan.

1

"Keep to your own," his mum and dad would tell him, but he never truly believed his parents' words. He had spent years ferrying tourists to and from the airport back in Pakistan and learned that most people are the same; some were rude, and some were nice; but they all were people with baggage trying to navigate through life. Meeting so many different people every day was a big reason for him moving to London. To the dismay of his parents, he wanted to explore the world and learn more about other cultures beyond his homeland.

His current fare wasn't much of a talker and the driver was eager to drop him off as soon as he could. He turned onto Ferry Lane, another minute or two until his final destination.

"Not long now my friend, we're almost there," he said.

The young man in the back gave the driver a simple nod and then looked back down at his Blackberry Curve.

The driver approached the cross junction before Tottenham Hale tube station and raced through the lights before they could change from amber to red. He flashed a cocky smile to himself in the rear-view mirror as he just made the lights and was seconds away from completing his fifty-seventh drop of the day. He heard a car horn beeping from behind him and he saw that a black car with tinted windows had sped through the red light. He was so fixated on the black car speeding up behind him that he hadn't noticed the second black car driving alongside him with the driver of the car screaming and gesturing at him to pull over.

The driver slammed on the brakes and was forced to the side of the road by the two black cars that had boxed him in. He was kicking himself; he was sure there were no police in sight when he had jumped the lights.

"How could I have been so stupid? I need this job and I can barely speak the language to talk myself out of this. I can't lose this job and disappoint my family even more," he thought.

Several men dressed in black from head to toe wearing large bulky vests which must have left them sweating buckets in the twenty-six degree heat, exited the cars and began yelling at him; but he struggled to understand what they were saying. When he noticed the drawn guns in their hands, he felt a cold shock push its way through his entire body. His hands were glued to the steering wheel and sweat began to pour from his forehead as he stared blankly at the men outside approaching his cab.

The sound of his rear door opening immediately snapped him out of his trance as he remembered his passenger in the back of the car. His fare had made a break for it and began running away from the cab, two bright flashes followed which oddly left a ringing sound in the driver's ears. Seconds after the flashes, his door was pulled open and he was wrenched out of his seat, dragged to the floor and made to look down at the ground next to the rear tyre of his car. The pressure of the man's knee on his back knocked the air out of him. The ringing in his ear worsened as the man pushing down on his back started shouting.

"Do not look there. If you move I will shoot. Keep your head down and do not look at the body!" screamed the police officer.

It was only when the man had mentioned the body that the driver realised the young man in his cab was laid out on the floor a few feet away from the taxi. He tried his hardest to avoid the blank and empty look in his passenger's eyes, but all he could think about was the poor family of the recently deceased Raymond Dwyer.

CHAPTER 1

7th August 2011, 07:37
Reynolds Drive, Harrow, London

As soon as Nick King's day began, he knew something was off. This wasn't because he was overly spiritual or had some greater knowledge of the universe. He had simply woken up in a weird mood, something he had put down to him being slightly hung-over. He woke up at 7:37am on a Sunday morning, which in itself was unusual as he often slept in on Sundays, especially after a heavy night out. He tossed and turned, trying to get those few much-needed hours of sleep but to no avail. His fiancée, who was able to sleep after a big night of drinking, had quickly become frustrated with her tall, dark and handsome fiancée knocking into her and keeping her awake. She usually loved his big rugby player like frame; but in that moment, she wished he hadn't been a spitting image of his South African father and more like his petite sister who resembled their tiny blonde mother.

She eventually kicked him out of bed and demanded that he make her usual breakfast – toast and black coffee with one sugar and one sweetener. He had become accustomed to his fiancée's odd taste, yet still felt uncomfortable making or ordering them. Especially her favourite drink – Malibu and coke mixed with a Southern Comfort and lemonade, which she had been throwing back the night before.

He picked up his Blackberry and checked his BBM and emails while he got breakfast ready. He flicked through Facebook and Twitter, liking and re-tweeting various comments and pictures that he saw. He fulfilled his marital duties by sharing, liking, and forwarding any and all of his future wife's tweets, messages, and comments on all of the various social media sites she had a presence on. He smiled at the picture of his dad on his fridge and thought back to the best advice his late dad had given him: "*Happy wife, happy Life.*"

While he was buttering the toast, he noticed a blinking light from the corner of his eye. He ignored it at first until the phone began vibrating and blinking over and over again, which was not an odd thing for his fiancées phone to do, but never this early, especially on a Sunday morning. He picked up the phone which continued to vibrate and flash in his hand as more notifications came through.

He told himself that it was okay for him to look through her phone because it clearly must've been an emergency. He also didn't want to wake her up in case it was nothing serious and she decided to kick him again. Nick often made a conscious effort to avoid looking at her phone, even though she didn't mind, as he always wanted to make sure he respected her privacy. This was partly because he was raised to respect others privacy by his father, but also because he hoped that it would ensure that she would respect his.

He entered her passcode, *051106*, the date of the first time they slept together. He often teased his fiancée saying that most people used dates as passwords from birthdays or a first date, not a date from the time she got lucky with a guy for the first time. She would bite back and explain that the 5th November 2006 was also the date that she realised she truly loved him.

"36 BBM messages and 15 emails before 8am, what is going on?" thought Nick. He looked through his fiancée's emails first, mostly junk mail and a few YouTube notifications, he then checked through her BBM. He scrolled through the older messages first; just some pictures her friends had sent her from the night before. He continued to scroll through and started to see a pattern emerge from all of the messages he was reading.

His hazel eyes dilated the more he read. He couldn't believe what he was seeing at first, but there was no way all of these messages could be fake. *"How had I missed this news when I was looking through my phone,"* he thought, perhaps wanting to get back to bed with the missus had distracted him from absorbing the bad news he had seemingly flicked past when he was making breakfast.

He opened Internet Explorer and checked all of the major British news sites – BBC, Yahoo, Sky News, The Guardian, and The Sun. They were all reporting the same thing. In that moment, Nick knew he had to say something to his fiancée but before he could; he needed a moment to himself to compose his thoughts. He knew that once he told her the news out loud, then it became real; and the moment it became real to him, he knew he had to go to work and his relatively peaceful life would get a whole lot less peaceful.

Now more than ever, he wished he could have had longer in bed that morning, so he could treasure the extra time he could've had with his woman. That strange, sinking feeling he had when he woke up, felt even stronger now; and he knew that things in the very near future were about to get much more complicated.

CHAPTER 2

3rd June 2016, 23:00
Unknown, The Independent State of England

"Gooood evening people of The Independent State of England, or the ISOE; that's an abbreviation I cleverly made up for the very lengthily named city we currently live in. Remember when it used to be called London? I dare you all to call it London in public. I dare you. Go on, live a little. I await reports back on how my little challenge goes.

This is your nightly announcement and reminder to take care when roaming the streets tonight, as always we have the gangs- sorry the "People's Police," out in droves again spreading the good word of The Boss and protecting the many boroughs of the city. Supposedly to maintain order but, as many of us know, what they actually do is maintain the chaos.

Today has been a particularly quiet day in the state. Only ten incidents of violence and gang related warfare has been reported. Perhaps our fearless leader has finally had a change of heart and has decided to bring some good to the city? Unlikely, I know; but one can always remain optimistic that pure evil can become good

9

once again.

This is your resident Master of Ceremonies, the Eye in the Sky, signing off, and of course, giving thanks to "The Boss" for uniting the people of this country and bringing us into her playground of destruction, hate, and isolation. Thank you for the new world you promised and failed to deliver.

We salute you, Boss!"

3rd June 2016, 23:13
Downing Street, City of Westminster, The Independent State of England

His bag had been packed for months but he couldn't bring himself to actually leave. For the longest time, Nick truly felt in his heart that he could change The Boss and get back to the original plan. Or at the very least, get them both out alive and rescue her from the world she had created and save her from the person she had become.

However, today was the final push he needed to make his escape. He only needed one more thing before he could leave, and it wasn't going to be easy to get. His sister had been locked away in the compound and was awaiting punishment for simply being seen talking to a person from one of the resistance boroughs. Nick had been telling her what to do her whole life and she would always listen to her big brother, but today she had been the courageous one. She did what nobody else had had the balls to do; stand up to The Boss. It was because of her courageous actions, however, that his sister Emily now faced an unknown fate. But he would not allow it to happen; she was all that he had left.

He had to get away from this place and now he finally had the motivation to do so. He had to get himself and Emily to safety and out of the city. *"Maybe that's why she finally snapped,"* thought Nick. Perhaps she put herself in harm's way knowing it would give him the kick up the arse he needed to make a decision. Regardless of why she did what she did, it didn't really matter anymore. All he knew was that his time was up.

Before he could take that first step towards his new life, he paused in his room and looked around at where he was and thought about how he had got there.

Years earlier, when his journey with The Boss began, he never dreamt that he would reach these heights. Not only had he supported her from the start, he had actively encouraged her to be the best version of herself that she could be. When she began her political campaign, he encouraged her; when she became Prime Minister, he encouraged her; and when she broke her promise and refused to take down the fence that the previous government had erected to try and keep order, he didn't stop her. It wasn't until he had seen the repercussions of her actions on the people in the city that he realised the reality of what she had done. An upheaval ensued and a battle for independence erupted, which resulted in those loyal to The Boss fighting anyone who didn't swear blind allegiance to her. The biggest losers of these clashes were the people she vowed to protect, who ended up scraping by on minimal rations and searching for purpose in her new world. The people had become trapped and isolated from the rest of the country.

He stood next to her as she made each bad decision, and he watched her slowly turn into a person she said she would never become, a corrupt and power hungry political leader who would do anything for her own agenda. He did everything he could to open her eyes to the chaos she had created. He pleaded. He lied. He tried to distance her from those who had been hissing in her ear. But she remained undeterred and stubborn, refusing to back down from her choices. He had run out of things to try and was left with no other options but to leave.

Working his way through the complex wasn't an issue for Nick and figuring out the routes and times of the guards that were on patrol would be a cakewalk for him. Being second-in-command came with some additional perks and knowledge, which included control over The Boss' security.

Despite there being eyes on him, as far as everyone was concerned, he was still The Boss' number two, which meant he could come and go as he pleased. He still had to tread with caution; the moment anyone realised that he was on his way to see his sister, he would be immediately stopped and sent back to his living quarters, or worse, to her.

Over the last few months, he had been spending

more and more time in the gym. This had become his only outlet to burn off his frustrations, so walking around with a large bag wasn't a peculiar sight. Everyone in Downing Street knew he often warmed up in his room before he went to the gym. So, the fact that he was sweating from nerves, could be excused – he hoped desperately.

Due to his high-ranking status, he rarely had to adhere to the proper security measures of the headquarters and he'd hoped today would be no different. He'd made it through the various metal detectors and checkpoints The Boss had insisted be set up in her own home and office. The paranoia and anxiety had worsened over the last year, and there were very few people she trusted. Nick had been by The Boss' side from day one, helping her in every aspect of her rise to power, but he despised what she had become. He'd never wanted to leave her. He shared her original message and ideas for the country, but she had finally forced his hand and he knew he could no longer serve under her. He pushed all memories of her, good and bad, out of his mind. He didn't have time to be distracted with any other thoughts, except for getting to his sister, escaping Downing Street, and leaving the city.

He was his normal charismatic self when passing the guards. He had hated referring to them as guards. These people were once his friends, many of whom he helped get into the position they were in now. However, in this moment, he couldn't think of them as friends; they were pawns he needed to manipulate so he could achieve his goals.

He continued through the complex and walked straight past the courtyard which was oddly quiet that night. "*That can only mean one of two things,*" thought Nick. "*Big Dave and Sarah are late for their shifts; probably having sex in the toilets again, or they've moved the guards from the courtyard to help cover Emily's room.* Nick crossed his fingers and hoped the horny guards were up to no good and that there hadn't been an increase in security where his sister was staying. The last thing he wanted to do was physically harm anyone stupid enough to get in his way. He had hurt enough people in the last few years and had no intention of doing it ever again - if possible.

He slowed his pace the closer he got to Emily and assessed the area surrounding her room. Fortunately, he had access to all of the security cameras in Downing Street, so he knew where all the blind spots on the base were. To cover his back and buy himself some extra time if he needed it, he borrowed a trick from so many TV shows and produced a make shift body of himself under his sheets using pillows, on the off chance The Boss ordered anyone to collect him from his room. He knew it was ridiculous, but it only needed to work for a short while, just long enough for him to make his escape.

A wave of relief came over him as he saw that there were only two guards standing patrol by his sister's room in the west wing of Downing Street. Unfortunately for him, however, the two guards were two of The Boss' best and two people he really liked. Knocking them out was not only going to be physically difficult but it was also going to sting him personally. He was hardly a brawler but he had recently upped his muscle mass and combat training, something he felt was necessary since living in a more violent world. He had also become a hot political target for the resistance boroughs that knew who he was, so he felt he needed to be able to protect himself if they ever decided to try and rebel against The Boss again. Despite how much time he had put in the gym, he wasn't overly confident that he could take on two trained soldiers, but he had hoped adrenaline, the element of surprise, and a strong purpose would help him.

There was no turning back from this. His decision had been made and he had to go for it. There was no other way to get to his sister except through the front door of that building and into her room. He had to get around to the side of the building which housed Emily and a number of other people who The Boss felt had wronged her, somehow take out the two guards, get to Emily's room, break her out, avoid any guards and all the security cameras, and escape from Downing Street.

"Piece of cake," thought Nick.

"Okay. Okay. Fuck it. Let's go," said Nick, psyching himself up before making the mad dash towards the building to attempt his daring breakout. However, before he had a chance to move, one of the guards in front of the building received a call on his radio.

Nick couldn't quite make out what was being said, but he was sure he heard his name which sent a number of worrying scenarios through his head. Had he been caught? Had they realised what he was doing? Had his stupid 90's TV show bed trick failed? If he was caught, what was going to happen to him? What was going to happen to Emily? Was this the biggest mistake he had made since encouraging The Boss to fight the machine and run for Prime Minister of London?

As quickly as those thoughts had entered and left his head, the two guards covering the building were gone. They had vanished in a flash, leaving a confused Nick to frantically look around the site to see where they had disappeared to. He waited for a few minutes before slowly walking towards the building, while keeping a wary eye out for the guards or anyone else in the area. He reached the door of the building and put his hand on the keypad. He checked his surroundings one more time and then entered the code that gave him access to the building and his sister. He was in.

"I'm either very lucky or something's up," he thought. But he didn't have time to worry about which it was. He went straight to Emily's room and opened the door.

"What took you so long?" hissed Emily who was standing in her room with a rucksack on her back. "We have to go now!"

He didn't say a word. He nodded at his sister trying his best to ignore her dishevelled long brown hair and the bruises on her face; a very different look than the beautifully prim and proper way she presents herself usually.

They left the building and the pair quickly ran back through the courtyard towards the gardens at the back of Number 10. They tactfully manoeuvred around the complex, avoiding the security cameras on the way to the gardens, and fortunately didn't encounter a single guard. The pair had to temporarily pass through the main building of Number 10 so they could get to the gardens and through to the secret exit Nick and The Boss had built when they first moved into Downing Street in case of an emergency escape.

They entered Number 10 through a side entrance which led to an empty hallway that Emily had always been desperate to add some flair to. She knew that it was only a short path to the beautiful gardens, but she had a knack for giving personality to the simplest of things. She had tried adding some plants to the hall but the guards on duty kept knocking into them and damaging them whilst on patrol. After a while, she stopped bothering.

The lack of guards patrolling tonight hadn't gone unnoticed by the siblings, "Something doesn't feel right. Where are all the guards? Do you think they're on to us?" asked Emily.

"If they are, it's too late to turn back. We've made our beds and now we have to sit in them," said Nick.

"I don't think that's the right expression," said Emily.

"I know it isn't, but I thought I'd annoy you one last time; just in case, you know," said Nick, trying to make light of their current situation.

"You're an idiot," replied Emily, smiling at her brother and then gently resting her head against his.

"You ready to get out of here?" asked Nick.

"Ready when you are!" Emily exclaimed.

Nick opened the door to the garden and peered out into the darkness. The garden had always been a place where he could get away from things. It was tightly secured with electrified barbed wire pinned to the tops of the walls which surrounded the entire garden. It was rarely patrolled or monitored, which meant it was peaceful, quiet and most importantly empty at night. Nick and Emily ran towards the back of the garden to a brick wall which was surrounded by bushes, flowers, and a dead apple tree Emily had attempted to grow when they first moved into Downing Street. The large bushes acted as camouflage in disguising the pair, while Nick searched for the human sized rabbit hole that he and The Boss had personally built in the garden. Nick kicked around for the hole until his foot hit a large collection of rocks which had been expertly laid to cover the hole.

"Found it. Okay, let's go," said Nick as he and Emily began moving the rocks and fake grass from the covered hole.

A deafening noise suddenly filled the garden, causing Emily to scream in fear. A bright white light followed and blinded the pair, turning the once gloomy garden into a supernova of light with nowhere to hide. Nick grabbed Emily who was holding her hands over her ears and yelled something at her. Through the noise of the sirens, she deciphered that he wanted her to keep helping him clear the escape tunnel.

Nick noticed the shadows of the guards scrambling through the building towards the garden and he practically pushed Emily down the escape tunnel once it was accessible. He didn't have time to think about how the guards had found them, but he knew that they must have been anticipating he would be up to something.

He had no time to waste. He continued through with the plan to escape from Downing Street, get past the Mountbatten Statue, and disappear into St. James' Park without anyone seeing where he was going. Nick jumped into the escape tunnel behind Emily. But before he could crawl through to freedom, he noticed a red flashing light hovering at the other end of the garden. He had seen enough drones in his time to know where the light was coming from. He didn't know whether to be annoyed at himself for missing it or hurt that The Boss had been spying on him.

He knew that he planned to escape the city and destroy the woman he had helped get into power, but her lack of trust in him and her having a response team on hand to apprehend him, was a real low blow. It was, however, the last push he needed to pry himself away from The Boss forever.

CHAPTER 3

4th June 2016, 23:49
George Street, City of Westminster, The Independent State of England

He never knew if he would ever go through with his escape plan, but he had made sure he had a rough idea of how he would travel through the city and where he would be going. Fortunately, he had spent a lot of time working in Trafalgar Square and spent many of his lunch breaks exploring the beautiful parks in the area. So, as soon as he and Emily had jumped down from the garden wall at number 10, he had planned to run straight for St James's Park.

He had made sure that he'd destroyed his and Emily's phones so they wouldn't be tracked by The Boss' communications team, which meant he had to rely on his memory and not Google Maps to navigate around the city.

The telecommunications in the city had been heavily restricted over the last couple of years. The Boss needed to maintain contact with the outside world to guarantee the city supply drops were made on time; she also wanted to ensure the gangs loyal to her were able to communicate with each other across the state. She had tried to limit access to those she trusted, but she soon realised that there were far too many hackers left in her city for that to be possible.

Before the pair could get lost into St James's Park, there was a small patrol standing on Horse Guards Road behind Number 10, forcing Nick and Emily to swiftly hide behind the stands surrounding Horse Guards Parade.

"How are we going to get past them Nick? Her people are everywhere and now they know we've escaped!" said Emily in a panic.

Nick had a hundred things going through his head. *"What the hell have we done? Is there any way we can get past these people? Are they gang members or are they soldiers of The Boss? If they're gang members, which gangs do they belong to?*

Nick had heard rumblings about some of the gangs loyal to The Boss recently uniting and joining forces, most would see this as a positive thing, but he had warned The Boss to be wary of these groups getting too organised and trying to rise up against her. He was The Boss' eyes and ears and would often advise her wisely to ensure that she would stay in power; the irony being that advice was now going to make it much harder for him to bring her down; something that was not lost on him.

His train of thought had been broken when he heard the static noise coming from a handheld radio nearby. He felt a tingle of fear wash over him as he suspected that they had been found out already. As soon as these gang members or guards found out that he and his sister had escaped, they would immediately begin covering the walls and roads surrounding Downing Street.

"What are we going to do Nick?" asked Emily.

"Piece of shit radio; I can't hear a thing on these things," came a female voice from the group on patrol up ahead.

The pair peered over the stands and saw a guard smacking her handheld radio to try and get it to work.

"I don't think their radios are working properly," said Emily optimistically.

She turned her radio on and off a few times but had no luck in getting it to work. "The comms signal has been playing up recently. My phone isn't working either. I can hear the alarm going off. Let's rendezvous with the crew inside and see what the problem is. It's probably another bloody drill," said the female guard.

The group hastily left the area and moved towards the rear entrance of Downing Street, walking past Nick and Emily. All it would've taken was for one of the six guards passing by to look to their left and the siblings would have been seen. Fortunately for them, the guards were in such a rush to get inside, they missed the two completely. He couldn't believe how lucky they were, but before he could take a moment to be thankful for their timely break, Emily was pulling him into the nightfall of St

James's Park.

Once they had hopped the fence into St James's Park, they ran and ran until they were well and truly in the heart of the fifty-seven-acre park. They had two choices while navigating through the park. They could rush through the open and dimly lit park, quickly with the hopes of not running into any of the Westminster gangs; or they continue going through the darker and more hidden parts of the park, taking their time and ensuring that they escaped Westminster via a much safer route.

Nick felt that it would be far more dangerous for them to stay out in the open, so he decided that they would take their time and use caution this early on in their escape. He had also hoped that by going at a slower pace and moving through the shadows, anyone who may be looking for them, would pass them by giving the pair free reign to escape the borough.

After running through the park for a few minutes, Emily grabbed Nick's arm. "What are we doing Nick? Where are we running to? Please tell me you have a plan?"

"Right now, I'm just trying to get us out of Westminster. We can't do anything while we are in her territory, and we're literally surrounded by people loyal to her. Some of them would die for her, and all of them will definitely kill for her. "The Westenders," "Star Gang," "The Soho Squares;" they all operate here and will be looking for us. We have to get as far away from here as we can."

She nodded at her brother obediently. As they locked eyes, he could see the fear in his sister's amber eyes and the sweat falling from her tan skin. Their whole lives no one ever thought the pair was related. He had inherited his dad's dark complexion and square jaw, whereas she was much lighter and had softer facial features like their mother. The only physical quality that united them was their mother's button nose. Despite their stark differences in appearance, the siblings had as close of a bond as anyone else they knew, and because of that bond, Nick refused to show Emily that he was just as scared as she was; until they were safe, he needed to be strong for her.

"Let's focus on getting out of her house alive and then we can talk about what's next. I know where we are going so catch your breath because we can't stop again; not until we are nearly out of the borough and closer to Camden," explained Nick.

They continued through the park, and by some miracle, the pair made it through the park unnoticed. They crossed over from St. James Park to Green Park which meant going past Queen Victoria's Memorial directly in front of the now vacant Buckingham Palace.

A year prior, The Boss had refused to bring down the fence and people began fleeing the city. Nick had wanted the team to move into the Palace, as he felt it would provide them with excellent security against their enemies who remained in the city. The Boss, however, had said that she didn't want to move into the Palace because she didn't want the people thinking that she was better than them. She hated the idea of class and hierarchy; she believed in earning your spot and your power through hard work and struggle and not because you were born into hegemony and wealth.

The Palace had been empty for a very long time, and the surrounding area had become a haven for the homeless. Once a bustling tourist attraction and place of Royal history, had now become a dilapidated show house. Aside from some stray cats and a number of homeless people who were either asleep or high, Nick and Emily were able to enter Green Park unnoticed. The homeless crisis was yet another one of The Boss' failings as supreme leader of the Independent State of England.

Nick knew exactly what his plan was and where he was going, but he didn't want to clutter Emily's brain with too much information in the likely case they had to improvise and change tactics. She didn't cope well when plans changed, and she wasn't the best at going with the flow. God help you if you suggested going to a different club or bar when she had organised a night out. She was often the butt of the joke amongst her friends who would tease her mercilessly about how anal she was. She would always take it in jest, but there was a much deeper and meaningful reason as to why she was like that.

She was only thirteen when their father died. She struggled to acccpt that hc was really gone. Nick, who was forced at the age of eighteen to become the man of the house, would often catch her waiting for their dad to return home from work with the film she had asked him to buy for her on the day of the crash. She had bugged him all day about picking up a film for her on his way back home from work, which meant her dad had to take a different route home than he usually did. To date, Emily still refuses to watch "Harry Potter and the Goblet of Fire." Her dad's death was never the plan, and she never stopped blaming herself for it. That guilt changed who she was. She became someone who had to stick to the plan, because if you stick to the plan then nothing can surprise you and nothing can go wrong; a mantra she had since abandoned after living in the new world she did.

Nick's escape plan had been nerve racking so far, but the pair were on the right track – *"break sister out, escape Downing Street, disappear into St James Park, continue through to Green Park, survive Hyde Park, and try and go unnoticed while travelling through the streets of Paddington with the hopes of collapsing somewhere near the Camden borough."*

Green Park proved to be a mostly easy venture for the pair; however, Emily swore that she had heard voices in the park. It wasn't until they could see Wellington Arch ahead of them that they had spotted where the voices were coming from.

Between them and Hyde Park was Wellington Arch. It was an impressive arch, but it was what was under the arch that was of real concern to the pair – seven men; all armed with cricket bats were loitering underneath the archway. If Nick had to guess, these men were members of the "Centuries," an all Sri Lankan gang with an affinity for cricket. They've been known to practice the strength of their cricket bats on human bodies, so Nick was feeling rightfully nervous after seeing these men. Luckily for them, the "Centuries" had only had a few men out that night, so Nick and Emily were able to quietly sneak around the arch and move on to Hyde Park.

The fact that nobody outside of The Boss' immediate team had been alerted of Nick's escape, meant that the pair had only encountered a few scares when leaving the park and moving through the streets of Paddington. They kept mostly to the smaller roads and back alleys as they neared Edgware Road, where they agreed to find shelter for the night.

While desperately trying to find somewhere for them to stay, Nick discovered a small block of flats with the front door to the foyer wide open. They closed the door behind them and managed to wedge the door shut with some loose blocks they found in the communal garden. The pair then broke into the ground floor flat by forcing open a slightly opened window which looked out onto the garden. Once inside, they immediately got to work in making sure the flat was secure and safe so they could hide out and get some rest, even if for a few hours.

The pair had been fleeing from Downing Street for just under three hours and had only made it as far as Edgware Road. Once they had escaped from Downing Street, their troubles had only begun as they had to navigate their way through the Westminster borough, an area entirely dominated with supporters of The Boss and with the highest levels of security and gang activity.

They decided to split up and make sure the rooms in the flat were empty and secure before they could pass out in their new temporary accommodation. The two bedrooms, the kitchen, the living room, and the bathroom were all empty.

"The bedrooms are clear, but one of the beds is covered in crap so we'll have to bunk up," said Nick.

"Do you mean it's covered in loads of rubbish or actual crap?" asked Emily.

"I'm not going to sniff it to find out if that's what you are asking," replied Nick sarcastically.

Emily collapsed on the sofa in the living room. Nick handed Emily a bottle of water and a packet of crisps. She snatched the food from Nick and inhaled the bag of crisps in seconds.

"Jesus, didn't you eat anything before we left?"

"Running for my life increases my appetite apparently," quipped Emily, wiping the crumbs from her mouth.

Nick sat down next to her on the sofa, "You should probably get some sleep. I can stay on lookout for a bit."

"There's no way I can sleep right now. You go, and I'll stay up?" said Emily who was full of adrenaline.

"You sure?"

"Yeah, I'll wake you if I start drifting off and we can

swap."

He rocked forward off the sofa and walked towards the back bedroom.

"Nick, before you go to sleep. Will you please tell me where we're going? What's our end game here?" probed Emily.

He walked back to his sister and crouched down next to her. He took her hand and looked her in the eyes. "We're going to bring that psycho down. Believe it or not. I've still got some friends left in Enfield and they're going to help us escape."

"And then what? We get captured by the government or the resistance outside of the City?"

"We have enough dirt on The Boss, and her regime to bring them both crashing down. I don't know if we'll be declared traitors, or if we'll be arrested or even killed once we're out, but I can't let her do this anymore," explained Nick. "We both know she has lost her mind and she needs to be stopped. Will you help me do that Em?"

She squeezed his hand. "You're bloody nuts, you know that? Of course, I will help you," she said grinning at Nick. "Now, bugger off to bed. One of us needs to be rested before we head out again."

He walked to the far bedroom of the flat and climbed into the freshly made double bed. He closed his eyes, and in that moment of silence and isolation, a thousand things floated through his head as he tried to comprehend what he had actually started. He had to commit to his plan and there was no turning back from it. He knew his only options were completion, death, or all of the above.

His eyes began to get heavy and he started to fall asleep, however, before that deep sleep could take him, he heard the creaking of floorboards. "*Probably Emily pacing around the living room,*" he thought.

The creaking continued and became louder and clearer. He wasn't sure why, but the sound of the creaking floorboards made him think about something he hadn't fully acknowledged when he first came into the bedroom. Perhaps it was pure exhaustion that made him miss it, but the bed he was laying on was perfectly made. Most flats and houses in The Independent State of England had been abandoned, evacuated, or taken over by gangs or civilians in hiding.

His eyes shot open as he felt a gentle but cold feeling pressing on his throat. It was a feeling he had only ever experienced once in his life before, but it was a feeling he would never forget because it was the first time, he thought he was going to die. Even in his half-awake state, he knew someone was holding a knife to his throat. He turned his head slightly and standing over him was an elderly bald Indian man holding a Stanley knife to his throat; behind him were two young girls who were both holding long screwdrivers.

"You picked the wrong house to break into son," came the raspy voice that Nick thought would be the last voice he would ever hear.

CHAPTER 4

4th June 2016, 03:05
George Street, City of Westminster, The Independent State of England

"I'm sorry I have to do this to you son, but I have people I need to protect," said the elderly Indian man who was practically expressionless while holding his knife to Nick's throat. Nick could see the ruthlessness and lack of caring in this man which told him that he would kill him without a second thought in order to protect his people.

He tried to speak but the pressure of the knife on his neck made it difficult, the man holding the knife must've been in his early 60's but he had the strength of a man half his age.

"Please don't hurt my sister. Let her go. Please!" gasped Nick.

"If she's gone by the time I'm done with you, she'll have a chance to live. But if she's still here, I'm sorry but I can't risk her revealing where we are," said the elderly Asian man calmly. He leaned in close towards Nick and looked him in his eyes. "She won't feel a thing, I promise."

Dread and anguish rushed through Nick as he prepared himself for the end. Before he could accept his inevitable demise, however, a loud clicking sound engulfed the room. "Let him go now or I'll shoot all three of you."

Emily was standing in the doorway of the room with a gun pointed at the man and the two young women. "Nick, get up," ordered Emily.

"Kill him Haresh. We can take this slapper!" screamed the ginger haired woman standing behind Haresh.

The other young girl, who couldn't have been older than fourteen, started to show signs of nerves as the screwdriver in her hand began to visibly shake. "She has a gun Haresh. She'll kill us all, or worse, if she shoots that gun the gangs nearby could hear it," said the young blonde-haired Aryan looking girl.

"Shut up Lara. We can take this skank out before she has a chance to even pull the trigger," said the other young woman.

"Try me, bitch," threatened Emily, pointing the gun at the young woman's head.

Haresh pulled his knife away from Nick's throat at the sight of Emily holding a gun to the young woman's head. "Please don't. Look I've taken the knife away," said Haresh.

"Haresh what the hell are you doing?" said the young woman showing no fear.

"This young lady has something to lose. Same as us. She will die trying to protect her brother and I will die trying to protect you girls. What's the point, if we all die?" explained Haresh.

Nick jumped off of the bed and stood behind his sister. She was furious when she noticed the small cut on his neck. "You're bleeding. You fucking cut him? Throw your weapons on the floor. Do it now!" ordered Emily.

Haresh threw his knife to the floor and nodded to his companions to do the same. Lara threw her weapon down but the young woman refused and stood her ground.

"Lucy, lay down your weapon," instructed Haresh.

She reluctantly threw her screwdriver down at Emily's feet. Nick bent down and collected all of the weapons. Once he had all the weapons in hand, Emily swiftly walked over to Lucy and punched her in the face knocking her to the floor. Nick pulled Emily away from Lucy before she could do any more damage.

"Don't you dare think about following us or I'll make sure I really hurt this bitch!" yelled Emily.

Haresh and Lara helped Lucy to her feet, "Please leave us alone, you have our weapons, now please go - quietly," asked Lara politely.

Emily quickly left the room while Nick slowly began backing away towards the door, not taking his eyes off of Haresh and the two ladies with him.

Haresh stepped in front of Lucy and Lara like a mother bear protecting its young. "Thank you for letting us live and I'm sorry again for the knife. I had to keep my girls safe. I hope you understand."

"I get it, but a bit of advice for next time, maybe try

and ask any intruders to leave first before threatening to kill them," said Nick.

"If I spent the last couple of years saying please and thank you to strangers I encountered, well my friend, I would not be standing in front of you today," laughed Haresh. "Riots, violence, and destruction are all around us. These are not the times for politeness."

"Trust me, brother, I know that more than anyone. But don't worry; things are going to change around here real soon," said Nick.

"What do you mean by that? What change?" asked Lucy who used her shirt sleeve to wipe the blood from her nose.

Emily hurried back into the room and tried to pull Nick away, "You've said enough Nick. We have to go. We're going to have to find another place to stay before someone catches up to us."

Haresh walked towards Nick. Emily instinctively pointed Haresh's knife at his face forcing him to hold his hands up in the air in an act of compliance. "You two obviously know how to look after yourselves. You don't need our weapons as well. Why don't you stay here for the rest of the night? We can feed you and we can keep you safe for the night, and in return, you give us our weapons back before you leave," said Haresh.

"Please, you can't leave us defenceless and if there are people looking for you, you're safer here than out on the streets," pleaded Lara softly.

"We're good. I'm not staying in the same building

let alone the same flat with that," said Emily pointing the knife at Lucy. "Let's go Nick."

Nick looked at Lara and Haresh and was overcome with guilt and sympathy for this small group of people fighting to survive. "Have you had many break-ins? How secure is this place and do you have much food to spare? We'll need some supplies for when we leave as well," asked Nick.

"Let me show you what we have," said Haresh.

Haresh led Nick, Emily, and the girls back to the empty kitchen, "We've checked all of the cupboards already and we couldn't find anything," said Emily.

Haresh smiled at Lara and Lucy and then knelt onto the floor and began pulling up some loose floorboards. Lucy and Lara joined Haresh and did the same. The group revealed a hidden goldmine of tinned and dried food.

"And people used to make fun of me for being a hoarder in my previous life," boasted Haresh, "We have plenty of food for the three of us and when we run out, we know how to get more; so please help yourselves. Stay with us tonight and when you decide to leave, you will return our weapons and be on your way. Agreed?"

Nick whispered in Emily's ear discussing their options; meanwhile Lucy pulled Haresh towards her and Lara. "How can you be sure we can trust these pricks?" said Lucy.

"I can't, but they are obviously running from something and I don't think killing three strangers is something they need to burden themselves with right now. For now, I think we're safe," said Haresh. He put a hand behind each of the girl's heads and gently pulled them towards him. "Nothing has changed okay. I'll look after you, you'll look after me, and we'll all look after each other. Understood?"

"Understood," said Lara and Lucy in unison.

After seeing Haresh, Lucy, and Lara embracing in an intimate moment of solidarity, their minds had been made up and they interrupted Haresh and the girls. "Okay. We'll stay with you, just until we get some rest, and of course we will return your weapons to you once we have left. You have our word," said Nick extending his hand out to Haresh, who returned his as the two shook on their new temporary alliance.

Emily pulled out a tissue from her pocket and offered it to Lucy as a peace offering. "Sorry about punching you in the face babe," she said.

Lucy snatched the tissue from Emily and wiped away the remaining blood from her face. "Don't worry bitch. It won't happen again," said Lucy, smiling at Emily. Emily laughed and smiled back, a smile of respect, and a smile that showed one another that they were two tough women on the same page.

Lara and Lucy took some tins of warm peaches and questionable canned meat into the living room and laid out a shabby feast on the broken living room coffee table, inviting Emily to join them. Haresh continued to show Nick around the flat and asked for his help in setting up some security measures.

In between bites of food, Lucy began fiddling with a broken wind-up radio. She jammed a small key into the back of the radio and unscrewed the casing.

"You have no idea what you're doing do you?" asked Lara.

"Not really, but it keeps me busy and ya never know, I may be able to add electrician to the list of skills I've acquired since we got stuck here. It'll go nicely with me being able to heat up tinned food with a lighter...and going nearly a year without getting any," joked Lucy.

Emily tried her hardest to fight back the laughter, but she couldn't contain herself. "Shit!" said Emily between laughs.

"What?" asked Lucy.

"I think I actually like you," she said, smiling at Lucy.

"I have that effect on people love, I'd certainly like you more if you were a bloke though, cause I'm not joking when I say that I seriously need to get some. Your brother single?"

"I wouldn't go there if I was you," responded Emily, "It's not me being protective or anything, it's just... very complicated."

They all laughed and the feeling in the room became much more cheerful.

Nick and Haresh were by the front door of the flat attempting to barricade and reinforce the door with some old mattress slats, a screwdriver with no handle, a pair of scissors, and a rusty hammer. "You should really be doing this to the main entrance of the building as well, the door was wide open when we got here and we walked straight in," said Nick, hammering a crooked nail into the door.

"We've been here for about year and this is the longest we've had a place to stay that we can call safe. We've learnt some tricks over the years when trying to hide from the gangs. Other places we've stayed in the past, we've always made sure that we boarded up all of the doors and all of the windows. We thought we were safe, but all that did was invite people in," explained Haresh.

"What do you mean?" asked Nick.

"Answer me this. If you were looking to round up people and steal from them, hurt them or even kill them, would you look in the place with the door wide open or the place that is entirely boarded up looking like it has something to hide?"

"People are still hunting people?" asked Nick in disbelief.

"Where have you been son? It's been like this for a while now. The three of us is all that is left from our original group," said Haresh. "Pass me those pieces of wood please."

He passed Haresh a collection of misshapen and damaged wooden slats which Haresh hammered across the front door, "Our group was full of people from all walks of life. People who once believed in The Boss, old and young that wanted what she wanted – unity. In a funny way, despite all of the mayhem, we got it. I, for one, never thought that I'd end up with a foul-mouthed ginger woman from

Leeds like Lucy and a shy blonde white girl from Hertfordshire like Lara."

"We can hear you, old man, and I'm not that loud," yelled Lucy from the other room, forcing Haresh to laugh to himself.

"Those girls are everything to me now. They are my family and I thank The Boss every day for bringing them into my life. Unfortunately, she lost her way and brought this world upon us as well. Pass the screwdriver please Nick," asked Haresh. "So, are you going to tell me where you two are heading?"

Nick paused momentarily. "Seeing as you were so honest with me, it's only fair I return the favour," said Nick, handing Haresh the screwdriver. "We're heading for Enfield. I have friends there and they're going to help me and my sister escape the city."

"And what will you do when you escape the city? Join the others?" questioned Haresh.

"We are going to take The Boss and her whole regime down," said Nick bluntly.

Haresh put down the screwdriver and stared deeply at Nick trying to figure out if this man was serious or not, "And who are you to accomplish such a big task?" he probed.

He opened his mouth intending to reveal to Haresh exactly who he was, when suddenly, the noise of radio static from the living room interrupted him.

"Holy shit I fixed it!" declared Lucy in disbelief.

She picked up the radio, wound it, and began searching for a working channel. Nick and Haresh walked back into the living room to investigate the commotion. Nick perched himself on the armrest of the living room sofa while Lucy continued to search for a broadcasting radio station. She had little success at first, finding either the old rolling public service announcement telling people to evacuate the city or extracts from The Boss' YouTube clips which had been played on a loop over the last couple of years. Hearing those old clips was painful for Nick as it reminded him of a happier time, a time when The Boss wasn't The Boss, ruler of the city, but his friend.

Lucy continued to search until the static on the radio faded away and turned to silence.

"What happened? Did it break again?" expressed Lara with concern. "I was hoping we could get some music out of that thing or at least some news from the outside world."

Lucy frantically continued to fiddle with the radio, desperately trying to get it to work. She wound it again, and out of nowhere, a voice began crackling through the radio. Lucy and Lara looked at each other with excitement and the group crowded around the radio; everyone except for Nick who remained seated.

"...100% the thing I miss the most is sports. Your Eye in the Sky has certainly not seen any gangs playing a nice game of footie in no man's land. For Christ sake, people from all over the world were killing each other in war and even they had the ability to put their nonsense behind them and have a kick about. If a game of footie doesn't bring people together, I don't know what will..."

Nick stood up from the sofa and leant in towards the radio, "What is this? Is this that Eye in the Sky Muppet? Turn it off. This guy chats so much bollocks."

"Your Eye in the Sky has some breaking news. This comes straight from my pigeons in The Independent State of England. It looks like we have ourselves an old fashioned man hunt. Apologies, that was sexist of me. We have ourselves an old-fashioned non-gender specific hunt. It's looking like there is some dissention amongst the ranks over at The Boss' Tower of Doom. Despite my not so subtle views on how I feel about The Boss, I am above all else a reporter first, and I will continue to reluctantly pass on her messages as to keep the people of the city informed. I've been told that her right-hand man Nick King, who some of you may recognise, and his crazy hot sister Emily...Damn it, I did it again. I'm sorry for yet another sexist remark; but she is beautiful though. Anyway, those two sad sacks have apparently fled The Boss' evil compound and are now wanted. Oh, and as an extra sting on poor Emily, Nick is wanted back alive and baby sister Emily is wanted back dead or alive - which if you ask me, is an absolute waste. For your efforts for catching and turning in either or both of these fools is, you get Carte Blanche, which for you simpletons out there means a blank cheque – you get whatever you want. Now, that's an enticing offer. Even I'm tempted to climb down from my perch and find them, BUT that would go against all my values of hating The Boss with my entire body. Good luck to you Nick, Emily, and to all the gangs in The Independent State of

England. Happy hunting and keep an eye on them so-cials for incoming images of Nick and Emily. In other news..."

Emily stood up and rushed over to Nick. Haresh, Lucy, and Lara were sat in awe around the silent radio which had finally run out of juice and died.

"You wanted to know who I am Haresh. My name is Nick King...and it's my fault The Boss took over this city."

CHAPTER 5

4th June 2016, 05:45
George Street, City of Westminster, The Independent State of England

"Nick, we have to get out of here. We need to go now!" yelled Emily.

Nick continued to look at a shocked and baffled Haresh who was staring right back at him.

"Nick, what are you doing? The whole city is going to be after us. We need to leave!" shouted Emily.

Lucy squared up to Emily. "We can't let them go. Can we?" she said.

Lara shot up as quickly as Lucy had and stepped in between her and Emily. "What are you talking about? These people haven't hurt us. They're friends here," said Lara defiantly.

Lucy looked to Haresh who was engaged in an intense staring contest with Nick. "These aren't our friends; we've known them for a minute. Haresh, if we turn them in, we can get whatever we want," stressed Lucy.

Haresh finally broke his gaze from Nick and gave Lucy a look that she had received hundreds of times before, a look she knew to mean, *I've said something incredibly stupid and now I need to shut up.* Haresh turned his attention back to Nick. "Take what you need, take it all if you must, but prepare yourself for what's coming next and get to where you need to as fast as you can," said Haresh.

Without hesitation, Emily collected hers and Nick's bags and began filling them with cans of food and bottles of water from Haresh's stash. Nick swiftly grabbed Emily by the arm and stopped her from packing the bags. He shook his head at her and took everything his sister had put in the bags and returned it to the counter. Haresh had given them more than he could've asked for; safe passage out of his home, which was enough. He looked over to Haresh and gave him the slightest of nods. Nick and Emily zipped up their rucksacks and walked past Lara, Lucy, and Haresh without saying a word.

Lara stuttered and struggled to say anything as she couldn't believe how quickly things had escalated and how fast the siblings were leaving. Besides the noise of wood being removed from the door, Nick walked out of the flat in silence, not even taking the time to say goodbye. Emily, on the other hand, took the gun out of her bag and put it in Lucy's hand. "It's a fake. Make sure whoever you point it at doesn't know that," said Emily giving Lucy a cocky half smile and then disappearing from the flat leaving no trace of them ever being there.

Once they had left, Lara began to sob; not just because she saw two potential allies leaving the group, but because she saw two new friends enter and exit her life in a blink of an eye like so many others had before them. Haresh, Nick, Emily, and Lucy understood that in the world they now lived, friendship was fleeting and opportunity where possible was short lived.

Haresh could see that Nick had the potential to make change, and although he has only known him for a few short hours, he believed Nick would do all he could to stop The Boss, or die trying.

CHAPTER 6

4th August 2012, 19:34
Gray's Inn Road, Camden, The Independent State of England

She still got butterflies before going into a big interview. In the last year, she had been on a variety of different talk shows and with the help of Nick and her team, she knew every step she had to take to get her point across and had perfected her skills in debating. Her heated back and forth Twitter battle and subsequent one on one interview with Piers Morgan, exploded on the internet and went viral. At twenty-five years old and with no full time job, The Boss made an experienced forty- seven year old journalist look like a child after he criticised her for her supposedly encouraging comments made about the continued rioting throughout London and other parts of the UK. The Boss, who had requested the one on one meeting with Piers, quickly shut him down by exclaiming that she would never condone violence, looting, and rioting; but she would always back freedom of speech and equality for all.

She had always had an intense passion about these

ideals but struggled early on in her life to properly vocalise herself on a public platform. Nick and those closest to her would have to constantly listen to her ranting about the unfair treatment against those who were trying to make something of themselves but received no help. She'd turn up to parties angry and annoyed after she would hear about politicians and the super-rich getting tax breaks and benefits on top of their insanely high salaries, whilst she and other hard working people were clawing away to get a decent wage to only have it slashed away by taxes. She would get frustrated when she would hear about immigrants coming to the country and abusing the housing and benefits system, whilst she was crammed into a studio flat paying a fortune for rent.

She wanted to make a change but had no way of doing so, or so she thought; "God bless social media," was a statement she frequently used.

Nick was her biggest fan and he lit up every time she walked onto set for a prime time TV show or spoke in front of a crowd of adoring people. Her enthusiasm, her passion, and her fight were all things he loved about her being in the public eye. He also had his own selfish reason for seeing and hearing her speak the words she spoke because many of the words she spoke were in fact his. The messages, the feeling, and the thoughts were all hers, but she had never been the best wordsmith when it came to scripted speeches. Nick had always had a knack for stringing words together. Hearing words he wrote being spoken on live TV was one thing, but hearing them inspire people, gave him a great feeling of satisfaction and purpose.

"Wish me luck," said The Boss.

"You never need it. Go cause some trouble!" said Nick enthusiastically as The Boss made her way onto the Channel 4 news set.

Nick made his way backstage to watch The Boss work her magic on the Channel 4 News when his phone started ringing; he knew it was his phone because the annoyingly catchy melody of Psy's "Gangnam Style" began blaring from his suit jacket pocket. He quickly scrambled to reach for his phone, as various production crew around him were either laughing at him or getting annoyed when his inappropriately timed ring tone played during a live newscast. He answered his phone and confirmed that he would be making his dinner reservations at the restaurant he had booked for later that night. He had been looking forward to this dinner for months. He had been so busy with publicity and touring the country with The Boss, that he had neglected his personal life. Tonight was the night he was going to finally sit down with his fiancée and have some much needed alone time with her. He hadn't been more excited for a dinner since the weekly Friday night kebab nights he used to have with his dad and sister when he was a kid.

He decided to watch the rest of the broadcast backstage in the green room so he could get the last of his work done before his big dinner date. He sat down in the green room, which to his dismay, was actually green for once, which meant he couldn't make his classic ice breaking comment about most green rooms in fact not being green. The VIP treatment he received no longer felt like a perk to him, as he had been privy to countless green rooms over the last year. Although, he did feel slightly uncomfortable when people waited on him hand and foot. The Boss, on the other hand, quickly got used to and enjoyed the preferential treatment that came with being a minor celebrity on the rise.

Nick helped himself to some fruit, opened his laptop, and began typing away whilst watching The Boss defend herself against the criticism she had been facing from a number of political figures in the city over the last few months. Many of these politicians had been openly vocal about The Boss and her alleged praise and encouragement of the continued rioting and acts of terrorism that had been taking place throughout the country since last year's shooting of Raymond Dwyer. She swiftly shot down these allegations and took aim at those people who had been trying to slander her name. She spoke to them directly by looking down the lens of the camera and telling them that if they had a problem with her, they should come and talk to her face to face. Those quick quips and intense camera stares from The Boss had always made Nick laugh, as she loved using her time on TV to experiment with new tricks and tactics to make herself look more intimidating and strong. Nick would tell her that it reminded him of an evil Disney villain talking to a piece of fruit before they were about to poison the princess.

Her segment had started to wrap up, and like she had been doing for the last year and a half, she dominated the interview; once again taking full advantage of her time in the hot seat. When she had finished, she returned to the green room followed by a couple of production assistants.

"Well done. You absolutely smashed that. This level of national exposure is going to do wonders for you!" said Nick praising The Boss.

"How many times have I told you, it's not about me. It's about all of us. Remember that or I'll have to keep saying cheesy stuff like that until it sticks in that skull of yours!" replied The Boss still buzzing from another successful TV appearance. "I'm thirsty. Where's that coconut water we asked for?"

She looked around the room and realised the two production assistants who escorted her into the green room were standing by the door.

"Perfect. Excuse me. Could one of you grab me a coco..." asked The Boss before being interrupted by the male production assistant who rushed towards her with such speed that the walkie-talkie strapped to his belt dropped to the floor. Nick instinctively stood up and stepped in between The Boss and the eager production assistant.

"Whoa, take it easy brother!" said Nick sternly.

"I'm sorry. I didn't mean to scare you. I'm such a big fan of yours. We both are. So, we had to speak to you," said the overly excited production assistant.

The Boss put her hand on Nick's shoulder and gently pulled him away from the two production assistants. The female production assistant walked over to The Boss in a much calmer manner than her co-worker had done and joined him.

"I'm sorry about my friend. He's a bit keen. My name is Rachel and this is Mo. We wanted to say that we are HUGE fans of yours. We've been following your YouTube videos and Twitter posts since you started back in 2010," said Rachel with an adoring smile on her face.

"Thank you. That means a lot to me. I always love meeting the people who enjoy what I do," replied The Boss, showing genuine appreciation to her fans.

"Here you go. I'm sorry again for charging at you. Sorry as well mate. At least I know you're well protected with this guy around," said Mo handing The Boss a bottle of coconut water.

"He does have his uses from time to time," said The Boss, flashing a smile at Nick who had sat back down in his chair. Nick ignored Mo and continued working on his laptop.

"Please pull up a seat and join me. Unless you'll get into trouble?" requested The Boss.

"Oh my god thanks," beamed Mo who immediately grabbed a chair and sat down so close to The Boss that their knees were touching.

"Mo, we can't. We have to get back on set," stressed Rachel.

"It's fine. I'll explain to your managers that I was being an unruly guest and required all of your time," said The Boss playfully.

Rachel sat down next to Nick who was ignoring everything that was happening in the room.

"So, you've really been following me from the beginning?" asked The Boss.

"Absolutely! Your posts and videos are incredible. They have me either crying with laughter or crying with sadness and anger. The way you tell stories always has me glued to the screen; whether it was about the police hounding your friends, or when you felt like you were getting ignored over the chavvy people in the job centre. I'd be listening to you talk and I'd be laughing so hard that it wasn't until after I finished watching you that I realised the stories you were telling were actually really awful. I couldn't believe the stuff you were saying was actually true!" said Mo.

"Unfortunately, all of them were. My friends and I would see and go through all kinds of crap, and it wasn't until I was forced to live in a tiny one bedroom mobile home after I was unfairly evicted from my flat and declared homeless, that I finally spoke up and took a stand against the unfair treatment I and so many others face every day," explained The Boss. "I was told because I was single with no kids that I'd only get the bare minimum. Meanwhile, on the news, I see that immigrants are being given housing over citizens, and not only that, they're abusing the housing system by renting out their council houses to their family members and friends who have come to the country illegally. It was the last thing in a list of many that led me to try and make a difference. Fortunately, I was able to voice my frustration online. God bless social media and YouTube, is all I'll say. I never dreamed in a million years that it'd get to this level though. Who'd of thought an unemployed short blonde girl with big thighs and big boobs from Harrow could make such an impact."

"Well you deserve it. It was hard earned," said Nick, softly interjecting his thoughts into the discussion.

"He's right, ya know. You do deserve it. We all deserve a person like you. Someone who speaks up for the hard workers who are stuck in the middle like me and Mo," said Rachel.

"What do you mean stuck in the middle?" asked The Boss quizzically.

"We work between ten to twelve hours a day here. Sometimes more when it's a busy week. Guess how much we get paid after taxes?" asked Rachel.

"Not a whole lot is the answer!" blurted out Mo. "I know our money goes to help fund the NHS and schools and whatever else our tax pays for. The problem is, we earn too much to get any extra help and support from the benefit system or the government, but we don't earn enough to actually enjoy our hard earned cash money and spend it on anything other than the basics after we've been raped of our taxes. I had to turn down a promotion last month because it would've meant I'd have been slightly over the tax threshold and actually worse off financially, despite having a higher salary."

"It's messed up I know, and I've been exactly where you guys are. The tax and help in this country is all backwards, and unfortunately, what that means is hard working people like yourselves can't quit your jobs because you need to live; but at the same time, you can't get up the career ladder quick enough to enjoy the money you are breaking your back to earn. You're right. It's bullshit!" agreed The Boss.

"It's so refreshing to hear someone like you actually agree with us," said Mo who was literally on the edge of his seat with excitement. "You'd be surprised how many political figures come on this show and ignore us when we've tried to speak to them before. All they seem to care about is their image. Rachel and I have always said that you'd make a great Prime Minister for this country,"

"Me? No way. I'm nowhere near that level," laughed The Boss, not taking what Mo had said seriously.

Rachel crouched down next to her. "Don't sell yourself short; you'd be surprised at how many people would actually support you. There are a lot of angry people in this country who don't feel like they're being heard and they are waiting for the right person to follow and get behind."

"I literally have no clue about politics. I'm just some minor YouTuber who vents about her first world problems in front of a webcam," said The Boss doubting herself.

Nick, whose interest had suddenly been peaked, leant towards her. "You are so much more than that, so much more. Look at these two. Sure, this one's a bit excitable..." said Nick gesturing towards Mo, "But they're right. You've reached these two people. Think who else you may have reached. Prime Minister! Why the hell not?"

She leapt out of her chair and began pacing around the room. "You can't be serious Nick. Give me an audience of young adults and a webcam and I'll give you all the powerful speeches and anecdotes all day long, but going up against the government, you must be mad?"

Nick walked over to her and put his hands on her shoulders. "Look where you are though. Channel 4 wanted you. We didn't call them, they called us. How many other news networks, talk shows, schools, and communities have wanted a piece of you? They all wanted you and you've bloody delivered every time, and not only did you deliver, but they all fell in love with you. Celebrities are tweeting about you; better yet, celebrities are beefing with you on Twitter!" said Nick causing The Boss to crack a smile. "If you can shut down the likes of Katie Hopkins and Piers Morgan, you can certainly do it to some random MP or politician who doesn't know a thing about the country they live in. You got this. I believe in you."

She put her hand on Nick's and squeezed it gently. "Let's do it."

"This is crazy Nick," said The Boss hugging him.

"I know, but we vibe off crazy, let's go and make history!" said Nick. "Now, first things first, does anyone know how the hell you become Prime Minister?"

"I have no idea," laughed The Boss.

Mo walked over to her and interrupted the pair with his phone in his hand. "Hold on, let me Google it," said Mo.

CHAPTER 7

5th June 2016, 19:36
St James Terrace Mews, Camden, The Independent State of England

She'd been up for hours after only getting a few hours' sleep; sleep that fell on her purely because she'd been awake for thirty-three hours straight and her eyes could no longer physically stay open. The pitch black storage garage she and Nick had hidden in after leaving the flat on George Street hadn't helped with keeping her awake either.

Nick had never had a problem falling asleep wherever he was, and no matter how busy or loud it was around him. Emily had always hated that about him. She recalled countless times when she returned home from school and she'd find Nick sleeping like a baby on the steps of the house with half of his school uniform on and the other half scattered at the bottom of the stairs. The first time she questioned him about not going to his bedroom to sleep, he said that he intended to, but he'd get tired halfway through taking his uniform off and would need a rest.

She remembered when times were hard and she needed her big brother to comfort her, but he would be fast asleep, and she didn't have it in her to wake him up. Like the time when their family was forced to move into a rundown council estate after their dad was let go from his job, and she heard her dad sobbing in the living room because he felt like a failure as a parent and provider. Or the nights when she could hear people fighting outside of their flat. These were the times she needed her big brother, but he would be asleep. Just like she needed her brother those nights, she needed him tonight as well.

After finding out that she was wanted, dead or alive, she needed her brother to comfort her; however, she knew that whatever fears were running through her head, Nick must've felt those fears a hundred times over and would likely be blaming himself for getting her involved in all of this trouble.

Once they had left the flat, the siblings ran. They didn't say a word to each other; they just ran as fast as they could and for as long as they could. The sun had been up for at least an hour when they left, so they had to move quickly. Fortunately, for the pair, it was so early in the day that the streets were emptier than usual. Nick had always said that nobody was ever out between five and six a.m., and luckily for the pair, that was still the case.

They stuck to their plan of travelling through the parks in the city as to minimise their visibility. They headed straight for their father's favourite park and a place they knew very well, Regents Park. Unlike their prior visits as kids, they didn't have time to admire the scenery of the park or stop for a picnic. Emily did catch a glimpse of the now dilapidated remains of London Zoo, which sent a rush of nostalgia and thoughts of her father through her.

Once they had exited the park, they headed towards Primrose Hill. However, after twenty minutes of sprinting on no sleep and with the sun beginning to fill the city with more and more light, they decided they needed to take shelter somewhere for the day and get some rest.

After searching the streets near Primrose Hill, all the pair could see around them were boarded up homes and a small row of storage garages. Haresh's advice, about making the place you're hiding in not look like it's trying to hide anything, had stuck with Nick, so he opted to hide in one of the storage garages. They had managed to crawl under one of the garage doors that wouldn't quite shut all the way and once they were in, they grabbed some boxes, sheets, and anything else they could find in the lockup to hide the gap between the garage door and the floor. Luckily for the pair, there were some old chairs and dusty sheets in the garage which the pair used to sleep on; unluckily for them, however, there wasn't any food or water in the unit.

Unbeknownst to Nick, Emily had "forgotten" to return a tin of pineapple chunks from her bag which she had taken from Haresh's stash. While he was asleep, she decided to help herself to the tin. She felt slightly guilty about not sharing the food with her big brother, but that pang of guilt disappeared as soon as she had opened the tin and devoured its contents.

She hid the empty tin behind some boxes at the back of the garage and that's when she heard what sounded like a bolt of lightning hitting a metal roof. She almost jumped out of her skin at the noise; her dread grew when she heard muffled voices passing by when a small group of people started banging on the storage garage doors and chatting loudly as they walked down the alley past them. She didn't know if these people were dangerous or not, but she was terrified nonetheless by the loud sounds and thoughts of what could happen if they were found. Nick had barely flinched when the group had walked past. She slowly manoeuvred herself over to Nick and laid down next to him. She draped her arm over him and closed her eyes as the small mob outside disappeared past them.

10th April 2009, 01:33
Hendon Way, Barnet, London

For a Friday night in town, the streets were very quiet. There were a few drunken lads sitting on the floor outside of a closing kebab shop, shovelling strips of a lamb doner meat into their mouths while they drunkenly giggled about the night's activities. A short African nurse in her late forties clutched onto her handbag as she walked past the drunken men. The nurse was returning home from a long shift at work. Her eyes were so tired and red that she could've easily been mistaken for someone who had been tortured with sleep deprivation. Fortunately for the nurse, the three lads ignored her; however, the same cannot be said for the nineteen-year-old Emily King who was wearing a short red dress, had her high heels in her hands and black mascara streaming down her face. Despite having a face like Alice Cooper, when she walked past the men, she still received the typical cat calls a young woman like herself would get from disgusting men when walking down the street.

"Boys, boys, look. Fucking hell, she's gorgeous. I'd give my right bollock to have five minutes alone with that," said one of the drunken idiots who thought he was whispering.

Emily did her best to ignore the men.

"Awww she's been crying. Oi love, did you get in an argument with your mates over a boy? Why don't you come over here and we'll look after you," yelled the man.

Emily turned to the men and gave them the middle finger and continued to walk bare foot down the street. She went to a nearby fried chicken shop and ordered herself some chips. The lone worker in the restaurant, who was as eager to get home as Emily was, said she could wait in the restaurant while he closed up. Emily took out her phone and began texting someone,

Hey, I'm in Hendon. Bad night. You awake? Was hoping that lift was still available? xxx.

A minute later her phone beeped and vibrated on the table. She opened the message which read, *Be there in 10 x.*

Nine and a half minutes later, the sound of a car horn beeping signalled to Emily that her ride had arrived. She'd recognised the car right away; the driver's door was the same pale silver that matched the rest of the car, but the passenger's side door was a much darker and matted silver. The original door had been taken off by a drunk on a moped, who drove straight into the open passenger door a few months prior. Fortunately for the moped rider, his head stayed on his shoulders; but he did suffer a broken leg, a £2500 fine, and six months community service doing voluntary work in a local charity shop.

At first, Nick was annoyed with the mechanics who told him that they only had a replacement door in a slightly different colour; however, as time went by, he found his mismatch doors to be quite the conversation starter and he grew to love them. He also took small pleasure in knowing that the slightly off colour of his car irritated his girlfriend. Emily and Nick would often tease her about the car and discuss what other outrageous adjustments they could make to the car to really make it sparkle.

Once Emily had gotten into the car, she quickly realised from the red lines in her brother's eyes that he was probably about to go to sleep when she texted him. How he had got in his car and drove to her so quickly was beyond her, but she was always grateful for how good and sweet he was to her. He never wanted to be a father figure to her; he only ever wanted to be her big brother, but somehow, he wound up being both. Fortunately, he always knew which hat to wear when he was with her.

Nick turned up the car stereo and drove away as the melodic lyrics of Damian Marley filled the car. Nick was always introducing Emily to new music. She'd often make fun of him for having such an eclectic and varied taste, but she secretly admired him for embracing his love of different things without a shred of embarrassment.

The pair barely said a word to each other during the journey; Nick could clearly see that Emily had been crying after a bad night out so he wanted to let her tell him what was wrong instead of trying to fish it out of her.

The pair pulled up outside of his flat.

"What are you doing? Aren't you taking me home?" asked Emily quizzically.

"Nah, you can crash here tonight. Plus, I can't be arsed to take you all the way home now. I'll drop you off in the morning," replied Nick.

"Are you sure I won't be in the way. Isn't the lady of the house working tomorrow?"

"Didn't I tell you? She quit her job. They kept asking her to work extra hours but they weren't paying her for it, so she refused. When they said she had to, she decided to quit instead."

"Are you serious? Did her contract say anything about extra hours?"

"No, we both looked it over and we looked online to see if it was legal but we couldn't find anything. The worst thing was the Job Centre. When she went down there for some advice, the guy we spoke to said she should have done what she was told as it was her job. Another lady said she'd have to wait twelve weeks before she could sign on because she quit. She's pissed. We both are," explained Nick.

"That's awful. Sorry about that Nick. I feel a bit silly for being upset now."

"Let's go inside. The missus will be asleep and we can grab a drink in the living room/kitchen/dining room/tiny shitty studio flat that I live in."

Nick walked into the living room with two glasses of Jim Beam and ice. He gave the least chipped glass to Emily and took a sip from his glass before collapsing onto the frayed futon next to her.

"Come on then. What's up? Why am I picking you up at one in the morning? Are you and Dan fighting again?" Emily took a long sip from her glass and avoided making eye contact with Nick. "I'll take that as a yes. What happened this time?" probed Nick.

"In all honesty, I don't know. We were out with his snobby rich city friends who he knows I hate, and whenever we are out with them, he becomes exactly like them and I always feel out of place. I tried my best to get on with them, but the same thing happens that always happens, they start making digs about me being a cleaner and say that I should try looking for a proper job. I couldn't bite my tongue anymore and I lost it with one of his douchebag friends. After that, Dan flipped out on me and ignored me for the rest of the night, so I left. I think we may be done," said Emily, not seeming overly upset at her revelation.

"Wow, really? Just like that? You don't think you can work on it? Trust me, I'm the last person who wants to keep seeing you get hurt. But, as you know, I'm a big romantic and I believe in working on a relationship. Me and madam in there have had our fair share of ups and downs, but we work on it and we always seem to come out stronger."

"Even when you refer to her as madam?" said Emily playfully.

Emily smiled at her brother and then stared pensively at her glass. She slid her fingers over the rim of the glass thinking about what Nick had said. She knew Nick had a good point, but unlike her brother, she wasn't a romantic. She'd had several boyfriends in the past few years that had all ended for the same reason; she was distant, and all of her previous partners never felt like she was truly invested in the relationship. She never knew exactly where her reluctance to be in a serious relationship came from. At times, she thought that it may have stemmed from being raised by two loving and caring men, which subconsciously made her feel like no man would ever be as good as her brother or father.

Nick broke his sister's trance when he poured more

whiskey into her glass. She looked back up at her big brother who was smiling at her. "You do what you need to do Em, as long as it's right for you. I'll back you no matter what. And if you need me to go and smack that boy around the ear for you, you know I will," said Nick before finishing his drink.

Emily was always pleasantly surprised by her brother, whenever she thought that he may not fully understand how she felt, he would reassure her and tell her that he would support her decision no matter what she decided. She finished her drink and cuddled up to her brother on the sofa.

"You better not fall asleep on me again loser. Falling asleep together as kids was cute but now it's just creepy," joked Nick.

5th June 2016, 22:44
St James Terrace Mews, Camden, The Independent State of England

It had been a long time since Emily had felt the cosy warmth of a really good deep sleep. She fell into such a deep sleep that she had unwittingly woken up her brother with her loud snoring an hour before she woke herself up. As she jarred forward and opened her eyes, she saw Nick standing in front her packing their bags and laughing at her.

"What's going on? What are you doing?" she asked rubbing the sleep from her eyes.

"It's time to go. The sound of your snoring has probably alerted half the city of our whereabouts," teased Nick. Emily gave him the middle finger and grabbed her bag, "Let's go."

After the nonstop chaos over the last forty-eight hours, the pair allowed themselves a moment of clarity and enjoyment by travelling through the dark paths of Primrose Hill so they could take in the breath-taking views of what used to be the famous London skyline. They realised the risk they were taking by standing on top of one the most popular hills in the city, but despite being in the midst of so much danger, they couldn't help themselves. The iconic sight of London the siblings once remembered was drastically different now; the buildings remained intact, but the lights that once shone from the BT Tower, the Shard, and the London eye now lived in the shadows of their former selves.

After a few minutes of peace and calm, the pair continued on their journey and walked down the hill towards Chalk Farm. When suddenly, out of the corner of his eye, a small flash of light in the distance caught Nick's attention. He strained his eyes towards the silhouette of the London Eye, certain that he saw a faint white light moving in one of the pods of the large Ferris Wheel, a light so small it could've come from a mobile phone or a key chain torch. However, as quickly as it had caught his eye, it had disappeared.

"Everything okay?" asked Emily.

"Yeah, I thought I saw something," said Nick. He rubbed his eyes and figured that the lack of sleep must've been playing tricks on him. "It's nothing.

I'm just tired. Let's get a move on so we can camp up somewhere safe and get some proper sleep."

By the time they had reached Hampstead Heath, they were dripping with sweat. They'd managed to do an hour and ten minute walk in less than thirty-five minutes. Nick led Emily half way through the heath, and then cut through a small wooded area which led onto Spaniards Road; a quiet but wealthy street filled with huge houses hidden amongst large trees and minimal lighting, a perfect place to hide out for the night uninterrupted.

Nick's insider knowledge of how the city had developed and was run over the years became a very valuable tool for the pair.

When the looting and rioting was at its worst, the biggest and most expensive houses and flats were ransacked early on in the rebellion and then were quickly forgotten about; likely because most people figured that there was nothing left of value to steal from these places. Many of the homeless communities found shelter in these mansions; however, Nick knew which areas were vacant and which weren't. He had made sure he considered even the most minor detail when planning his escape.

Spending a few days in one of these expensive houses not only gave Nick and Emily the sanctuary they needed, but it was also Nick's way of surprising his sister and fulfilling a dream she had always had of owning a huge house in Hampstead. Growing up in a tiny two bedroom flat in Harrow always left Emily pining for more in life. Her aspirations were often material and she would constantly tell anyone who would listen that she was going to be a famous celebrity who lived in a huge mansion in Hampstead, with a swimming pool and her own personal bar. Her wants in life had since changed over the years; whereas, before she sought out fame and celebrity, she now yearned for something much simpler but just as unattainable. She pined for freedom and a quiet life. Every time he looked at his sister, he was reminded of the fact that he took away the simplicity of her life and filled it with dreams of wanting to escape from the horrors in the world.

His knowledge of the streets hadn't failed him when they arrived to a quiet and deserted road. The pair could take their time in deciding which luxury multi million pound flat or house they could camp in for a few days; however, exhaustion outweighed desire, and the pair decided to pick the first house on the street which happened to be a six bedroom detached house with a rooftop terrace and an indoor swimming pool.

Nick and Emily stood in awe of the grand house.

"It's nice and all Nick, but couldn't you have picked a house with great white pillars in the entrance way? It's like you don't know me at all," said Emily playfully.

The pair climbed over the front garden fence, scaled the house using a ladder Nick had found in the triple garage and climbed onto the rooftop terrace. Despite how useful ladders and toolboxes were in times like these, nobody ever seemed to take them. *"Far too heavy to lug around,"* thought Nick.

Once they had climbed onto the terrace above the garage, Nick lifted the ladder up onto it and the pair entered the flat through a smashed patio door. After their most recent encounter with breaking and entering, they were much more thorough in scanning the house for threats. It took them forty-five minutes to survey the entire house and ensure that they were safe. Among the wreckage and mess in the house, they managed to salvage a decent stash of food and a couple bottles of what they could only presume was expensive red wine. "Rich people in rich houses must have rich wine," deduced Emily.

The view from the rooftop terrace didn't quite compare to the sight from atop Primrose Hill, but it was a beautiful view of Hampstead Heath, none-theless. Even the slightly burnt pub and abandoned cars in front of the Heath didn't take away from the view of the night sky. With it being a beautifully clear and warm night, Nick and Emily decided to drag a partially torn king-sized mattress onto the terrace and sleep outside. Neither of them had said a word to each other; they just lay on the mattress gazing up at the stars.

Once again, Nick was the first to drift off to sleep; however, this time it didn't take long for Emily to follow. Her eyes began to get heavy and she finally let sleep take her and give her the rest she had been so desperately looking for.

Shortly after she had fallen asleep, unbeknownst

to the pair, a particularly dangerous gang had ventured further out of Westminster than they should have and were ransacking the nearby pub only a few hundred meters away from the sleeping siblings.

CHAPTER 8

6th June 2016, 03:08
Spaniards Road, Camden, The Independent State of England

She was wanted by the most powerful and dangerous person in the country, yet she was not only able to sleep, but she was able to dream. Being under the stars, allowed her to take a moment and bask in her past triumph over The Boss and the embarrassment she must've felt when she openly defied her. When The Boss had found out that Emily had been secretly involved with someone from a resistance borough, she knew The Boss would finally take action against her after she had spent months trying to get under her skin. She had been chipping away at The Boss in hopes that Nick would see that nobody was exempt from The Boss' wrath, even his sister. It was quite the gamble, but she took solace in knowing that her brother would do the right thing if it meant the safety of his sister. She had some guilt towards the poor fool she was using for her plan, and she tried not to think about what had happened to him; all she wanted to do was get her and her brother away from the madness.

Her mind was free to wander and for the first time in a long time there were no nightmares, only a tranquil dream. She was flying. She was soaring through the clear blue sky looking down at a big empty field with not a person, plane, or bird in sight. She quickly realised, however, that she wasn't flying in the traditional sense, but she was falling, peacefully gliding down to earth. The large parachute backpack strapped to her was so light that she hadn't even noticed it was there. The fall felt eternal. She had all the time she wanted to look out onto the world, to be above everything, to admire the beauty of the land and feel the emptiness of her surroundings and the clarity in her head. After what felt like hours of drifting through the sky, she began to get closer to the ground, and decided she should finally pull the cord of her parachute and gracefully touch down onto the floor below.

She tugged the release cord but nothing happened. She pulled it again, and again, and again, but nothing; there was no movement, not even a rustling from the parachute. She was approaching the floor at an alarming speed, faster than she had been travelling during her entire descent.

Panic began to set in as all of those thoughts of happiness and lucidity were replaced with anxiety and an uncontrollable fear. No matter how many times or how hard she pulled the release cord of the parachute, it refused to open. She was left with two options – continue to frantically try and release the chute or accept her fate with the knowledge that despite the very real feelings of fear and dread coursing through her, people can't die in a dream. She opted for the latter and stared her fate head on; with open eyes and a free mind, she accepted that the world was about to collide with her, and she was ready.

When she smashed against the ground, she was proven right, a person cannot die in their dream; however, the sound she heard when she impacted with the earth's surface was not the sound she had expected to hear. Instead of a splat or a thud, she heard the sound of smashed glass.

"Am I made of glass in my dreams?" thought Emily.

The blue sky hovering over her began to turn black and she heard more glass smashing around her.

"Is someone laughing?"

She opened her eyes and sat up from the mattress. The parachute on her back had disappeared, but the sounds of smashed glass from her dream remained and echoed throughout the night sky over Hampstead Heath.

Nick was dead to the world. *"The man could sleep through an explosion,"* thought Emily.

She stood up and slowly peered over the small brick wall on the rooftop terrace to try and see where the noise was coming from. A loud crash caught her attention and directed her to the source of the noise; however, when she looked towards the half-burnt pub, she couldn't see anyone or anything there. *"It must be a wild animal,"* she thought.

She turned to go back to sleep, hoping that her dreams of falling would be replaced with something more enjoyable; but when she sat back down on the bed, she immediately stood back up again as the very clear noise of a door being thrust open and a group of people laughing and yelling drew her attention back to the pub once more.

She rushed over to the wall and peered over it again to see who was loitering at the pub. She knew she was fairly well hidden, but she remained cautious, nonetheless. She couldn't quite make out any of the faces, but she counted six people outside of the pub and could hear a few more inside. *"Probably stealing alcohol left over in the cellar,"* she thought.

There were four men and two women outside. One of the men had a head of bright florescent orange hair which she had only ever seen on one other person before. During her stay at Downing Street she was introduced to all manner of people, at the beginning it was mostly celebrities, politicians and other high profile people; however, as things descended further into chaos, she would be introduced to up and coming gang leaders who worked for The Boss.

She didn't remember all of the gang leaders she had met, but for one obvious orange reason, she remembered one man. She often referred to him as "Mr. Pumpkin Head." Not only was his hair and face bright orange but his head was as empty as a hollowed out pumpkin. His name was Ron and he was also the leader of "The Westenders" gang, one of the more violent gangs that operated throughout the Westminster borough.

Ron and his gang were treading on territory that wasn't theirs. *"Probably out looking for trouble,"* thought Emily. The Westenders worked very closely with The Boss. Ron believed it was because he offered something unique to The Boss, his muscle and loyalty. However, the truth was, The Boss knew she could manipulate that pumpkin headed fool with a simple bat of her eyelids and a few bags of coke. Emily had only heard passing comments about The Westenders and what they were capable of, but it was enough to know that they were dangerous. They couldn't risk being seen or caught by them; they had to leave and fast.

She looked back at Nick who began to stir from the noise the gang was making. She realised that they weren't just yelling amongst each other for fun; but they were yelling and laughing at two members of the group, a woman and a man.

Ron grabbed the woman by the hair and shoved her to the floor; the man next to her leapt towards Ron and took a swing at him, however, before he could make any contact with Ron, he was hit over the head with a half full bottle of whiskey. The couple were pulled to their knees and surrounded by the other gang members.

"Oh my god!" said Emily out loud.

She suddenly felt the calloused hands of her brother covering her mouth and pulling her to the floor.

"What the hell are you doing? If that moron sees us, we are done for. He has a direct line to The Boss, and he will not take us back before getting a few blows in first," whispered Nick.

"There are people down there that need help. We have to do something," replied Emily.

"We don't have to do anything. We have our plan and we are sticking to it. Those people down there have nothing to do with us. We don't get involved," said Nick, who went back to the mattress and began packing his things.

"We can't do nothing. You know better than anyone what these gangs are capable of, especially Ron and his lot. How can you watch more innocent people get hurt? He could kill them!" stressed Emily.

Nick ignored Emily and continued to pack his bag.

"Isn't this why you're doing this? Isn't this why you escaped, to end all of this? To change what this place has become? After The Boss, you have the most blood on your hands. You want to save people, well go on then. Down there are two people who need saving," continued Emily.

Nick zipped up his bag and threw it over his shoulder.

"I have the power to end this. I'm thinking of the many, which means, I can't sacrifice everything for the few – meaning those two down there. They were stupid enough to get themselves into trouble so now they are on their own. Trust me, there is a much bigger picture at play here."

Emily looked back at the couple, who were surrounded by The Westenders, she was unsure if she should listen to Nicks' logical thinking or to her instinct to help someone in need.

"We have to go now while they're distracted," demanded Nick.

The woman on her knees let out a painful scream as she watched her male companion being repeatedly punched in the face, her screams sent a cold chill down Emily's spine who could no longer bare the sound of her cries of agony. It had become a sound she had been all too familiar with over the last few years.

"You're right Nick. You do have the power to end this all, so why don't you go and do that. I'm going to do what's right and try to keep what's left of my morality," said Emily before grabbing her bag and jumping off of the rooftop terrace to the soft grass below.

"EMILY!!!" shouted Nick in alarm.

Nick rushed over to the edge of the roof and watched as his sister ran through the back garden of the house and disappear towards a fight she couldn't win alone.

"For fuck sake Emily!" said Nick, feeling exasperated with his stubborn sister.

Nick looked over to the floor below and jumped onto the grass hoping he could catch up to his sister before she got herself killed trying to do the right thing.

CHAPTER 9

6th June 2016, 04:17
Spaniards Road, Camden, The Independent State of England

The sound of his head hitting the floor was a repulsive noise to all who could hear it. Fortunately for Will, he didn't hear this noise, instead he heard more of a muffled tone emanating through his ears.

"STOP IT. You're going to kill him," screamed Izzy.

Tara, the only other woman present in the gang, walked over to Will's girlfriend Izzy and slapped her around the face so hard that she fell to the floor. A large red mark instantly appeared on her pale white cheek. Tara pulled her back to her knees by her long jet-black hair and screamed in her face. "You'll go first if you don't shut yer fookin mouth pet."

Ron laughed maniacally as he watched his reliable gang of psychopaths go to work on Will and Izzy. He picked Will up off of the floor in a much gentler way than Tara had done with Izzy and carefully wiped the blood out of his brown and sunken eyes. He thanked Ron by spitting a large amount of blood onto his white Adidas trainers. Ron looked down at his now blood stained trainers and laughed to himself again.

"This lad has some serious balls on him. Oi Tara, you seen the size of the nuts on this guy?" asked Ron.

"He looks like a little long-haired top knot pussy from where I'm standing pet," replied Tara.

"You hear that? She thinks you're a pussy. I say she's wrong. I say you're a man with great big balls. But guess what, friend? I eat guys with balls twice the size of yours for breakfast," said Ron.

"You eat guys' balls for breakfast? That's cool dude. Its 2016, you'll get no judgement from me. You must be the daddy though right? And that must make your boy over there the bitch? Although, from the way you hit, you could easily be the bitch," said Will defiantly.

Ron smiled at Will and grabbed him by his shirt, he pulled his huge fist back with the intention of knocking Will out, however, before he could swing his fist towards Will's face, he was distracted by a loud crash and the sound of smashed glass coming from inside of the pub. Ron pushed Will to the floor and turned to one of "The Westenders" standing behind him, a dopey looking man with a powerful physique and an impressive upper body, but who had unquestionably skipped his leg day workouts.

"Jay, get your big dumb arse in there and shut those idiots up will you. I'm trying to work out here and I want to be able to hear my fists hitting this pricks face. If you have to hurt them to shut them up, do it. Just keep them quiet," ordered Ron.

Jay slowly wandered to the back entrance of the building awkwardly manoeuvring his massive frame through the small pub door.

"You cannot get the staff anymore, am I right mate?" said Ron, who crouched down next to a battered Will. "Listen mate. I'm going to be honest with you. I like you. You're a tough bastard and a funny fucker. I could use a man like you. What you reckon? You want to join us? We do what we want, when we want, and The Boss absolutely loves me. You'll be set for life."

Will looked towards his frightened and dishevelled girlfriend.

"Sorry fella but this offer is only for you, not for your little bit on the side," explained Ron.

Ron gave a nod to Tara who took Ron's cue and kicked Izzy in the face, instantly crumpling her to the floor. Will jumped to his feet as a surge of passion and adrenaline came over him and he ran towards Tara with his fists drawn. He got a few feet away from her before he was clotheslined to the floor by one of Ron's lackeys. Ron let out a big sigh of frustration and slowly strutted over to Will who was gasping for air on the floor.

"I wish you had made a better choice. What's was your name again? Come on, don't be shy. You can tell me."

Will struggled to speak after being knocked to the floor. He continued to struggle when Ron pressed his large foot down on Will's stomach and leaned in towards his face.

"I said, what is your name? I only ask so I can tell everyone the name of the idiot I destroyed who refused to join me," explained Ron.

Will continued to cough as he tried to sputter out a sentence.

"Will, my name is Will, and I'd rather die than join someone who blindly follows that crazy bitch," gasped Will, as blood began to spill out of his mouth and onto his dark curly beard.

Ron waved his hand to Tara and ushered her towards him. She handed him a spotlessly clean and shiny nine inch knife. Ron grabbed Will by his collar and dragged him over to the floor towards Izzy, he threw him down in front of her, and held Will's bloodied face inches away from her as she sobbed in front of the love of her life.

"I gave you a chance Will, now you get to watch your little lady friend die. And as she takes her final breath, she'll get to see you die too," whispered Ron sadistically in Will's ear.

With tears in her eyes Izzy begged for Ron to stop. She screamed in pain again when Tara yanked her head back exposing her neck. Ron held the knife to her throat forcing her to close her eyes in fear.

"No, no, no, sweetheart, you have to watch him watch you die, now open those pretty green eyes for me," whispered Ron.

Tara squeezed Izzy's face until she opened her eyes. "Why are you doing this? You don't have to do this for her. Please let us go," pleaded Izzy.

Tara squeezed Izzy's face even harder. "This isn't

for her you dumb cow, this is for us. We don't have to do this, we get to. She gave us this world and now we get to run it, you understand me pet. We're the strong and you are the weak. Do her Ron. I'm getting bored and want a drink before those idiots finish it all," demanded Tara.

Ron winked at Izzy in a final show of disrespect and wickedness and pressed the knife hard against her throat. Will kept his gaze locked on Izzy who looked back at him with tears in her eyes.

Will's attention was diverted momentarily when he saw a bright blaze of fire reflected in Izzy's big emerald eyes. Ron and Will both turned around and saw that the back entrance of the pub was engulfed in flames. Everyone was in stunned silence as the merry laughter coming from the rest of "The Westenders" inside of the pub had now turned into screams of horror and distress. Before Ron or anyone else could react to what was happening inside the pub, a flaming bottle soared through the air which narrowly missed Ron and landed on the chest of the gang member standing next to Tara. The bottle smashed and exploded into a great ball of fire setting him alight.

An enraged Ron looked around the car park, trying to see who would dare attack him, but the area was dimly lit and surrounded by tall trees and bushes. Besides the bright flames coming from the pub and his recently deceased companion, he couldn't see anything around him. The bottles had flown in from two different directions, so Ron had no idea how many people were out there; not that it mattered to him. Ron believed brawn was better than brains, and he refused to ever back down from a fight.

"Come out you fucking cowards and show yourselves. Do you know who I am?" shouted Ron.

Tara ran over to Ron, dodging the flaming pile on the floor that was once her friend and frantically began pulling at his arm to wrench him away from the bedlam around them. Ron locked-on to a bush by the side of the car park when he saw a small flash; perhaps the sparks from a lighter struggling to catch light.

He pushed Tara off him and began marching towards the bush. As he neared the bush, he heard a familiar voice calling his name; it was a voice he knew all too well. He even once considered that voice to belong to a good friend. Their relationship was always one sided; Nick never considered Ron his friend. Like The Boss, he humoured him and manipulated his simple mind into getting him to do whatever he needed doing. Nick often joked with The Boss that for a guy like Ron, a few bottles of vodka and a few grams of coke would go a long way; little did he know, she would actually use drugs and alcohol as a method into manipulating the senseless bully. When Nick confronted The Boss about her questionable methods, she justified it by telling him that Ron and his kind represented the scum and laziness of this world, so it was okay to use them and help them kill themselves.

Ron turned around and glared at Nick who was

now standing out in the open with the fires he had created, slowly burning out around him.

"Oh shit, so it's true. You ARE a traitor. I guess I owe that poor kid I almost killed an apology; I lost my cool when he told me you had betrayed her. I thought he was spreading vicious lies about my good friend, and you know how much I hate liars," said Ron.

"You know she was always playing you mate? We both were. She thinks you're a fool, she gets you to do whatever she wants while you think you're actually making a difference, it's a win-win for her," said Nick.

Tara shoved Ron causing him to break his focus from Nick. "What are you waiting for? Do him in. He's a bitch, and with him out of the way The Boss will make you her new number two," said Tara excitedly.

Ron looked back at Nick and smiled his crooked smile. "You fucked it mate, and she's right. With you gone, I can step up," said Ron, pointing his knife at Nick. "Sorry to do this to you pal. I always really liked you."

He took a step towards Nick but was immediately halted when he heard the smashing of glass followed by the unconscious body of Tara suddenly at his feet.

"Oops, it looks like she's had too much to drink," said Emily who was stood next to Ron with a broken glass bottle in her hand. "And yes, I did just say that."

With Ron briefly distracted, Nick charged at him

and tackled him to the floor, frantically trying to get his arm around Ron's throat so he could choke him out. Emily ran over to help Will and Izzy back to their feet.

"Are you guys okay?" she asked, offering her hand to Izzy.

She reluctantly took Emily's hand and pulled herself up; the pair worked together and helped Will to his feet as he struggled to stand by himself.

"Who the hell are you guys?" asked Izzy.

"We're the good guys."

"Did you really just say that?"

"Yes, I did. I'm so freaking hyped right now and I can't stop thinking of tacky one liners to say," said Emily, with a big cheesy grin on her face.

The ladies put Will's arms over their shoulders and started to walk him towards the tall trees of Hampstead Heath. "Wrap it up Nick, we have to go," shouted Emily.

Nick struggled to keep Ron, the much bigger man restrained on the floor; he tightened his hold on Ron's throat until he began to fade away. His eyes became heavier and heavier as he struggled to get any air to his tiny brain, but when his eyes began to shut for good, a burst of adrenaline came over him and he began pounding on Nick's legs with his huge gorilla like fists. Nick did his best to keep his hands clasped together and not lose his grip around Ron's thick neck, but Ron's power was much greater than his; something Nick was very aware of having sparred with him in the past. He continued to repeatedly hammer down on Nick's legs until he could no longer take the pain and loosened his grip from around Ron's neck.

Ron crawled on the floor after falling out of Nick's arms breathless; meanwhile Nick tried to get the feeling back into his legs. Ron got to his feet first and quickly mounted Nick; he put his huge hands around Nick's throat and returned the favour by squeezing the life out of him. Feeling the pressure of Ron's hands on his throat made him realise that he had massively underestimated how strong Ron actually was. He began to fall asleep much quicker than Ron had; he fought for breath and tried his hardest to keep his neck as stiff and tight as he could.

From the corner of his eye, he could see his sister running towards him, a sight that filled him with even more panic as he knew Ron had always had a thing for his sister; and with nobody to stop him he would have his way with her, one way or another.

Emily charged at Ron and cracked a bottle over his head. The bottled didn't break on his large pumpkin like cranium and the impact barely fazed him. Izzy grabbed the bottle from Emily's hand and had a go at hitting Ron over the skull. The bottle remained intact but left the big man wobbly and dazed. It took one final blow from Will that finally smashed the bottle over Ron's bonce and knocked him to the floor in a heap. Will fell on top of Ron and unleashed a fury of fists on his face until he was no longer moving. Nick and Izzy had to pry Will off of Ron and drag him back towards the darkness of Hampstead Heath, leaving behind them a scene one would usually find in an old Western film after an epic saloon fight.

"All I wanted to do was give my sister a decent night's sleep," thought Nick, realising that his already impossible mission was going to be a lot more trying than he had originally thought.

CHAPTER 10

13th February 2012, 18:00
Woodcock Hill, Harrow, London

Her social media presence had blown up over the latter part of 2011, and her YouTube videos had been racking up huge numbers. Most of the appearances she'd been invited to had been fairly low key and the shows or events she was on were with young twenties-something hosts who she felt at ease with. She had started getting used to people admiring and praising her, though this certainly wasn't something she thought she'd ever experience. The only admiration she had received like this before was when her closest friends had peer pressured her into mounting the lion statues at Trafalgar Square without wearing any underwear on a night out.

Although she was on her home turf, she felt uneasy walking into Kenton Hall for the "Fresh and Wise" event she had been invited to. The low-key event hadn't been hugely publicised. It was mostly aimed at the fifteen to twenty-five-year-old residents of the Harrow borough and was promoted as an event that would educate the younger generations on

British politics and how the government affected their lives. The event was sold as a way of giving the younger generation a voice and allowing them to express how they really felt about the city they lived in; however, The Boss was sceptical that it would go down that way. Nonetheless, she'd hoped by showing up she could make a difference. Her motivation for beginning her blogs, vlogs, and endless social media campaigns was to point out that there were large groups of people in the country and city who wanted to speak up, but were not able to vocalise themselves on a platform in which they would be heard. She wanted to act as their representative and speak for them.

Nick, who usually attended these events with The Boss, couldn't accompany her that day due to being stuck at work on a mandatory training day that he didn't want to be at. She had no family, so in Nick's place, The Boss had asked her other friends to come along to support her. However, she knew that the real reason they came was to get as much free food as they could, and hopefully get the chance to mingle with some celebrities. *"Great friends they are,"* thought The Boss.

Nick had organically filled the role as manager to The Boss, a role which meant that she could focus her time on her content; while Nick dealt with the organisation of her many appearances, phone calls and emails. Unfortunately for Nick, the role of manager to a D-list YouTube star didn't pay as well as he'd have liked, which meant he had to continue working at his full-time job simultaneously.

The venue was a tiny place. It was mostly used for gaudy wedding receptions or sweet sixteen birthday parties. The stained carpet was a combination of both sticky and wet, and the entire building had a damp beer infused aroma that lingered in the air. The only thing overpowering the stench of stale booze was the high intensity strength urinal cakes coming from the bathrooms. The smell immediately took The Boss back to her days with her second foster family and all those late nights she spent at her foster dad's cricket clubhouse over the summer. She was convinced that the urinal cake smell was intentionally made to be that strong to trick the regulars into thinking that they were actually drinking in a clean establishment.

Her friends were being steered towards the main crowd before the show began leaving The Boss by herself backstage. Even though she always went out on to stage or on to a TV show by herself, she always felt at ease knowing Nick was with her backstage, keeping her composed and going over what she was going to say. This time was different, and his absence was notable. She took a deep breath and reminded herself that this was no different to any of the other appearances she had done before; the only difference was that instead of a zany celebrity hosting the show and mildly flirting with her, she was sharing the stage with a local politician who was different to her in every way – in class, in education, and in stature. His cloth was cut from that of rich parents, top quality schooling and Ted Baker suits; whereas the closest thing she had to a suit was a pink tracksuit with the words 'JUICY' scrawled across the back of the trousers.

Councillor Suresh Nehete was already sitting backstage in his three-piece suit. He looked composed and calm which meant The Boss could add another thing to the list of things that made them different. He stood up from his chair and greeted her. They didn't have time to chit chat, as they were swiftly escorted towards centre stage. The host was already onstage thanking everyone for coming before introducing The Boss and Suresh to the stage. The Boss continued to breathe and tried her best to calm her nerves behind the curtain. Suresh noticed how uneasy she was and felt he should say something to her.

"It'll be okay. The people have come here tonight because they knew we were going to be here. They're here for us, so be yourself and you can't go wrong," he whispered.

She smiled at him, shocked at the notion of a nice and caring politician. Perhaps she had judged this man too soon. "Thank you," she said politely.

The pair received their cue and walked out onto stage. Suresh, the more confident of the two, took the lead and entered onto stage first to a barely audible applause. The Boss walked out a few paces behind and instantly had had her breath taken away from her by the deafening cheers and applause of five hundred people who filled the hall. The Boss stopped in her tracks, and was overcome with emotion and taken aback by the ovation she received. Those feelings of nervousness and trepidation she had felt prior to walking onto stage, had been replaced with an overwhelming feeling of gratitude, excitement, and most importantly acceptance. Acceptance from the people of her borough.

She waved to her adoring crowd and it became very apparent that the crowd was there for her and not for Suresh. Suresh looked to The Boss and smiled at her as she lapped up the crowd's approval, however, inside he was astonished at the reaction she had gotten.

Despite his confidence, Suresh wasn't used to crowds of this size. He had spoken in this venue many times, but he had never seen it filled with more than a hundred people at any one time. People were literally spilling out of the doors and trying to cram into the room so they could get their eyes on The Boss. The elderly members in the crowd who were sat in the front rows of the venue were less impressed; Suresh felt comfort in knowing that the older people were there for him and that he wasn't completely outnumbered. Past the first three rows of the hall, the crowd consisted mostly of young people ranging from thirteen to thirty-five, which was no surprise to The Boss as her videos were aimed at that demographic.

Suresh and The Boss sat down on the stage, and in turn, the cheering audience settled down as the event got under way. The host of the evening, Carl Rice, a former Harrow Councillor turned local businessman, acquired The Boss' contact details through his various connections, and he had personally invited her to speak at the event. He had hoped she would be able to speak directly to the younger people at the event about a variety of topics, including the benefits of voting, getting more involved with local politics, and to give her thoughts on the continued and sporadic rioting happening all over the country since Raymond Dwyer's death. When she first spoke with Carl, she was sceptical about his intentions; but after listening to him speak at length with her about her YouTube channel and the content she was producing, she knew that this man had not only done his research, but he made it very clear that he shared similar opinions to her. He struck her as a logical man who looked at the whole picture before making any snap decisions.

After doing some Googling of her own, she discovered why Carl was now a former Councillor; he was not a quiet man. He would openly criticise the internal politics that came with his job and all of the red tape he would have to deal with when trying to make any kind of change. After feeling like he was banging his head against a brick wall, he had taken some time away from politics and developed a much more distant relationship with the government.

He explained that the point of this public event was to have an open discussion, but he warned The

Boss to be prepared for a debate because chances are it would turn into one. The idea of debating was something that really worried her, but Carl reassured her that he would try and keep things on topic and help her in any way that he could if he felt like she was in over her head. Carl reintroduced the pair on stage, which gave The Boss another little ego boost when she received another huge round of applause. He then began running through an agenda of what would be discussed at the event. He opened up the floor to The Boss and Suresh for opening remarks and further discussion.

Suresh, being used to this type of atmosphere and questioning, dived straight into the conversation with his rehearsed spiel. He spoke about the mania and unlawful actions associated with the continued rioting in major cities all over the country, how he believed they were being organised by groups and weren't entirely random. He blamed social media sites for allowing such organisation, and he openly laughed at the notion of young people getting involved in politics or even voting.

"People like us are actively trying to encourage young people to get out and vote, however, there are many, including Raymond Dwyer, who would rather skate through life and encourage others to do the same," said Suresh.

A roar of boos erupted at his comments towards Raymond Dwyer and his implication that young people don't care. The Boss couldn't believe how different this man was presenting himself, when only ten minutes earlier, he seemed like a caring gentleman. When performing in front of the people, he came across as stubborn, biased, and reluctant to see any alternate views. *"How could someone be so welcoming one minute and so dismissive the next,"* thought The Boss.

Once he'd finished, Carl thanked him for his views and looked to The Boss for her rebuttal. She soon realised that it wasn't just Carl who was looking at her to speak, it was everyone; all eyes were on her, all but Suresh's.

"Now that we've heard from Suresh and his thoughts on these matters, let me invite you to share your views with the crowd. I'm sure I speak for everyone when I say that we are all on the edge of our seats in anticipation at what you have to say. The stage is yours Boss," said Carl.

The Boss licked her lips and opened her mouth ready to speak; however, before she could start, she was rudely interrupted by her counterpart on stage.

"Ha, Boss? Is this a joke to you people?" said Suresh loudly, "Boss? What is she the boss of? Discussing matters she has no earthly right in discussing and riling up the youth of today even further with her dangerous rhetoric?"

He looked out to a crowd of angry faces.

"In all honesty, I'm surprised you actually bothered to turn up today," continued Suresh. "Yes, when you are in front of a web camera or prancing around on TV talking about fighting the system or taking down "the man," and complaining about how unfair it is for people like you to get ahead in life, you have people succumbing to your drivel and actually believing what you're saying. But the problem with that is, when these people put their trust in you and then they realise you haven't got the faintest clue about how the "system" works, they will be left worse off after your fifteen minutes of fame has run out."

The large crowd began to murmur in disagreement.

"They will be left feeling even angrier and feeling even more helpless and they won't blame you, they'll attack people like us. Because instead of educating them on how politics and the government works, you blame everyone else and encourage them to blame everyone else as well. You're encouraging them to riot on the streets for days on end with no real cause except to bring anarchy to the country. I've tried to watch your videos, but after a few minutes of laughing to myself, I turn it off because I don't need a lecture from a little girl who knows nothing about unfair treatment of those seeking benefits, or the state of the NHS, or racial and sexual discrimination. I refuse to keep quiet when I see people like you acting like you know what goes on in this country, when in reality, you simply act like the pied piper and are luring people away from real help to a land of hopelessness and false promises," said Suresh in a fanatical speech.

The Boss was left gobsmacked after Suresh's epic tirade.

"There you go sweetheart. If you want to get involved in politics, you've learnt a very valuable lesson in how to call someone on their BS," whispered Suresh patronisingly.

The crowd erupted into a chorus of boos directed at Suresh, forcing Carl to leap back onto centre stage to try and calm down the hostile crowd. The Boss looked out to the crowd and realised that many of the people who were cheering for her when she first walked out on stage had now gone silent.

"Was what Suresh saying about me true?" thought The Boss. *"Am I a fake? Am I leading these people into a land of false hope and even harder times?"*

She allowed doubt to creep into her head, but only for a moment when she suddenly remembered something he had said in his verbal attack against her, something that took away the doubt and instead sparked up a white hot rage inside of her.

"Encouraging?" she whispered to herself, "Encouraging?" she said slightly louder, but was only faintly heard by Suresh as the shouting and anger in the room continued to drown her out. She clenched her fists and directed all of her attention to Suresh. "How dare you accuse me of encouraging the acts of rioting and looting that are happening around this country!" yelled The Boss.

The room fell silent.

"You claim you tried to watch my vlogs - perhaps if you actually took the time to listen to them properly you'd know that I have nothing but animosity and resentment towards the animals that roam the streets and harm innocent people. Looting from local businesses and causing complete mayhem in the country that I love. Yes, I've said and will continue to say that I understand why some people are fighting and have fought; fought being the key word. Fought for what they believe in. But in no way does that mean I condone the actions of these rioters. You talk as if you understand these people; you don't live in the same world as they do, so how could you understand? You say we are our own worst enemy, how the hell would you know?" snapped The Boss.

The quiet crowd began to rally behind The Boss once again.

"I'm a white female and I struggled for a long time to progress in this world, so how hard do you think it is for non-white people, or immigrants trying to make something of themselves; for people who could only go to state schools or talk using slang because that's all they were exposed to growing up. You don't know because you aren't one of us. Your lot pretend there isn't a divide, but the people rioting on the streets would beg to differ. And those who aren't rioting, people like me who are handling things peacefully, they know that there is a divide. But instead of rioting, we use our words. But guess what happens, we get laughed at or ignored by the likes of you. You could've come out here and debated with me or spoken to me with respect, as equals, but instead you accuse me of encouraging chaos. I'm sure I speak for everyone here in saying that people like us, are fed up of being looked down on by people like you."

"Okay everyone. Let's try and calm things down here and remember that we are here for the youngsters and not to take jabs at each other," interjected Carl.

Unfortunately for Carl, his words only made The Boss realise that many of the younger audience members were filming her on their phones, and she decided to get up out of her seat and talk to them directly.

"Thanks Carl, but I don't think this is a time for calm. I think we are a long way from calm in this country," said The Boss who had gained a newfound confidence.

He nodded at The Boss and sat back down next to Suresh, who for the first time during the event was dumbstruck.

"For all of you filming me, do me a favour and make sure what I'm about to say now, above all else, is posted and shared everywhere you can. I cry for my country and what it has become; not the destructive mess it is heading towards due to pissed off rioters and idiots with nothing better to do. But I cry for the people who are trying to live their lives. People who can't get a job because of uncontrolled illegal immigration and lack of regulation on people coming into our country and abusing the benefits system; exhausting hard working nurses and doctors whose time is taken up with people who contribute nothing to this country, but want a free hand out while hard working people are suffering and dying and losing what matters to them," exclaimed The Boss, whose eyes began to fill with tears at the thoughts of what her country and city had become.

It felt like the air had been sucked out of the room. Everyone, even those who disagreed with her, couldn't help but be drawn in by her passion.

"I may come across as preachy, but all I've ever done is speak about what I know and what I've seen and the equality that I believe does NOT exist in this country. I'm tired of fighting to be treated like a human being. I never wanted fame or followers; all I've ever wanted was a simple life. But issues in this country, which are out of my control, prevent me from having a simple life; like it does with millions of others that live here. I never thought people would listen to me, but for however long I am in this position and people are listening to me, I WILL act as the voice of the voiceless. I will be my own Boss, and if you like me or you don't, at least I speak my truth, which is more than I can say for people like Suresh and the people he represents."

The Boss looked back at Suresh, who finally seemed like he was listening to her.

"So, do me a favour Mr Nehete. Next time you go out and publicly speak to "your people," remember that you don't know a thing about your people, and if you ever need a lesson in relating to the people of this country, you be sure you come and pay a visit to The Boss."

The Boss throws the microphone towards Suresh, who fails to catch it, and then walks off stage.

Once she was backstage alone, her mind began to race. "*Oh my God. What have I done? Have I ruined it all? I laid into a politician in front of hundreds of people. People were filming. This is going to go viral in a heartbeat and I'll become a laughingstock,*" thought The Boss.

The fear rattled around her head. A loud humming noise broke her train of thought, however, she quickly realised that the humming noise was coming from the crowd in Kenton Hall who had exploded onto their feet and were cheering and applauding her, louder than she had ever heard before.

A huge smile appeared across her face when she recognised what was happening and she broke out into a hysterical giggle of pure elation. Her friends found her in this state of joy backstage a few minutes later. "Oh my God, that was unbelievable. That was nuts! You went up against that dickhead of a councillor and made him look like a fool," said one of her friends.

"Yeah," replied The Boss jubilantly.

"Yeah? Is that all you have to say?" said her friend who began to laugh.

"I saw red when that arsehole spoke to me like that. The guy has no clue what he represents. He pretended to be nice to me when we were back here, but then attacked me when we were in front of the people," said The Boss.

Her friends continued to laugh amongst themselves; they signalled to The Boss to look over her shoulder. Standing behind her was Suresh, who had been booed off of the stage. The Boss could hear Carl wrapping up the event and she faintly heard him apologising to the wild crowd for her walking off and the abrupt ending.

"Well young lady that was..." began Suresh, struggling to get his words out as he adjusted his tie, "... that was fantastic!" he finally said, to The Boss' surprise.

"Excuse me?" replied The Boss.

"It was incredible. I'm absolutely humiliated, of course; but you showed me and the people an honest and very real desire that lies within you. More importantly you have given me a tonne of free publicity, once the footage from those videos hit the internet. People are going to be talking about me. I'll be flooded with invitations to speak on the radio and on television to defend myself and give my rebuttal. This is excellent exposure for the both of us," said Suresh, unaware of the hatred she had developed for him.

"You are unbelievable," scoffed The Boss.

"Come on, you are clearly a very clever woman. Sometimes you have to play the game to get ahead and take any opportunity you can to get over. You know, you'd certainly make an excellent spokesperson for the Conservative party. That young and raw passion could make such a difference if it was channelled correctly. What do you say...Boss?" asked Suresh as he extended his hand to her.

Carl came backstage and interrupted the pair before The Boss could properly refuse Suresh's offer. "Wow, did you hear that ovation. Those people love you. You have a genuine following behind you, Boss. I don't know what you plan to do with all of this momentum, but don't waste it," said Carl.

She stared at Carl with an expression of irritation at the choice of words he had used when speaking to her. "Waste. What do you mean waste? I don't waste a thing. What is it with you lot today; is it 'speak down to women day' or something? You know what Carl, thank you for inviting me here today, but I really didn't appreciate you trying to speak for me out there. I can speak for myself and I certainly don't need your advice," said The Boss, who then turned her attention to Suresh.

"And you, I love how you think all of this is a game. What you do affects people's lives; people who are struggling every day. Let me make something clear, I am not an act and this is not a performance, and the sooner you lot realise that, then and only then, will I ever consider talking to either of you as equals."

Her phone began to vibrate in her pocket, "Excuse me gentlemen," said The Boss with a smug smirk.

As she walked away to answer her phone, her friends approached Suresh with their phones. "Hi, Mr Nehete, mind if we get a quick selfie with you?"

The Boss went to a nearby bathroom and saw that Nick was calling her.

"Hey, how did it go?" he asked.

She smiled to herself, "I'd say it went pretty well."

CHAPTER 11

9th June 2016, 15:50
High Rd, Barnet, The Independent State of England

Will had been in and out of consciousness over the last three days; Izzy and Emily had done their best to keep him alert and fed. During his recovery, Nick had spent his time making sure the abandoned cinema they were hiding in was secure and safe for as long as they needed it. He'd told Izzy and Emily that he had to keep busy so he could ensure that they were all safe; however, Emily really knew that he was trying to keep his distance from the group because he wasn't happy about being stuck with Izzy and Will.

He wouldn't dare show it, but he was thrilled to be hiding out in the cinema. When everyone had begun illegally downloading and streaming movies, leaving cinemas struggling for business, Nick had prided himself on paying full price to watch the latest releases on the silver screen. He made the effort to enjoy movies as they were intended to be viewed – especially when he got the cinema nearly all to himself.

Despite him secretly loving his temporary hide-out, he knew the few remaining bags of popcorn, sweets, and fizzy drinks would only sustain him and the others for a few more days and he was eager to continue on to Enfield. He was focused on the mission at hand, and all he wanted to do was lose the extra baggage he had accumulated and get him and his sister as far away from The Independent State of England as he could.

He was upstairs in the office spying through a small gap in a boarded up window, watching the citizens of the neutral borough of Barnet. The civilians that lived in the neutral boroughs and the resistance boroughs would often make sure they were well within their own territories and indoors when the sun went down. While the rioting had settled down over the last year, mostly because there was nothing left to loot, gang warfare and violent policing took over and it became increasingly easy to get caught up in a feud between rival gangs.

East Finchley was on the border of the neutral borough of Barnet, so more often than not some of the Camden gangs would try their luck with the locals in Barnet by harassing them or attempting to rob them. These gangs were small in numbers and were run by halfwits who were rejected by the larger gangs in the Camden borough. Nick had heard about these gangs, but as they were fairly harmless, he never felt the need to alert The Boss about them. He feared what she would do to them if she knew they were crossing into the neutral zone; although he despised these gangs, he didn't want to see people hurt if it was avoidable.

They had hoped that by allowing these neutral zones to operate separately from the other boroughs in the city, it would paint The Boss in a better light and change the perception of her as evil dictator to humble and fair leader. Unfortunately for her, the resistance groups didn't buy it. Nonetheless, she continued to allow the neutral boroughs to remain separate from the normal rules of the city, as long as they remained neutral; something she made crystal clear to anyone who joined the neutral communities and to the mayors who ran their respective boroughs.

Nick felt safe in Barnet, but he knew he had to get further into the borough to truly be out of harm's way. If any of these smaller gangs found him, they wouldn't hesitate to sound the alarm. "*What better way for one of these minor gangs to make a name for themselves by bringing me and Emily back to The Boss*," thought Nick.

"What you looking at?" asked Emily.

"I'm just people watching. I hate this; these people have no idea what to do with themselves. They're all just getting by, barely surviving," said Nick. "Speaking of surviving, how long until the new tag along is up and running?"

"Will, his name is Will and I'm no doctor, but Izzy and I think he's recovering well. We found a first aid kit and did what we could. I think he'll be okay. Look, I was thinking..." began Emily before being interrupted by Nick.

"Great. That's good to hear. Give it a few more days and then we can part ways with them."

"Nick. We can't abandon them here. They're in no condition to be left alone, even in the neutral zone."

"What do you want me to do Em? I can't let every stray we find come with us. I'm trying to get us out, me and you; anyone else will delay that from happening."

"It's two people. The least we can do is help them get further into Barnet so they're safe. That Izzy seems pretty tough, and Will can definitely take a punch or two, even if he does have a big mouth."

"They'll get in our way, trust me," said Nick stubbornly.

"I do trust you, but you also need to trust me. Your biggest problem has always been trusting others; you've always seen other people as delays, as objects in your way. You find it so hard to see the value in other people. You say they'll get in our way, I say they can be of use to us. We know people are after us, so why not have some backup. You may not want to admit it, but they aren't the only ones who need help. What you're trying to achieve is massive and we need all the help we can get," argued Emily.

He contemplated what Emily had asked, but before he could make a decision, he was drawn to the office door by the sound of creaking floorboards outside. He put his finger to his lip, gesturing to Emily to be quiet. He crept towards the door and with a quick pull, swung the door open and saw Izzy scurrying away from the office. She stopped running after being caught eavesdropping and turned to face Nick, her pale white skin had turned bright red as she was flush with embarrassment.

"I'm sorry. Will is waking up again and I needed your help moving him," Izzy said.

Emily stepped out in front of Nick who was staring at Izzy. "We'll be down in a sec," said Emily.

"Thank you," replied Izzy. She started to walk back down the stairs but stopped when she reached the top step. "I didn't mean to listen to you two talk. I didn't hear much of what you said so don't worry. But I wanted to tell you that we aren't weak. We are strong, and we don't get in anyone's way," explained Izzy assertively before going back downstairs.

"You just got told boy!" laughed Emily.

The siblings entered the dark cinema room to the sight of Izzy anxiously looking around the dimly lit room. She had a tight grasp on Will's hoody which he had been using as a pillow when he was resting on a large VIP cinema seat, but now he was nowhere to be seen.

"Where is he?" asked Nick with panic in his voice.

Izzy ran up and down the aisles frantically looking for Will. Nick and Emily headed up to the cinema screen and looked behind it. Izzy left the cinema room to see if Will had hobbled out to the bathroom or to the concessions stand. Nick and Emily came out from behind the screen and stood in front of it looking out onto what appeared to be a very dark and empty cinema room, both feeling baffled as to the where Will could've possibly got to.

"Oi you two, down in front. I'm trying to watch the movie" came a voice that neither Emily nor Nick were familiar with. The pair looked around the room to see where the voice had come from. They pin pointed it to a corner of the cinema which was much darker than the rest of the room due to the lights in that corner being smashed.

"Oh no way. He did not say that. I heard this movie was savage, but holy shit, I didn't think my boy Robby Downey Jay would be so harsh," came the voice again, shouting at the black screen.

Will gingerly stood up from the back row of seats and began clapping. "What a fantastic ending, and I tell you what, I did not see that twist coming. Well done Mr M Knight," said Will.

Nick walked down the centre aisle in the room and slowly approached Will.

"Are you a complete idiot or did that baboon hit you really, REALLY hard on the head?" questioned Nick.

"Listen mate, just because you didn't like the movie, it doesn't mean you have to get all pissy with me. How's about you get me some sweet and salty popcorn. Yes I like both kinds; so what?" said Will with a smile on his face.

Will carefully limped out from the back row and walked towards Nick and Emily. "I don't think I've officially had the chance to properly introduce myself. My name is Will; Big Willy to you."

Nick couldn't help but laugh to himself, "Yeah, I'm

not going to call you that," responded Nick.

"You're right. You can call me Will. Only my loved ones get to call me Big Willy. Speaking of which, where's my beautiful girlfr…" before Will could finish his sentence the saliva in his mouth had suddenly been knocked across the room and onto the wall next to him. Fortunately for him, the lack of lighting in the room meant that Izzy wasn't able to connect her fist with his face as well as she would've liked it to. Emily and Nick leapt towards Izzy and restrained her from hitting Will again.

"You stupid arsehole, I was worried sick about you!" shouted Izzy.

He wiped the blood from his mouth. "I'm sorry baby. I couldn't help myself. This guy was all like 'OMG where has he gone' it was hilarious," laughed Will.

"Get the hell off of me!" yelled Izzy, pulling herself away from Nick and Emily. "You're an idiot."

Izzy leapt towards Will again, but this time she wrapped her arms around him and kissed him on the exact spot she had punched. Nick looked away when the couple were kissing. Will noticed how uncomfortable Nick was and pulled away from his girlfriend.

"Slow down Izz, my man over here clearly isn't a fan of public affection," said Will

"Don't worry about him, his fiancée used to say the same thing," said Emily.

Will limped over to Nick and puts his hand on his shoulder. "Fiancée, wow. Who's the lucky lady? Is she upstairs? I'd like to thank her for saving my arse as well."

"Will, no," said Izzy quietly.

Nick shrugged Will's hand off of his shoulder. "She's dead. She died a few years ago. I lost her when this country went to hell."

"Oh man, I'm sorry mate. I had no clue." said Will mournfully.

"No, you didn't have a clue, so maybe keep your stupid jokes to yourself and mind your business," said Nick, before he walked to the exit of the cinema room.

"Was it The Boss? Did your fiancée die because of her?" asked Will.

Nick stopped walking and rushed over to Will. He grabbed him by his already ripped shirt and held him against the wall. "Listen to me idiot, the best thing you can do right now is shut your damn mouth and stop talking about things you have no clue about," threatened Nick.

Izzy pushed Nick off of Will and stood in between them. "We are all here for the same reason; we are all here because of her. You are obviously not a fan of her either. If you were, you wouldn't have helped us," said Izzy with authority in her voice.

Emily pulled Nick away from Will and stood face to face with Izzy. "You're right, we are all in the same boat and all we are trying to do is get to somewhere safe, somewhere we can survive. What are you two doing?" asked Emily.

Izzy peered over Emily's shoulder and saw that

Nick looked as if he was ready to burst into tears at the mere mention of his fiancée. She stepped back from Emily and took Will's hand. The couple looked at each other, and without saying a word they realised that there was more to Nick and Emily than they were letting on. They didn't know what they were hiding but they knew they owed them both for saving their lives and the least they could do was tell them who they were.

"I found a case of beers at the back of the storage cupboard when I was looking for my idiot of a boyfriend" said Izzy, "I'll go and get them and we can talk. I think it's time that we all get to know each other a little better."

CHAPTER 12

9th June 2016, 17:27
High Rd, Barnet, The Independent State of England

It had been relatively silent inside the cinema since the four of them had sat down to talk. The only noise that could be heard was the distinctive and very loud gulping sound coming from Will's throat as he chugged down three bottles of beer one after the other without saying a single word. Nick was both impressed and concerned with Will's drinking abilities and from the expression on Izzy's face, which resembled that of a girlfriend who thought, "*Yes this is the man I love despite the mad and stupid things he does.*" It told Nick that she was used to this kind of behaviour from him.

"Finished?" asked Izzy, breaking the silence in the room.

Will put the third bottle of beer down next to the other empties and immediately opened another one. He looked over at Izzy who was not so subtly shaking her head at him. He rapidly downed his fourth bottle of beer, let out a very loud burp, and put the bottle on the floor.

"Yes, I'm done, for now. God, I've missed beer. It's insanely warm and a bit flat, but it's been a while since I've had one; so right now it's the best thing ever," declared Will.

Emily picked up a bottle and opened it, "Is that what you two were doing in that pub? Looking for alcohol?" asked Emily.

"That wasn't our original intention, but when we came across the pub we thought we'd get a few in. We were doing what we've been doing for the last couple of years, surviving," said Izzy.

"Finding that pub was a bonus. Everything was fine until, ya know, I nearly got murdered by that bear of a man," joked Will.

"It was pretty stupid of you going into Camden alone; the gangs in her territory can barely stop fighting each other, let alone people they don't know," said Nick condescendingly.

Nick wasn't the least bit worried about being discreet in expressing his feelings towards his new cohorts. He didn't care about them. He had somewhere to be and something to achieve, and these two had cost him three days, which meant three days longer under her rule. Despite his hard headedness, he knew that having some allies wasn't a completely bad idea. These two had shown that they were tough and just the right amount of crazy to help get him and Emily to Enfield in one piece.

Will opened beer number five. "We don't really have a plan in all honesty; we've kind of been drifting around for the last couple of years trying to find somewhere to fit in. Before all of this, we lived together in Stratford. Like everyone else, we were fed up and stuck. We worked in a crappy fast food restaurant and spent our days at work together or in our crappy flat. We didn't go out much because whenever we did, Izzy would usually attract trouble," said Will.

"What do you mean? What kind of trouble?" asked Emily.

"My surname is Bozkow," answered Izzy. "My parents are from Poland and I was born there, but I've spent the last eleven years in London. I worked, I studied, I contributed, yet because of my accent and the way I look, I have people telling me to go back to my own country and to stop stealing their jobs; which is stupid, because those same people seem perfectly happy sitting in the pub and drinking on a Tuesday afternoon instead of looking for work. If they want my job in Fast Burger, they can have it."

Izzy took the open beer from Will's hand and took a big swig.

"The irony of all of that hatred towards Eastern Europeans is that these lazy English xenophobes stereotype us as being lazy, when all they do is sit around all day and complain. There is a reason why immigrants take these jobs and that's because the people here think they're too good to do them," continued Izzy.

"So, is that why you stayed here when The Boss isolated the city from the rest of the country? To get away from hateful people?" asked Emily.

Izzy took a sip from her beer. "Yes, amongst other reasons," she replied.

"We met each other at work and fell for each other pretty quickly. We didn't even consider me being English and her being Polish to be a problem. Why would we? When we first heard the stuff The Boss was saying, we bought into it like everyone else did. She was so on the ball; everything she was saying was so relatable. We'd never seen anyone speak for us the way that she did," said Will.

"What I loved about her was that she represented everyone. You could see that race, gender, sexuality or class didn't matter to her; it was about her message and her passion. You must have seen what happened at Kenton Hall? That changed public opinion of her in a matter of hours; so many haters began to love her, young and old. I'm guessing the same thing happened to you two?" asked Izzy.

Emily looked over at Nick who was playing with the label on his beer bottle. She could see that talking about The Boss was bothering him. Perceptions of The Boss had changed dramatically over the last few years and Nick knew that she had lost the respect of the people; but knowing and hearing were two different things. Hearing about the hardships she had caused the people first-hand, was a hard pill for him to swallow.

"I guess our story is pretty similar to yours," said Emily. "We got swept up in what The Boss was saying, and when it came to whether we should stay or leave, we decided to stay because we thought she was going to make a difference. We figured we could hold up in some abandoned mansion near Westminster for a while, sort of hide in plain sight; but that didn't really pan out, so we thought we would find sanctuary in the neutral zone."

Izzy noticed that Nick had distanced himself from the conversation and had refused to make eye contact with anyone.

"What about you? What's your take on all of this?" asked Izzy.

Emily tried to help her brother out by speaking for him but before she could say a word he put his hand on her shoulder and squeezed it gently to stop her from talking.

"What would you like to know?" asked Nick. "That me and my sister have been on our own for years, long before any of this happened. That our mum left us when we were kids, that our dad died when we were teenagers, and we've had to raise ourselves ever since. We believed in The Boss like you did; like everyone else did. She had a message and beliefs that meant something to us. But the same thing happened that always happens, she let the power go to her head; wrong decisions were made. She listened to the wrong people and we were the ones who suffered. Do you want to know about all the horrible things we've seen? Do you want to know what she did to my fiancée? Is that the kind of shit you want to know?" said Nick as tears began to fill in his eyes.

Nick had always maintained that he was a man's

man and he would never show his emotions in front of people. He didn't know, however, this was a defence mechanism he used due to his own insecure attachment issues which he blamed on his mother leaving him in his youth.

When he was around those he loved and trusted he was a man who was entirely emotionally open and he had a great sense of self-awareness about himself. The Boss often said that Nick should've become a counsellor as he had the type of face and character that people would gravitate to with their problems. She told him early on in their friendship that his welcoming personality was the main thing she liked about him when they first met at University. She was able to unload on him about anything and he would sit there and listen. Those qualities were why he became such an important asset to her. She could seek honest counsel from him or simply use him as a vessel to clear her mind and think things through.

Eventually, this stopped happening and she began to listen to others around her who had wormed their way into her inner circle. The moment The Boss began working with these kinds of people, was the moment that Nick began to no longer recognise her as the person he once knew. He tried to warn her that no matter how righteous your intentions may be, nobody is immune to corruption and the lure of power.

Nick stood up in frustration and left the cinema room and went back to the upstairs office. Emily left Izzy and Will and followed after her brother. She walked into the office to the sight of her brother trying to punch a hole through the wall. She offered him another beer as he stood panting with anger in the middle of the room with a bloodied hand.

"Take a minute and cool off. Once you have, we need to go back down there and figure out what we are going to do with those two," said Emily.

Meanwhile, Will and Izzy were cuddled up on the floor of the cinema room enjoying some alone time together.

"Jesus, that dude is seriously stressed out. Maybe he needs to get laid or something," joked Will.

"Speaking of which," said Izzy before pushing Will to the floor and climbing on top of him.

"Be gentle with me, my precious Eastern European flower. It's my first time," said Will in a frail child-like voice.

Izzy started to kiss him passionately and then felt something hard pushing against her leg.

"Hello mister. I know it's been a few days but I didn't think I could get you excited that quickly," said Izzy with a look of delight on her face.

He reached into his pocket and took out his mobile phone. The phone was in awful condition. He had a long history of breaking and losing his mobile phones, an issue he had been dealing with ever since he upgraded his phone from the Nokia 3310 years ago.

"Oh that reminds me," said Izzy as she climbed off of Will and picked up her backpack. She pulled out her phone, which was in a much better state than Will's, a phone charger, and a piece of paper.

Will sat up and leant against the wall. "Oh nice, mines been dead for weeks."

"I found the internet router earlier when I was looking for you. The Wi-Fi light was on, but I have no idea if there's any signal."

She found a plug socket at the back of the cinema room and plugged her phone into it. The couple sat around the phone and watched the battery bar slowly fill up. She tried to turn the phone on but it didn't quite have enough juice to switch on yet. While they waited for the phone to charge, Izzy sat in between Will's legs and rested her head on his chest.

"So, what do you think of those two? Do you think we should ask if we can go with them?" asked Izzy.

"She seemed pretty cool," answered Will. "But that dude needs to learn to smile once in a while. They saved our lives. They didn't have to do that, and that kind of thing doesn't happen anymore, especially on her turf. Whether they want us to go with them or not, we owe them big."

Izzy's phone sprung to life and the bright light of the phone lit up in the cinema. She entered her security password and navigated her way to the phones Wi-Fi settings. She entered the Wi-Fi code, and after a few seconds the phone connected to the internet. It began vibrating and pinging repeatedly as all of her missed notifications began flowing onto her phone. After fifteen seconds of nonstop buzzing and beeping, the phone was silent. She began flicking through Instagram, Facebook, and Twitter to catch up on all of the notifications she had missed over the last few weeks.

"Nothing out of the ordinary," thought Izzy. The same old images and videos had been posted, gang members posting about their most recent activities, all the trouble they were causing and the women from the gangs flashing their tits and arses online for everyone to see.

Hundreds of videos from the rest of world had been shared, which had become the norm, as it was the only real connection the people within The Independent State of England had with the outside world. Most of the videos shared were click bait videos, but the occasional video showing some real news from the world beyond the fence would come through. The Boss had tried her best to keep communication from outside of the city restricted; however, the odd video or post would break through the firewalls and be immediately shared and saved by everyone in the city, much to her annoyance. After the city was separated from the rest of the country, The Boss refused to allow her city to be infected by what she deemed "fake news," and she certainly didn't want news or stories about what was going on in her city to seep out into the wider world, although she knew this was an impossible task to achieve.

It wasn't until the couple had started seeing the more recent posts on the various social media platforms that their interest suddenly peaked. Post after post was being shared across all platforms about two escaped traitors who were both wanted. One of them, a mixed raced male who was wanted back alive, and the other was a mixed raced girl who was wanted back dead or alive. Will and Izzy checked as many different social media sites as they could to make sure that what they were seeing was true. They looked at it each with concern as they had read from multiple sources that there was a city-wide hunt for two of the most wanted people in the state, Nick and Emily King, The Boss' second in command and his sister.

Before the pair could say a word, they heard Nick and Emily coming back into the room. Izzy quickly turned off her phone, but not before taking a screen shot of one of the posts revealing who Nick and Emily really were. When the siblings returned, Will and Izzy had got to their feet, uncertain about what was going to happen next.

"Nick and I have been talking, and we think that it would be better if we all went to High Barnet together. We think it's the safest option for all of us. We need the numbers, and it's probably not the best idea for you two to be walking around alone after the arse kicking you took."

"Charming! We thought you might bring this up and we appreciate the offer but we don't know," said Will hesitantly.

Nick stepped closer to Will and Izzy. "Come with us to High Barnet, we can find whoever it is that is in charge over there and ask them if we can stay. After that we don't need to see each other again and we can go our separate ways. If you need me to say that we need your help, then fine, we need your help, just like you need ours. So, let's stop dicking around, get our shit together, and get moving," said Nick.

Will looked to Izzy who gave him a slight nod.

"Okay, we'll come with you. We owe you for saving us, but once we get to safety, we are even," said Will. "But I have one condition. We leave tomorrow, and tonight we get super wasted. It's been a hell of a few days and I think we all deserve to chill out."

Will picked up a beer from the floor and offered it to Nick, but he put his hand up and refused it. "No thanks, if we are going to drink let's drink something good. I found a bottle of whiskey in the office upstairs," said Nick, "But before I get it, I've got a condition of my own. We don't talk about her. Deal?"

Izzy and Will smiled, "Deal."

CHAPTER 13

10th June 2016, 06:39
Downing Street, City of Westminster, The Independent State of England

The sun had been up for over an hour and was beaming through the small tear in the curtains in The Boss' room. The sun rays were hitting the flat screen TV, creating a distorted rainbow effect on the black screen. She had been staring at the light effect for the last half an hour, while it moved slowly across the screen like a seventh century sun dial. She'd been awake for hours; it had been a long time since she had slept through the night, and most nights she would be lucky to get more than three hours sleep. Her focus on the sunlight on the TV screen was interrupted when her phone alarm went off and the rhythmic beeping echoed throughout the room.

Despite being awake for hours, her alarm going off signalled that her day had officially begun, and like most days, she had no idea what the day was going to bring. After her normal morning routine of showering, having breakfast alone and catching up on social media, she made her way to the first of many meetings that day. Per the norm, when she walked the corridors of Downing Street, half of her staff made sure they greeted her with over the top pleasantries, while the other half avoided making any eye contact with her entirely. Every member of her staff was afraid of her, but they expressed that fear in these two different ways, both of which annoyed her.

When she began her campaign to become Prime Minister, in an effort to show that she wasn't like all of her predecessors before her, she refused to move into Downing Street as she didn't want to be seen as thinking she was better than anyone else. However, Nick and many of her other advisor strongly suggested that Downing Street was the safest place for her to be while in power. The decision turned out to be the right call when she refused to tear down the fence and more and more resistance groups began to form against her.

Most of the rooms in the building had been renovated, and the traditional, outdated décor that once lined the walls had been replaced with some modern flare, something that better reflected the new leader of the Independent State of England. She also got rid of the names of the various rooms in the building; rooms like the "Terracotta State Drawing Room" and the "Pillared State Drawing Room," became "Meeting Room 1," "Meeting Room 2," and "Meeting Room 3." She was never the most creative person when it came to these things, but she didn't think it mattered. All she cared about was eradicating any memory of the old regime she felt had plagued the country. Emily had begged her to let her come up with some cool names for the rooms, but she wasn't interested. She'd named them for their purpose. She acknowledged the history of the country and what it once represented, but she was also aware of the huge change that was happening in the state; and she wanted to make it clear to everyone, that it was out with the old and in with the new.

The first meeting of the day was always the same. The Boss' cabinet would give her a rundown of the activities and goings on in the state from the day before. The Secretary of Defence updated her on the movements of some of the resistance groups in the state, which he confirmed was nothing to be concerned about. He then informed The Boss that there had been no major updates on what was happening beyond the fence in the rest of the country; besides from the regular supply drops in and out of the state there was still radio silence.

She remained firm on her decision to distance herself from the rest of the country. She felt disrespected and mistreated by those who fought against her, and she made it clear to them and the rest of the world that if they wanted to speak with her again, they would have to come to her. She gave respect where it was due and praised those who ran the country outside of the city for agreeing to continue to provide supply drops to the Independent State of England during these trying times. She knew they would not let the people in the state starve and to her credit, she found a way to keep her people fed.

On the rare days where violence and crime were low, the Independent State of England was actually a bearable place to live. Unfortunately for the residents of the state, those days were few and far in between.

Her first meeting ran over, which meant she was running late for her next one. She had always been forty-five minutes late to wherever she was going. Nick learnt very quickly that he would have to tell her to be ready to meet him an hour before she needed to. However, in recent times, she had become someone full of double standards and would bite the head off of anyone who wasn't in the meeting room before her.

After Nick escaped; her usual responsibilities had left her feeling more drained than ever. She no longer had anyone to unload on to and felt Nick's absence in more ways than one. Not having Nick with her in her countless meetings, left her thinking about him once again, and she pondered about what he was doing, what he was going to do next, where he was, and worst of all, why he had abandoned her.

Her next meeting was supposed to be about an update on the fence and the numerous sensors around the fence malfunctioning, however, when she walked into Meeting Room 3, she was met by Ron who was holding up one of her cabinet members against the wall by his shirt while the rest of her team watched on in fear. Given it was Ron, this wasn't an uncommon sight; he had always been a brute.

"Ron, how nice to see you," said The Boss as she sat at the head of the meeting table barely batting an eyelid.

Ron hadn't come alone and there were a number of his gang members in the room with them.

"Before we get to whatever it is you want to discuss, would you be so kind to put Mr Ali down? You know I don't do business unless everyone is sat around my table," continued The Boss.

Ron was covered in cuts and bruises and looked as if he hadn't washed since his run in with Nick. He put down Mr Ali and then sat down at the table opposite The Boss. Mr Ali ran out of the room in a panic. "*Take me with you*," thought The Boss; she was in no mood to deal with Ron today and she wasn't sure if she could stop herself from openly gagging at the stench of fire smoke, vodka and, body odour coming from his direction. Unfortunately, she understood that the cost of having Ron work for her was that she would occasionally have to humour him. She learnt very quickly as a ruler that sometimes she would need people in her life to do her dirty work for her. Nick had made it clear that he disapproved of her methods when dealing with Ron; unfortunately, drugs were the only currency that he and the Westenders responded to.

"How can I help you Ron? Shouldn't you be out patrolling your turf? I didn't call for you and I thought we spoke about you muscling your way in here. I have nothing for you right now. If you are looking to pick up, need I remind you that I'm not a fucking drug dealer. If you can't wait for your fix, I suggest you go elsewhere," said The Boss firmly.

Ron waved his hand in the air and signalled to The Westenders in the room to leave him and The Boss alone. With a slight nod of her head, The Boss gestured to the rest of her team who remained in the room to leave as well. Once the room had been cleared, Ron made himself at home and puts his filthy feet up onto the table.

"I'm here for my reward," said Ron.

She remained unfazed by Ron, "And what reward would that be?" responded The Boss.

"The reward for bringing that bastard Nick and his gorgeous bitch of a sister back to you," said Ron bluntly.

"You caught them?" asked The Boss, showing some intrigue in what Ron had said for the first time since she'd met him.

"Not yet, but I promise you after what they did to me, they're dead. Well, she certainly will be at least. You'll get Nick back alive, but barely. He took out a few of my guy, so I think it's only fair that the rest of the Westenders get there licks in before I hand him over to you," said Ron with a sick smile on his face.

The Boss stood up and poured herself a glass of coconut water.

"Drink Ron?" offered The Boss.

"Yeah, but none of that hipster piss. You got any vodka?" responded Ron gruffly.

She opened a hidden cabinet in the wall and took out a bottle of vodka, she poured a large glass for Ron and walked over and sat on the table next to him. She gave him his drink and they clinked their glasses together.

"What makes you think you'll catch Nick? He's already gotten away from you once. Where exactly did you run into him?"

"Over in Hampstead Heath, near Spaniards Road," said Ron, knowing full well that he shouldn't have been in another gang's territory.

"And what was the likes of you doing in such a nice area?" said The Boss playfully.

"Me and the lads were out for a late-night walk, staying out of trouble, and keeping our heads down."

She felt the vibration of her mobile phone in her pocket. She took it out and looked at the message on the screen. She quickly responded to the message and put her phone back into her pocket.

"Show me where you found him," she ordered.

She escorted him to the master surveillance room which she had had custom built on site at Number 10 so she could act as 'Big Brother' to the city. Her original intentions for this level of surveillance was so she could fulfil her promise of watching over her people and keeping them safe, however, like with so many others exposed to too much power, temptation and curiosity eventually got the better of her, and this advanced technology became a tool for her to keep tabs on people.

The surveillance room was manned by a handful of tech-savvy people who would report back to The Boss directly on any unlawful activities going on in the state, specifically those that posed a threat to her. Many of the resistance gangs had been successful in disabling the cameras in their boroughs and many of the cameras she controlled didn't always work, but she had her spies everywhere and other methods of keeping track on those who opposed her. Unfortunately for her, Nick not only knew the city like the back of his hand but he knew about the surveillance room, which meant he knew where not to go in order to avoid being seen by The Boss.

"Jesus Christ. I heard rumours about this place, but I didn't think it was real. How much did all this gear set you back?" asked Ron in awe.

"Bring up the footage from the cameras around the Spaniards Road area in Hampstead Heath on the sixth June between twelve a.m. and five a.m.," ordered The Boss.

It didn't take long for the woman behind the surveillance control panel to locate three cameras near where Ron had his altercation with Nick. She began scrawling through the footage; unfortunately, none of the three cameras had good visibility of the pub, so they had to use all three cameras to piece together the events that went down a few days prior. The footage showed images of Ron, his gang, and four other people at the pub. Ron did his best to describe the scenario as it played out, although The Boss felt as though he was embellishing certain parts of the story in a vague attempt to cover up the fact that he was bested physically.

"It took four of those pricks to get the better of me; even then, I was only down for a minute," exaggerated Ron.

She had stopped listening to him as she tried to focus on the footage in front of her. She noticed that the group had escaped into Hampstead Heath.

"Give me any cameras at the northern exits of the Heath," commanded The Boss.

The woman controlling the surveillance was able to locate a handful of potential exits in which Nick and his assailants may have escaped. One of the screens showed three figures running out of an exit near Kenwood House while holding up a fourth figure who was unable to walk. The Boss moved the woman's hand from the panel and took control of the system. She was sat on the edge of her seat as she intently focused in on the footage. She froze the picture and delicately turned a dial which moved the image forward one frame at a time. She released the dial and zoomed into the four figures on the screen, she hit a few more buttons as Ron stood behind her dumbfounded wondering what she was doing. She enhanced the image and once she had found what she was looking for, she slumped back into her seat with a feeling of achievement.

"There you are," said The Boss, finally finding what she was looking for.

On screen was a clear image of Nick, Emily, Izzy and Will fleeing from Hampstead Heath following the fight with Ron and The Westenders.

"I told you I found them," boomed Ron, making The Boss jump in her seat.

"Who are the other two?" asked The Boss.

"A couple of 'randoms' who got in my way."

"What were you doing with them?" quizzed The Boss.

"You know!" said Ron, avoiding the question.

"No, I don't. Enlighten me."

"Huh?" said Ron with a look of confusion on his face.

"Tell me what actually happened you moron," said The Boss, becoming increasingly frustrated with Ron.

"They were in my way and I was dealing with them," answered Ron abruptly.

"I see. Correct me if I'm wrong, but is the CCTV near East Finchley still out of action?" asked The Boss.

The control woman stepped forward to swiftly answer The Boss' question.

"Yes ma'am. In accordance to the Neutrality Treaty, there is no surveillance in or around the neutral zones. I could try and get some more footage of the escapees, but it wouldn't be much more than what we already have."

"That's fine. Chances are, they fled towards the neutral zone. Thank you for your help," said The Boss calmly.

The Boss took out her phone and began typing a message. She hit send, put the phone in her pocket, and then stood up from her seat.

"Give me the word and I will drag that prick back here for you," said Ron enthusiastically.

She gave Ron a pitiful half-smile. One she often gave him whenever he opened his mouth.

"Ron, you've been a valuable asset to me for a long time haven't you?"

He opened his mouth to answer, but she quickly interrupted him.

"You don't have to answer that. I've given you what you want and for the most part, you've done your job. Now, I've not always agreed with how you get things done, but it's just been another one of those things that I've had to put up with and let go," she said, gesturing for him to follow her as she left the room.

"I think we've finally reached a point in our relationship where I can be truly honest with you. I think I owe you that much," continued The Boss.

"I knew we were cool, Nick tried to tell me that you were using me. I'm going to make him pay for hurting you. I promise," said Ron feeling reenergised and motivated to prove himself to The Boss.

She opened the door of the surveillance room and put her hand on Ron's back, leading him out ahead of her.

"You're right Ron; for the first time in your life, you're right. Nick will pay for what he's done. Like everyone else who has let me down," she said with malice in her voice.

They both left the surveillance room and standing

in front of them were eight of The Boss' security team. At their feet were the barely conscious bodies of the Westenders. Ron froze at the sight of his fallen comrades, and after a few seconds of silence, he turned to The Boss unable to speak.

"Oh, my God, I think this is the longest I've ever seen you silent. This day is full of surprises isn't it?" said The Boss. "Let me explain it to you as simply as I can. You are done. You are a useless mouth-breathing Neanderthal who would be better suited living in medieval times than in civilised society. Granted the world we live in has become more like Westeros than Downton Abbey, but that is in part to feckless meatheads like you. You had your uses; but now, well look at you; you can barely keep your own team in line. You had Nick and Emily in the grasp of your hand and you let them go. That is not acceptable."

She stepped over the Westenders on the floor and stood directly in front of Ron.

"I'd like to thank you for your help over the years Ron, but your services are no longer required. I'd wish you well in your future endeavours, but your future doesn't look like it's going to be overly prosperous for you or particularly long for that matter."

She turned her back on Ron who was stuck trying to comprehend what had happened. His eyes widened and he stared a burning hole into the back of her head as an intense rage took over his entire body. Before he could take a single step towards her, with the sole intention of crushing her throat, her security team didn't give him an inch and knocked him to the floor and proceeded to beat him repeatedly with large black batons. Ron was able to get in a few good hits and even managed to dislocate the jaw of one of her guards, but he was soon overpowered, and the numbers became too much for him to handle.

With no remorse in her heart The Boss walked away from the carnage and the sounds of steel hitting skull. A member of her communications team approached her with a tablet computer. The team member flinched every time he heard the sound of the batons hitting the men's bodies behind him. He made the mistake of looking back at the beaten bodies, and after seeing the blood splatter into the air, he struggled to keep down the vomit that was bubbling in his stomach.

"Boss, I've got Bray Michaels from the Instagrammer Nazis on a video chat for you as requested," said the team member.

She took the tablet and accepted the video call. Bray Michaels, the leader of one of the most vile and vicious gangs in the state, had managed to manipulate his way into The Boss' inner circle. His gang had become famous for their brutal acts of punishment and redemption for crimes against The Boss. They prided themselves on their work, so much so that they would post images of their corporal punishment and violent attacks on Instagram as a message to anyone who thought about crossing them or The Boss. The Boss had never been thrilled about consorting with this group, especially when they decided to change their gang name from the "Insta-grammar Police" to the "Instagrammar Nazis," but Bray became a necessity to her campaign in gaining the votes she needed.

When the video call connected, she pointed the camera towards the lifeless bodies of Ron and the last remaining members of The Westenders gang.

"Impressive...seeing your face was the nice treat I anticipated but seeing THIS has most definitely given me that funny feeling down below," said Bray as he revelled in the sight of Ron dying in front of him.

She turned the tablet back around to face her. "The Westenders are no more," said The Boss coldly.

"It was about time that you dropped that useless prick. Any chance I can get a picture of him once your thugs have finished with him. I'd love to take credit for taking him out?" said Bray with a perverse smile on his face.

"What I did to him I can do to all of you. I want that to be crystal clear," said The Boss. "Nick was spotted four days ago near Hampstead Heath. He was with Emily and two unknown people. I've heard a few murmurs from people claiming they've seen him, but nothing definite. He was never someone who made friends willingly, so chances are he was being a hero and rescued some poor civilians. He's prob-ably headed to Barnet. I need you to do what you do best and take care of it."

"I love when you talk business Boss, you sound so

sexy when you use your big boy voice," teased Bray.

"Do I need to make another gang disappear today Bray? With the mood I'm in, if I was you, I really wouldn't test me. Remember that there are plenty of people who can take your place. Can I count on you or not?"

"Consider it done sir," replied Bray.

"Good."

"On one condition," snapped back Bray.

She gave him a steely glare but he continued nevertheless.

"I want Nick's old spot."

Her eyebrows shot up and she paused for a moment to consider the request.

"Fine…but I want him brought back unharmed and if that means you have to keep his sister alive for the time being, then so be it."

"And what about his new friends?" asked Bray.

"What friends?" replied The Boss callously.

She turned off the tablet and handed it back to the nauseated member of her communications team.

"Call the clean-up crew and tell them they have some bodies to dispose of and relay this message back to the comms team. I want them to spread the word to all corners of the state about what has happened here today. I want you to tell them that I want Nick back and that failure is not an option. Tell them what has happened to The Westenders and tell them that Nick was the one who killed Ron. I want this message everywhere. Get it on social media and wherever else your team can think of. I want my followers to know that Nick is dangerous and unstable, and that I'm doing all I can to stop him. And I want the resistance to think that he will go through them as well, if he must. I want Nick and his little gang stopped before they get any further away from me, by any means necessary."

CHAPTER 14

11th June 2016, 00:30
Unknown Location

"Good evening to all of the wonderful and not so wonderful citizens of The Independent State of England. Wow that name really is a mouthful isn't it? I, for one, loved the old name of this once great city, but let's not open that can of worms again shall we?

Here are your nightly headlines and current affairs of the day straight from my pigeons on the street.

The Lambeth brothers are still grumpy with each other and the borough remains divided. One of them loves The Boss, one of them hates her. Personally, I think there are some mummy issues at play here, but who am I to judge?

There are continued posts and reports of gangs invading the neutral zones of Barnet and Greenwich, antagonising the locals and trying to cause trouble. If things weren't bad enough, these dicks are now harassing people who have been made exempt from any form of gang interaction or unlawful interference by The Boss herself. Doesn't it strike you as odd that The Boss no longer seems to have control over her own people. It's almost as if she has no earthly idea what she's doing.

In other news, the resistance boroughs continue to be all bark and no bite. They pose such little threat to The Boss that she has pulled her troops away from these boroughs to focus on her other evil plans.

Gang war-fare in the south has decreased, however, it continues to escalate in the east, and from the looks of their Snapchat videos, the "Catford Cats," worst gang name ever by the way, and the Hoxton Squares have formed some sort of alliance in an effort to unite the East into giving The Boss its full support. It's nice to know The Boss continues to have people out there willing to fight for her, even if they are backing a vicious dictator. Bless.

Final update of the night, I'm getting reports from my tweeters and twatters that Nick King and his sister Emily King were spotted in the Hampstead Heath area four days ago. It seems Nick, Emily, and two unknown attackers were able to topple the mighty Westenders Gang. Yes, you heard that right, the leader of The Westenders, Ron, was beaten up, taken out, and is no more. The only thing that ape could do was beat the shit out of people and he couldn't even do that properly. The Boss would have you believe that Nick took out Ron, but I think we all know who was really responsible. And for those of you who aren't clear as to what I'm getting at, let me spell it out for you, if you don't give The Boss what she wants, you don't get to live.

Yet another subtle message delivered from our fearsome leader in a thinly veiled attempt to hide her image as evil tyrant.

The search for Nick and Emily continues. Good luck

Nick, the world is coming for you.

This is your eye in the sky with your nightly update. Till next time. I'm out."

11th June 2016, 19:06
High Rd, Barnet, The Independent State of England

Nick, Emily, Will and Izzy had all finally woken up after a mammoth drinking session which had delayed the group from leaving the cinema by an entire day. Nick was in the upstairs office with his head in the bathroom sink drinking water straight from tap. He wiped his mouth and collapsed on the sofa in the room. Emily walked into the office with a smile on her face as she sees her brother struggling with his hangover. She throws a packet of paracetamol at him which he didn't even attempt to catch due to a pounding headache and exhaustion.

"You are getting old big brother. How are you still hung over? It's been almost two days," teased Emily.

He popped two paracetamol, slowly walked back to the tap, and swallowed the pills. He staggered back into the room and laid his head on his sisters' shoulder.

"Whose idea was it to play poker?" asked Nick.

"Izzy, but you insisted we make it a drinking game. She really didn't look like she'd be good at poker but she absolutely crushed you."

"Be wary of the innocent looking ones, they're the worst. I should've known she was scamming us with the way she shuffled those cards, that and the fact that she suggested we play poker. And while we're at it, the fact she's been carrying a deck of playing cards with her this whole time!" said Nick.

The pair went back to the cinema room where Izzy was sat alone. "Where has Will gone now?" asked Emily.

A sudden noise of clanking glass bounced through the room and Will jumped up from the floor through a pile of empty bottles, "Hello, I'm here. I'm awake. I was just resting my eyes. What are we doing? Are we leaving?" asked Will in bewilderment.

Izzy hopped to her feet and walked past her boyfriend. "Yes stupid. Let's go." Izzy threw his bag at him and the group walked towards the rear fire exit.

Will stopped walking when a beam of light through one of the boarded-up windows caught his eye. "It's pretty bright outside, do you think it's alright to walk around in broad daylight?" he asked.

"I think we're safe. We'll go out through the back exit and down the alley past the houses. I've been scouting the streets for the last few days. It seems pretty quiet out there, mostly civilians. The further into Barnet we get, the safer we should be, in theory anyway. If for some reason we do get into any trouble, well, the race is on," said Nick with a smile on his face.

"Wow, was that a joke? And did you smile. I knew I'd break through to your warm chocolaty centre after several hundred drinks," laughed Will.

The group left the cinema together. They took half

a second to scan the high street to their left and the residential road to their right; luckily, they were both clear. They made a beeline for the alley across the road, and once they navigated through the small alley, they walked back onto the main high street and did their best to blend in with the civilians on the street. Izzy noticed that Nick and Emily had put their hoods up over their heads, seemingly trying to be extra cautious about protecting their identities.

"I think we're alright guys. Nobody knows who we are, and I don't think any gangs are going to be hanging around the streets this early," said Izzy.

"Better safe than sorry," said Emily as the group picked up their pace. "I'd feel more comfortable the further into Barnet we get."

The group continued through the High Street and remained unnoticed. Despite the huge change that had fallen upon the city, the people living here still didn't acknowledge each other or exchange pleasantries to people they didn't know; if anything it had gotten much worse over the last few years. It became less about people ignoring each other because they were being rude, and more about people ignoring each other because of survival. Nick had actually missed that awkward social interaction between strangers who were forced to speak to each other; however, in that moment, he was happy to be living amongst the socially awkward. It was safer that way.

The group passed by boarded up shop after boarded up shop, examining what was left of the street; this was a similar sight all over the city. All that remained open on the High Street were a handful of ration distribution stations in poor condition. Despite her many flaws, The Boss had kept her promise to keep the people she presided over fed. When word got out that the Ration Officers she had assigned to the ration stations were stealing supplies and in some cases refusing to dole out any rations, she had them removed and made examples of. The people of the city could attack her for all of the wrong she had done, but she would never allow them to call her malevolent by letting the people on her streets go hungry.

"You know what I miss, the little things," announced Will, louder than he should have for someone who was trying to lay low. "I miss drunkenly wandering into a crappy fast food restaurant and going face first into a messy kebab or Subway sandwich. World peace and a safe place to sleep, meh, a sloppy meatball sub at three in the morning, yes please. When I used to work in a nightclub, I would get so bored on the night bus home that I would count how many Maccers or Subway restaurants I could spot before I got home. I swear to God, I counted seventeen Subways between Leicester Square and Camden, seventeen. Isn't that nuts?"

At this point, everybody had stopped listening to Will. Everybody just felt hungry for sandwiches and processed meat. Nick considered going to one of the ration stations and getting some food, but he couldn't risk anyone recognising him. He took out some slightly squashed protein bars that he had stolen from the mansion in Hampstead Heath and shared them with the group. He gave Will an extra protein bar, not because he had started to like the guy, though he had, but because he wanted him to stop talking; he figured the longer Will ate, the less he would speak.

Amongst the closed down shops and ration stations, the street also had a number of rundown flats, a boarded-up library, and an abandoned school on it. School and education had been another thing The Boss had promised to redevelop and reinvent, but like everything else she'd promised, it fell by the wayside. During her early run as Prime Minister, she had a particularly passionate stance on education and trying to make learning fun. She felt that the education system had failed her in the past and she didn't want any more children to suffer the same thing. However, with a civil war brewing in her state and her refusing to take down the colossal electric fence that surrounded the city, some of her more righteous goals had slipped through her fingers and were never able to be rectified.

Libraries had become a dying industry, so she never bothered to invest her time into them. Her experience of libraries was a place you go to in order to get drunk, high and felt up – and only when it was raining or too cold to do it in the park. When it came to school, her focus was on people. She really wanted to keep knowledge alive in people. She wanted to make learning lively and fun, and she felt that she had spent a big part of her life not knowing anything and wanted to knock the normal curriculum of learning on its head. Unfortunately, once the dust had settled after years of rioting, after the great exodus of London and the separation of the state from the rest of the country; the type of people left in the city had a "Fuck you" attitude to education and her ideas on education reform came to nought.

The sun began to set in East Finchley and the streets had become relatively empty. The group continued through the town with the hopes of making it to High Barnet within a couple of hours. They approached Islington and Camden Cemetery when they noticed a small group of people converging on the road up ahead of them. They were facing away from Nick and the rest of the group, so they couldn't make out if they belonged to a gang or not. It looked as if they were crowding around something or someone.

"What is it? Do you think someone is hurt?" enquired Izzy.

Gradually more and more people joined the crowd, seemingly appearing from the surrounding flats and side roads next to the cemetery, one by one they appeared and all with their backs to the group.

"Hold on, something doesn't feel right," said Emily who sensed trouble.

"Do you think we should see what it is? Someone could be hurt," asked Will.

The small group of people that had originally been

formed of three people had now amassed to a collection of at least twenty to twenty-five people in a matter of minutes.

"I don't think anyone is hurt, but if we don't get out of here now, we will be," said Nick.

The four of them turned around slowly, but like a deer in headlights, Nick, Emily, Will and Izzy were simultaneously and suddenly struck with a blast of fear that took over their bodies. The road behind them, which was empty mere moments ago, had now been filled with another crowd of people staring directly at them. They were trapped.

Unsure of what to do next, Nick and the group turned back the other way in hopes of finding an escape route, but all they could see were the glistening eyes of the first mob they had encountered who had now turned around to face them. Nick looked to his left for escape, but a block of flats prevented any movement. He looked to his right and noticed the broken gates leading into a dark and isolated cemetery. It would be a risky move, but they could certainly lose the mob in the open darkness of the graveyard when or if the opportunity arose.

While he contemplated what the best move was, a man walked out of the crowd and began strolling towards Nick and the group. Even on this peculiarly dimly lit summer evening, Nick immediately recognised who the man was, with his gelled back bleach blonde hair, his burly well-trimmed beard and his immaculately clean dark brown Timberland Boots; Nick had no question about who was walking towards them.

"Now, I know what you are thinking. Can me and my group of rag tag misfits make a dash into that creepy little cemetery over there and outrun this incredibly dressed and stylish man and his band of merry men and women?" boomed the man in the deathly silent street. "The answer Nicholas, is no. Sure, you can try and make a run for it, but I wouldn't want you and your little gang to be all sweaty for the ever so artistic pictures we are going to upload of your beaten and broken bodies. We can't have the people of this fine city thinking our work is sub-par can we?"

The blonde man raised the baseball bat in his hand and pointed it at Nick. "Don't worry Nicholas. I'm not talking to you; just your friends. She wants you back prim and proper, however, that being said, for my own personal enjoyment, I will have to tell her a few little white lies about how you got those bruises and cuts all over your face and back. You'll corroborate my story, won't you? We can't have her thinking we're both treacherous liars," continued the man.

Will and Izzy gave Nick a quizzical look, "Who is this man Nick? And how does he know who you are?" asked Izzy, no longer able to stay with her confusion.

Nick and Emily didn't take their eyes off the man. Without turning, Nick croaked, "This is Bray Michaels, the leader of the Instagr...."

"Whoa, whoa, what was that? That's how you

introduce me? With that lacklustre twaddle? Take a seat you quadroon and I'll show you how it's done," interrupted Bray, who then audibly and unnecessarily cleared his throat. "Ladies and Gentlemen, children of all ages, it's my esteemed pleasure to proudly introduce to you, the Sultan of Swag, the Immaculate Entity, the maestro of maestros, the founder, CEO, president, King, and leader of the most brutal and selective gang in all of The Independent State of England, The Instagrammer Nazis, the one, the only, Braaayyyy Michaels."

A round of applause and cheers filled the now orange sky as The Instagrammer Nazi's loudly celebrated their sadistic leader.

"Thank you, yes, yes. I know I'm great," said Bray, before raising his hand in the air signalling to his gang to stop applauding him, "BOOM. That is how you introduce ME Nicholas. Always great with the pen but never with the tongue, isn't that right?"

Bray turned his attention to Izzy who still had a confused expression on her face. "Now that you know who I am young lady I can now answer your second question. How do I know Mr King? Funny story, we actually go way back, don't we?"

"What are you doing here? This is a neutral zone. You shouldn't be here. If she knew you were..." said Nick before being interrupted by Bray again.

"Who do you think sent me here?" said Bray condescendingly.

Nick knew in that moment that The Boss would go to any lengths to get him back, not only had she sought out Bray and The Instagrammer Nazis for help, but she had allowed them to breach the borders into a neutral zone. He could've kicked himself for thinking that she would stick to her word about sending gangs into the neutral zones after she had broken so many of her other promises already.

"Seriously Emily, who the hell is this person?" asked Izzy.

Emily was in a state of shock at the sight of Bray. She had seen first-hand what he and his gang were capable of. She had seen the violent and grotesque pictures Bray and The Instagrammer Nazis had posted online and she had hoped that she had seen the last of this nasty man.

"I'm sorry miss. Did you not hear my awesome introduction? I can hear that you have a little bit of an accent there. Perhaps your stupid Polish brain can't decipher what I said? Let me try and break it down for you. Hello, yes, please to know my name is Bray Michaels. You vant vodka and potatoes or only to take job from English person?" mocked Bray.

"What the fuck did you say?" said the usually exuberant Will, who clenched his fist and took a step towards Bray.

He began walking towards Bray with the sole intention of putting his clenched fist through his face, but before he could take another step, Emily quickly grabbed his arm and trembled out one word, "Don't."

"You should listen to her boy. Emily knows exactly what I'm capable of. Oh, and FYI, you are an absolute disgrace, mixing with these Eastern European scum; your loyalties are all wrong brother. Take care of your own first, remember that," said Bray, pointing his bat towards Will. "Emily, my beautiful sugar tits, God, even without those pretty little dresses and all that make up on, you still look incredibly smashable. Unfortunately for you, you've gotten on her bad side one time too many, so I cannot promise you that you'll be coming back to her looking as good as you do right now or coming back at all for that matter. You know I've got a soft spot for you, but some of the crew don't feel the same way. I pleaded with them to take it easy on you, but sometimes my loyal crew don't always listen to me. So, for what is about to happen, I apologise."

The street fell silent once again; Bray was at his most comfortable when he was in an awkward environment, especially one he had created.

"Not even going to try and talk you way out of this one then eh Nick?" asked Bray.

"No point mate. You've never listened to me before and I'm guessing nothing has changed."

"When you're right, you're right," laughed Bray.

Bray looked at his gang and gave them a slight nod. The Instagrammer Nazis took the order from Bray and began marching towards Nick, Emily, Will, and Izzy. The foreplay between Bray and Nick was over, and Nick knew he had to think fast, or he and his group would be done. He signalled to the others, and then looked towards the cemetery, knowing that it was their only chance of escape. Will, Izzy, and Emily nodded back at him, all making a non-verbal agreement that although it was suicide, they had to make a run for it. As the group were about to run into the blackness of the graveyard, they saw another large group of people running towards them from the cemetery.

"Shit, they've surrounded us. We should've made a run for it when he had the chance. They are going to kill the others and take me back to her," thought Nick.

"What do we do Nick? What do we do?" asked Emily in a panic.

He looked at Emily and took in the beautiful sight of his sister's face. He squeezed her hand and closed his eyes without saying a word. Will and Izzy saw what was happening and hugged each other as tightly as they could before they accepted their fate.

"STOP!" shouted Bray, ordering his gang to cease advancing on Nick. "Who the hell are you lot?" said Bray, staring towards the cemetery.

Out of the cemetery came a large group of men wearing turbans. A man with an orange turban and a wispy black beard stepped out in front of the group.

"Bruv, you know who we are," said the bearded man.

Bray looked around at the rest of The Instagrammer Nazis hoping someone would verify who this bearded man was.

"Honestly raghead. I've no clue who you are?" said Bray.

"Really?" asked the bearded man looking slightly

deflated, "I know who you are, and them two as well. Nick, Emily, you know who we are right, you must do?"

The siblings stared at each other unsure what to say and in perfect symmetry they both shrugged their shoulders at the man in the turban.

"*Haramzada.* My name is Anand and I'm the leader of the Sick Sikhs," bellowed Anand in frustration.

Bray stared blankly at Anand for a few seconds and then unexpectedly burst into a fit of hysterical laughter. He had tears running down his face and was hunched over in stitches. Anand, despite feeling incredible embarrassed, tried his hardest to maintain the cool persona he was so desperately trying to portray.

After a minute or two of gut wrenching merriment Bray had finally stopped laughing, he wiped away the tears from his eyes and composed himself as best as he could.

"Fuck me! Anand was it? Wow, you're a funny bloke; I mean, for a Paki at least," said Bray, immediately bringing the awkward tension back into the air.

"Enough of this, we've come for Nick and the reward on his head. It's time for the Sick Sikhs to leave their mark on this city. We are loyal to The Boss and we deserve recognition."

The Sick Sikhs took out their weapons and raised them above their heads. Anand pulled out a switch blade he had hidden in the fabric of his turban and pointed it directly at Bray.

"Stay out of our way Nazi boy or I'll cut you a permanent smile," Anand said menacingly.

Being at the receiving end of a threat from someone he considered so beneath him, wiped the grin from Bray's face.

"You five, subdue the cargo and dispose of the rest, everybody else, with me. It's time to prove why the whites are the superior race," ordered Bray.

The numbers in the two gangs were about the same. The Instagrammer Nazis led by Bray marched towards Anand and the Sick Sikhs. Both gangs were tooled up and had weapons ranging from homemade shivs to bats with nails in them and everything in between. The experience in street warfare had to go to the much wealthier Instagrammer Nazis. Bray, being the son of a lord, had surrounded himself with likeminded and equally well-off individuals. That wealth brought the luxury of them being able to buy whatever they wanted, which included the purchase of illegal weaponry and the ability to be trained by the best hand to hand combat specialists in the country. The Sick Sikhs were no pushovers either; the gang had fought their way up from nothing and their determination to be seen and heard made them a force to be reckoned with.

The two rival gangs collided in what can be best described as a glorified bar fight, meanwhile five of the Instagrammer Nazis on Bray's orders bolted towards Nick, Will, Emily and Izzy who were readying themselves for a battle. Not having any time to think, Nick picked up a slab of concrete that had come loose from the pavement.

"Find what you can to protect yourself and get ready. The moment you find a chance to escape you take it; if you get free, we'll regroup in Victoria Park," said Nick hastily.

The five members of the Instagrammer Nazis reached Nick and the group and stood in front of them ready to fight.

"Let's not make this harder than it needs to be, alright Nick," said one of the gang members.

"Sorry mate, I only know how to do things the hard way," said Nick, before swinging his arm around with the cement slab in his hand, and with as much power as he could muster, smashed it over the gang members head. The gang member fell to the floor in a heap. Nick had no idea if he had killed this person, but he didn't have time to think about it. He was in survival mode.

Before the dust from the cement slab could settle, Emily, Will and Izzy lunged towards the remaining gang members robbing them of any opportunity to attack them first. Nick shook off the pain that was radiating from his hand and joined in the fray. With chaos ensuing around them, everything to lose and A LOT of luck, the group collectively took down the remaining four attackers. With the gang members either dazed or unresponsive, Nick signalled towards the graveyard. He looked out to the on-going battle and saw that both gangs were so enthralled in the fight that him and his group could likely slip past the ruckus and escape into the darkness unseen. He couldn't spot Bray or Anand so he had to pray that they had taken each other out or were at least keeping each other occupied.

"We have to move, stick to the plan. We'll regroup in Vicky Park and then move forward to High Barnet," yelled Nick, while he pushed through the fighting crowd with Emily, Will, and Izzy following behind him.

Fists were thrown and some aggressive shoving took place as the group cleared a path to the cemetery. The group managed to get past the gate and into the cemetery with only a few bumps and bruises. Once everyone was past the gate, they took off into the gloomy night.

After choking out one of the Sick Sikh's with their own turban, Bray looked amongst the chaos to see that the five gang members he had assigned to take care of Nick were struggling to get to their feet, while Nick and the others were nowhere to be seen. He turned to the graveyard and caught the faintest glimpse of Nick and his group escaping into the distance. With the Instagrammer Nazi's dominating the remainder of the Sick Sikhs, Bray was about to signal to his gang that they needed to go after Nick; however, before he could make his command a numb tingling feeling radiated across his back which strangely sent him to his knees.

He looked over his shoulder to see Anand smiling over him holding a large steel pipe. Bray spat out a wad of blood and with the help of his bat, he got back to his feet. He wiped the blood from his mouth and smiled a crimson and villainous smirk at Anand.

Meanwhile, Nick and the group ran away from the mania as fast as they could and didn't dare to stop and take a moment to look back.

CHAPTER 15

Nick, Emily, Will and Izzy were laid out in a playground deep within Victoria Park; all of them exhausted, sweating profusely and feeling dehydrated. Typically, the journey from East Finchley to Victoria Park would have been an eighteen-minute walk, however, the group were forced to run and hide around most of East and North Finchley to evade the Instagrammer Nazis. Being chased by a blood thirsty gang who are trying to cash in on the bounty on your head, made the usually short trip substantially longer to achieve, several hours in fact.

Once they had reached the park, they hopped the fence and took cover amongst the bushes. There had been no sight or sound of the Instagrammer Nazis or the Sick Sikhs in that hour of hiding. Nick had hoped that the rival gangs had killed each other off, but he knew that Bray was a survivor. The man was a cockroach; he would stay alive until only the strongest and biggest boot could stomp him out.

Once the coast was clear, the group slowly crawled out of hiding and reassembled in the playground. Will and Izzy headed to the public bathroom in hopes of salvaging some water. Once they had returned from the bathroom, Nick knew he was going to be barraged with questions, questions he wasn't ready to answer.

Nick and Emily were sat on the swings. When the couple returned, they walked straight over to Nick and stood in front of him.

"Well, are you going to tell us or shall we keep pretending?" said Izzy with a scornful look on her face, "We know who you are idiot."

Nick jumped off of the swing and let out the smallest of chuckles. "Listen here tough girl, I don't have to tell you a thing, so why don't you get out of my face."

He pushed through the pair and shoulder barged Will when doing so. Unsurprisingly, Will grabbed him by the collar and pulled him backwards forcing him to trip over the swings. Will jumped through the swings and pinned Nick down. Will was the smaller of the two and he knew Nick was much stronger than him, but he had somehow mustered up enough strength to restrain him to the floor. However, he didn't realise that Nick wasn't putting up much of a fight because he had no intention of hurting Will.

Emily leapt from the swings to her brother's defence, but Izzy stepped in her way and pushed her back preventing her from interfering.

"If you touch me again, you and your boyfriend will be lying on the floor," threatened Emily.

"I'm sorry, but from the moment we met you two, you've been lying to us," said Izzy in frustration.

She took her phone out of her pocket and hit play on a YouTube video she had downloaded. She handed the phone to Will who held the phone in front of Nick's face.

"This is you, isn't it, standing next to her on the day this all started? That's you holding hands with her. Is she the fiancée you were talking about? Is she? Who the hell are you?" shouted Will.

Emily pushed past Izzy and shoved Will in an attempt to get him off of her brother. Will's beef was with Nick not Emily, so he reluctantly listened to her and got off of Nick. However, he made sure he continued to hold the phone with the video playing in front of Nick. Nick didn't get up off of the astro turf floor; he remained there in silence and watched the video of The Boss giving her first speech as the newly elected Prime Minister of the country, with him standing by her side, holding her hand, as they walked into No. 10 together.

He hadn't seen the footage of this momentous day in a very long time, and he had spent the following years blocking out any memories he had of it. After seeing the video, he was able to recall every minor detail of the day and every feeling he had when she was officially put into office. He remembered feeling a mixture of emotions throughout the day –

happiness, pride, frustration, and fear. All of these emotions rushed back to him all at once and paralysed him to the floor, making him unable to move.

Once the clip had ended, Izzy snatched the phone away from Will and the two backed away from Nick, allowing Emily to peel her comatose brother off of the floor.

"We've known who you are since the cinema. You guys have been plastered all over social media for the last week. The only thing we don't know is why The Boss is after you, and we wanted to give you the opportunity to tell us yourself? You were what? Her second in command? Her fiancé? And then you ran out on her?" asked Izzy.

He didn't say a word. He quietly walked over to a nearby bench and sat down. He looked up at the stars and took a deep breath. Still in a rage, Will stomped over to him, but before he could verbally attack him again Emily grabbed his arm.

"Stop it. You have no idea what we've gone through. It's not as simple as you might think," said Emily, defending herself and her brother.

"We've all gone through bad times," yelled Will, yanking his arm from her grip. "Look around, the only difference between us and you is that you two had a front row seat to the chaos and you did nothing to stop it. Your brother is literally holding hands with the enemy. He doesn't get a pass just because she put a bounty on his head."

"Emily. Come here," said Nick softly.

Emily walked over to her brother and sat down

next to him. Will and Izzy followed, keeping their distance. They remained unsure if they could trust the siblings.

"They're right. I had so many chances to stop her but I didn't, and seeing that clip proves that I let it all happen. I stood by her even when I knew what she was doing was wrong and now look where we are. You two, you want to know who we are. Well sit your arses down and I'll tell you," said Nick.

Will and Izzy huddle around Nick with open ears, hoping to finally get the truth.

"Yes, I was a part of her team. I was the team," began Nick. "I was her manager, from when she was a minor YouTube star all the way up until she was the Prime Minister of the United Kingdom and then The Independent State of England. I was not her boyfriend, her fiancé or lover; she was my friend, she was my best friend. We met at university in our first year and became mates instantly. The cracks in our personal and professional relationship began to show when her passion and ambition outgrew mine. In the beginning, we both wanted the same thing, equality and fair treatment for the workers and the people who keep this country running, the people who were hit with the most injustice. But she took that to the extreme. It never crossed my mind to leave her. I always thought if things got too bad, I could maintain the madness. I've tried to block out the day she became PM, but after seeing that video, I know I can never forget it. It was the day I truly realised that she had big plans in mind, plans bigger than I or anyone else could've ever imagined; and because of those plans and her determination, she ended up getting into bed with people she never ever should have."

14th July 2014, 13:37
Downing Street, The City of Westminster, London

The Boss and Nick were sitting in the back of a black Volvo XC90 Hybrid with tinted black windows. The Boss had her window opened wide and was hanging her head and half of her body out of the car window like an excited dog as she greeted her adoring public.

The car turned into Downing Street to deliver the pair to the front door of No. 10, but The Boss had other ideas and tapped the driver on the shoulder and asked him to let her out at the gates.

"What are you doing?" asked Nick.

"The people came to see the person they appointed as their leader. I've not disappointed them before and I'm not about to start now," she replied with a huge smile across her face.

Before he could say another word she had already shot out of the car to greet the people who chose her to be ruler of the nation. Nick had always been the type to celebrate grand moments and achievements in private, but even he couldn't contain himself, not today. He leapt out of the car just as quickly as she had so he could be involved with the celebrations. He may not have been the face of this operation, but he was as big a part of it as The Boss was; he was the man behind the curtain. Although she wanted to give him the credit he deserved for playing such a crucial role in her rise to power, he knew that it looked better for her image if she was perceived to have done most of the work herself. However, despite only occasionally being in the public eye, it hadn't stopped Nick from garnering a minor cult following of his own, a group who referred to themselves as "The Kingsmen." It was a group mostly filled with teenage girls who fancied him. He didn't admit it openly, but a little part of him enjoyed having a small group of fans who idolised him.

The streets were filled with supporters, young and old, abled and disabled, mixed ethnicities and people from different economic backgrounds. This is what she had achieved in the country; she had done what no other Prime Minister, President, or King had done before, and that was to unite a huge collective of diverse people under one leader. Of course, she had those who voted against her and those who resisted her; but with those people, she made sure she was overly hospitable to them. She welcomed their arguments and debates with respect; she only ever lashed out against those who tried to take her or other's voices away from them.

She spent almost thirty minutes working the crowd, which meant she was late for her first day of her new job, a thought which made Nick laugh. He had known her for a long time and he knew she was the kind of person who would be late to her own funeral, so he wasn't the least bit surprised at how long she had spent with her supporters. After taking selfie after selfie and eventually losing the feeling in her hands from the incessant high fiving, she eventually walked away from the crowds and towards her new office and home.

They walked side by side as they approached the podium, waiting for her in front of No. 10. Once they neared the podium, Nick began to pull back from The Boss as he felt it would look better if she walked into her new role by herself; however, she was having none of it and she grabbed him by the hand and pulled him next to her.

"Where do you think you are going? I want you right next to me for the whole world to see."

The pair hugged and Nick took his rightful place behind her, ready to watch her make her first public address as the new Prime Minister of the United Kingdom.

She stood in front of the fifty to sixty flashing cameras and red blinking lights, which were broadcasting and streaming her message to the country and to the world. For the first time in her life, there were no nerves. She had the world on her shoulders and power in her hands, yet she felt no nerves, only relief. She knew her work had only begun, but she had made it – an orphaned girl who dropped out of secondary school and was told by her teachers that she would be lucky if she made £10 an hour, a young girl who was bounced from care home to care home, foster carer to foster carer, who made her own way through university, and who tried to better herself but had life constantly kicking her down and knocking her back to reality. She was now on top and she had decided there and then that this is where she belonged; and she would never fall to the bottom ever again, no matter what it took.

She had forgone her usual deep breathing exercises she usually needed to compose herself before a big speech or appearance; instead, she took out her notes and swiftly threw them in the air.

"Apologies for the dramatics. Very unlike me, I know" she said sarcastically. "I've been stressing and planning about what I was going to say today for months, but now that the day is here and I am standing here, I realise I should do what I've done since day one and that is shoot from the hip and speak from my heart. What started as a series of videos and blogs from a frustrated and frankly pissed off young woman who had felt beaten up, victimised and abandoned by this country, is now the person in charge of it. I know most people in my position reflect on the good that their predecessors have done for the country, but as I've made it widely known, I have no good feelings or thoughts towards the old regime and their restrictive and unequal ways of dealing with the people they swore to help. Before today, politics in this country meant abusing expenses and taking excessive salaries, cutting taxes for themselves but raising them for the poor, blaming the rioting on the lower and working classes, instead of looking at why they were happening; ignoring the rising immigration problems and not supporting or rewarding the people that work hard in this country to keep it afloat. Issues on race, sexual orientation, and class were all ignored and treated like minor issues; but never again. My upbringing, my feelings, and my opinions have always been public knowledge and I've never shied away from speaking my truth."

A round of applause broke out interrupting The Boss' fervent speech.

"For those of you in the rest of the world who may not know much about me, I would never define myself as a patriot. I care about my country, but it's the people that I love, and I know that the people of this country are capable of greatness when given a chance to prove what they're made of. This country has tested me like it has tested all of you, but it has also put me in the position that I am in today and it has given me the ability to speak to the people around me now, the backbone of this nation who know they're worth so much more."

She turned to Nick and flashed him her beautiful white smile, he returned her kind gesture with a wink.

"When the continuous rioting took over this city and other major cities around the country, places like Birmingham, Liverpool, and Manchester, what did the old regime do to try and contain this madness? They built a fence around London to try and maintain the chaos and stop those who supported me from flocking to the city," continued The Boss. "I, on the other hand, encouraged those who believed in free speech, equality, and fighting for what is right to enter the capital in droves, to stand up in arms with their fellow brothers and sisters and show those who were oppressing them what they were capable of. This is our city and I will keep the promises I have made to you all. I promise to tear that fence down and have an unrestricted country. I promise to reward the hard workers and those who contribute to this country. I promise to start showing you what I am capable of and I will start doing that right here and right now in the capital. This city will run as efficiently as if it was its own independent state. I continue to welcome you all to my city; to our city. To our Independent State of England."

A mammoth round of applause roared through the sky as the people in attendance were enraptured and elated with The Boss' first speech as Prime Minister. Even the journalists and production teams present couldn't help but get caught up in this momentous and historical moment. The Boss stepped away from the podium with a huge sense of achievement and pride. Nick, with chills radiating all over his body grabbed her hand, and in a feeling of pure jubilation, he raised her arm in the air as if she were a wrestler who had been crowned world heavyweight champion of the world.

She gave out her final waves and air kisses before taking her firsts steps into her new office. When the door of Number 10 shut behind her and the loud cheering of the crowd continued, she allowed herself a moment to truly absorb the reality of what had happened. She leant against the closed front door, slid to the floor, and buried her head into her knees.

"Hey, what's the matter?" asked Nick with concern as he crouched down in front of her.

He gently lifted her chin and saw that she had tears in her eyes and a smile on her face.

"I did it Nick. I really did it," said The Boss with a gleam in her eye.

He helped her back to her feet and embraced her. "Fuck yeah you did. Come on Boss, you have a country to run."

The pair walked through Number 10 and absorbed their new surroundings. Nick led The Boss to the gardens where they were greeted by members of her inner circle who were all eager and ready to serve her, but most importantly to celebrate with her. After some initial pleasantries, Nick split away from The Boss to get some drinks. She was left to mingle with her guests and her trusted cabinet members. She spoke openly with those closest to her, allowing herself to enjoy the moment and adoration before the hard work began. She was trying her best to avoid talking about anything too political with her guests; she had years ahead of her to discuss her plans for the city and the country, so tonight, she wanted to enjoy herself.

She found an empty bench in the garden that had

the least amount of people near it so she could have a minute of quiet and peace to herself. She had needed a moment to compose herself from the madness and absurdity of what was going on around her. The Boss had about forty seconds of peace before she was approached by someone who had been a tremendous help to her in her road to victory as Prime Minister, however, it was someone she had hoped she could avoid speaking to for as long as possible.

Bray Michaels walked over to her, jumping at the opportunity to be alone with her while avoiding everyone else around him. His reputation had preceded him, and he wasn't shy in boasting about the underhanded things he had done in his life to usher people into powerful political positions. Many of The Boss' closest advisors were unhappy with her for allowing Bray to aide her, but she knew the value he had and the people he could influence. She knew it was a risk working with him but fortunately for her, the gamble had paid off.

She wasn't naïve. She knew what he represented and where he came from; he was a man born and raised into money and wealth, born to parents who had never worked a hard day in their lives, yet had plenty of political pull in the country, especially with the older white upper classes. He was a man with radical ideas on race and economical privilege; principles he had inherited from his parents. However, the difference between him and his parents was that he was much smarter than them and he saw the value in others and what they could be used for. He felt that he was better than most, but he knew how to manipulate people into thinking he was their equal. He understood that there was a large population of diverse people in the country that was ever growing, and he wanted to make them all think that he was their ally, when in reality he was using them. He exploited people into doing his dirty work for him, to get him drugs, women, and insider information; and then when he got what he wanted, he would throw them under the bus and use them as scapegoats. He was an intelligent man with incredible foresight, but he was also pure evil.

Bray sat down next to The Boss with a glass of Champagne in each hand. When he sat down, the waft of his oddly sweet aftershave came off his suit and invaded her nostrils. The fragrant scent briefly replaced the horrible thoughts she had of Bray with ones of lust. Although she despised him, she was still a heterosexual woman, and even she couldn't deny that he was a good looking man with a confident swagger about him. *"If only he wasn't such a massive self-entitled prick."*

"For you, Prime Minister," said Bray handing The Boss a drink which she reluctantly took.

"Thank you Bray. Nick is actually getting us some drinks, but thank you anyway."

"How are you feeling? Powerful, I bet. This is just the beginning for you. All that stuff you said you'd do, now you'll actually get to do some of it," he said before taking a sip of Champagne.

"It's not stuff Bray; it's what me and millions of others believe in. And I won't be doing some of it, I'll be doing all of it," said The Boss already feeling annoyed with Bray.

"Bless your cottons. It's cute that you think you're any different from any of those other filthy liars. I thought you were a realist, despite your various affiliations with the lesser people in this country. Your grasp on what can and needs to be done is one of the many reasons I like you. You know bullshit when you smell it and you aren't afraid to do what needs to be done to get what you want; damn the consequences," said Bray taking another sip from his glass.

"I'm nothing like you Bray and don't delude yourself into thinking that I am," bit back The Boss.

"Of course you aren't, you are better. You believe in what you say, and you believe that you will make a difference. Your only flaw is your compassion. People are shit; all of us. We are unreliable, scared, angry, untrusting pieces of shit. The people will never unite, you wait and see. All these people may follow you now, but it's only a matter of time until the whispers begin and the doubt sets in. I hope for your sake, when that day comes, you continue to do what needs to be done. No good deed goes unpunished, remember that," said Bray finishing the remainder of his drink in one gulp.

"Showering us all with your infinite wisdom again, are we Bray?" said Nick who was now standing over Bray.

He turned his head slightly towards Nick, barely acknowledging his presence. "I'm simply giving our new glorious leader some advice from someone who has actually grown up in this crazy world that we call politics. What was your background in again, Nicholas?" sniped Bray.

"My background? Media Studies. Yet, isn't it interesting where our paths can take us. You, a product of British politics, wealth and money; me, a self-raised Media Studies student who graduated with a 2:1 who went on to became the Prime Minister's number two, while you with all of your money and connections, sit at the kids table desperately trying to get your plateful. Hey, at least you're at the head of the kids table, even if that table only serves white bread," retorted Nick with a smirk on his face.

Not many people could get under Bray's skin quite like Nick could; he hated him for so many reasons. In fact, his mixed ethnicity was at the bottom of that list. He shot up out of his seat and stood nose to nose with Nick. He leaned in towards him and put his mouth next to his ear. "Stay close to her half-breed. It's only a matter of time until you slip up and I take your spot. I will show her things you never could and I don't just mean politically," whispered Bray.

The Boss stood up and separated the pair. "Not here, do you understand me? Not here and not now," said The Boss gritting her teeth in anger.

Bray backed away from Nick without taking his eyes off of him.

"My apologies Boss, too much Champagne. Very good Champagne might I add. Only the best for you. I'll leave you to enjoy the rest of your day. Nick," said Bray, raising his glass before turning his back on him and walking away.

"Bray. Until next time," responded Nick who raised his glass in return and then downed his drink.

He didn't take his eyes off of Bray until he left the celebrations. The Boss fell back down onto the bench where Nick joined her.

"Did you have to do that? I know you hate him but that could've been really bad for me. How'd you think that would have looked?" said The Boss chastising Nick.

"Let's not do this today, okay? Today is about happiness and celebration. I don't want to talk about that man again, ever again if possible," said Nick struggling to let go of his pent-up anger.

"I didn't want to talk about him today either, but you hardly bit your tongue," said The Boss.

"And I never will. It's one thing having to see him all the time, knowing what he has done for you professionally, but I refuse to keep quiet when I see that racist twat drooling over you like a school boy with an erection," said Nick, not being able to let go of the anger that only Bray could bring out in him.

"For god sake Nick, how many times have we gone over this? You know I didn't want to have to go to him for help but to get the votes and support from the people he represents; I had to play his little game. I despise myself for it, but unfortunately it's one of those many immoral choices I've had to make. I'm fed up of you acting like you haven't done anything questionable – the riots, the manipulation during the estate fires, the propaganda we fed to the youths trying to join the army. We made an entire generation turn on the government and follow me, and yes, we did it for the right reason, but it was hardly ethical. We had to do what we did then and I have to do what I need to do now, so don't decide which way your moral compass points when it suits you because that's not fair!" fumed The Boss who stood up from the bench with her once jovial mood being replaced with resentment and sadness "Thank you for bringing this up today like you said you wouldn't. This is all I've...no, all we've been fighting for and we finally have it and you're still not happy. Get it together Nick because we've only just begun. Thanks for ruining this for me."

When she realised people had begun staring at them, she decided to walk away. She felt exhausted and fed up at yet another argument the two have had, another in a long line of disagreements they had been having over the last few months. Nick had put the increasing tension between them down to the stresses of her running for Prime Minister, but now that they had achieved their goal, he didn't know what was to blame for their continued bitterness. Everything had been affected by the campaign, their friendship, their values, their goals, his relationship with his sister and even his love life. He had hoped that now she was in power, they would begin to rebuild their rapport and make amends for all that they had endured, but in that moment, he'd realised that it wouldn't be that easy and he had this horrible feeling that things were going to get a lot worse before they would get better.

11th June 2016, 23:58
Victoria Park, Barnet, The Independent State of England

"So, there you go, that's who I am. I'm Nick King and I'm The Boss' number two, her go-to guy. I managed her from humble beginnings to a crumbling end," said Nick feeling emotionally drained.

Will and Izzy, who were both sat on the warm astro turf in front of the siblings, were speechless at the story they were regaled with. Izzy tried to speak, but nothing other than some "umm's" and "ahh's" came out of her mouth. Will stood up and began pacing around on the spot with his hands on his head, desperately trying to contemplate what he had heard and what he and Izzy were going to do next. He had no idea if Nick was telling the truth or not, all he knew was that he and Izzy were in danger by being associated with him.

"So, what are you doing here? Both of you, why are you here?" asked Will in a panic.

"What do you mean? Didn't you hear what my brother has been saying? We had to get away from her. She went crazy!" stressed Emily.

"Yeah, I get that. It's all very well documented

that she went crazy. We are literally living in her crazy, but it's all a bit too little too late don't you think? After hearing that story, it sounded like your brother decided to grow a conscience when it suited him, so what I'm asking him is, what are you doing? What's your plan? Because if you think you can run away from her, you must be as mental as she is," said Will, "The entire city knows who you are and everyone is after you, both of you. Luckily for him though, she wants him back alive, but not you. If they catch you, you'll be dead. So, I ask you again. What are you doing here?"

"I was her number two, which means I know EVERYTHING, I've done EVERYTHING, and I've been through EVERYTHING" said Nick who began walking over to Will and Izzy. "I've seen her manipulate groups of people into following and supporting her. In most cases, she didn't actually have to try that hard; so many people were fed up with the world they lived in and she was the voice that spoke for them. I've seen her use tragedy and chaos as a tool to get what she wants. I had to watch as she made anyone who resisted her or gave her any trouble "disappear." I watched her speak from the heart to the point of tears when she saw the injustice happening in this country. I watched her get red with rage when discussing illegal immigration or people who abuse the benefits system or corrupt CEOs and politicians who got preferential treatment and a fat pay cheque over those who get by with the bare minimum. I saw her suck the life out of this country, out of me and, out of my fiancée when she took her away from me..." stuttered Nick as his voice began to break and tremble.

He tried his hardest to fight back the tears brewing in his eyes when he mentioned his fiancée. He had been fighting so many battles for so long, and after all of this time, his mind and body could no longer fight this battle anymore and the tears began to fall from his face. The tears had beaten him and he had finally let them out, but he refused to let them take over and he refused to be broken down by them, not yet.

Izzy and Will watched on as he poured his soul out to them; all of that anger and frustration Will was feeling suddenly disappeared and was replaced by guilt and sorrow. Seeing Nick, a man who was on top of the world, who had come from nothing and rose to a place of great power, who was now broken and crying in front of them after losing everything, Will started to realise that maybe he was trying to right his wrongs and that he was trying to rescue the world he had helped destroy.

Overcome with remorse, Izzy tried to reach out to console him, but before she could touch him, Emily pushed her hand out of the way and hugged her big brother. He wiped the tears from his eyes and let go of his sister so he could address the couple again.

"All of this has happened and I can't change that. I had the power and knowledge to stop it then, but I didn't. I still have that knowledge and now I CAN stop this," said Nick. "So, to answer your question of what am I doing here, I'm going to leave this hell hole and I'm going to get help from the people beyond the fence. I will tell them everything I know about her and when the time is right I will bring that dictating bitch down and I will restore this city to what it once was, for better or worse, but without her."

CHAPTER 16

Another sleepless night meant she was up early and had been back to work from the crack of dawn. By 8am she had been sat in a meeting regarding petitions received from both the resistance groups and those loyal to her asking for the rebuild and renovations of basic facilities across the state, such as hospitals and schools. Along with these renovations, the petitions also asked for appropriate staff who would be rewarded for working in these vital roles, which would consist of medical personnel, teachers, and anyone else who could help to rebuild the damage in the city. She had dropped the ball on matters such as these in recent months with much of her resources being delegated to the fence being maintained; making sure there was enough security around the vital deliveries from outside of the state and ensuring that the people in her city were fed.

Despite being separated from the country, she had several connections with the new government that had been established beyond the fence, as well as some alliances with some other countries in the rest of the world. These connections aided her in importing the goods she needed into the state, and in return for their support, she exported weaponry to these countries; many of which had questionable ethics when it came to the use of firearms. This was yet another immoral decision she had made which Nick disapproved of. She tried to justify this decision by telling him that in order to prevent the gangs in the city from arming themselves with deadly weapons, she had to get rid of them. The last thing she needed were trigger happy gangs running around her city like a bunch of wild cowboys.

There were some concerns amongst her team about these petitions; not about the petitions themselves but concerns over the rival boroughs seemingly working together for the betterment of the state. If these conflicting boroughs could agree on matters like these, what else could they agree on? The last thing The Boss needed was another mutiny on her hands. She knew all about starting a rebellion and deep down in her heart she knew that one day karma would rear its ugly head. With Nick no longer by her side, she found it increasingly difficult to ignore the very real possibility of an uprising against her, and although she wouldn't dare show it, those thoughts terrified her.

The meeting already had an air of tension when The Boss had severely scolded a member of her team who felt it was an appropriate time to discuss the team receiving bonuses for their hard work over the turbulent year. She had made it clear at the beginning of her political campaign that anyone who was a part of her team had better be there with the goal of fairness and equality as their main priority and not for a big pay out. This particular cabinet member was feeling extra confident that day and felt that it would be a good idea to make a snide comment about the hypocrisy of The Boss apparently caring about equality, while she sat in a world of luxury and privilege as the world beyond Downing Street had become a violent cesspit. The moment these words were uttered from his mouth, he knew he had made a terrible mistake. Over the last year, The Boss had transformed from a welcoming and friendly person to someone who was easily agitated and lost her patience with people very quickly.

She had never been a physical person and she'd never personally dealt with someone who she needed to "disappear," but she very nearly made an exception for this particular cabinet member, instead she allowed the man to leave the room on his own two feet with the caveat being that he pack his bags immediately and leave her team forever. The Boss and everyone else in the room considered this gesture a show of mercy, however, what her team didn't know was that she had her security team on standby to rough up the cabinet member before he left to ensure that he never made the mistake of challenging her again.

Due to the incident with the cabinet member, the meeting ended earlier than expected, which fortunately for The Boss, meant she had time to return to her room for some time to cool down with a drink and perhaps even some yoga.

She tried her best to concentrate and follow along with the yoga video on her tablet, but she couldn't find that Zen she so desperately needed. Her mind would not stop racing with thoughts of Nick and of all the things going wrong around her, so she decided to forgo the yoga and opted for a long hot shower instead. She always said that a hot shower is where she found the most clarity and thus got her best ideas from; a theory Nick often teased her about and said that her getting clarity was actually a euphemism for giving herself a bit of "self-love," a phrase that still made her cringe but also smile when she thought of him saying it.

The shower had helped for a moment, but after a few minutes of standing in front of a half-steamed mirror, she caught a glimpse of herself and the millions of thoughts and emotions came running back to her and hit her like a bolt of lightning. She could've cried, she could've smashed the mirror, she could've run, but she didn't, she wiped the condensation off of the mirror and continued to dry herself off.

Her attention was suddenly drawn back to her bedroom where she was certain she had heard footsteps coming from the other side of the door of her en-suite bathroom. A thought popped into her head; in her eagerness to be alone, she had forgotten to lock the door to her living quarters. Despite being in one of the most secure places in the city, the paranoia she had begun to feel on a daily basis was very real; and in this instance, she was right to have been worried. Being highly paranoid wasn't always a bad thing. She had made sure her room was sufficiently equipped with plenty of weapons, should she ever need them. She reached into the toilet cistern and pulled out a waterproof sealed bag with a 7mm handgun inside of it. Guns and heavy artillery were never something Nick had any personal interest in, but after being introduced to the world of firearms by Emily of all people, The Boss had grown to love them.

Emily had spent her youth as an air cadet, and part of this after school activity, besides the constant marching, was getting to go on field trips which included trips to gun ranges. Before she had become The Boss, Emily was the first one to ever take her shooting and it was something she instantly fell in love with. The power to destroy something in front of you was an exhilarating feeling for her and it became an excellent tool for her to express and vent the rage she would feel prior to her starting her YouTube channel. Emily and The Boss bonded over their love of shooting things and there was a flicker of guilt from The Boss when she thought back on how things had turned out between her and Emily; once upon a time she considered Emily to be a close friend of hers.

The thoughts of Emily had exited her head as quickly as they had entered, and she prepared herself for what was on the other side of her bathroom door. *"Is today the day someone finally tries to take me out,* thought The Boss, *if it is, they will not take me quietly."*

Both parties on either side of the door knew where the other one was and The Boss was not going to allow the person on the other side to make the first move, so she pushed the bathroom door open and pointed the gun at the figure sitting on the edge of her bed.

"Easy sweetheart I come in peace. Jesus, even with a gun pointed at me, you turn me on," said Bray with a sleazy smile on his face.

"What the fuck are you doing in my room, Bray? How did you even get in here?"

"You standing in front of me in nothing but a towel is literally a recurring fantasy I've had, gun included. But I am going to need you to lower that thing, and by that thing, I mean the gun not the towel... well, maybe the towel later."

"I don't think so. You seem to have forgotten who I am. Perhaps a bullet or two to the kneecap will remind you to never enter my room without my permission," said The Boss lowering her gun and pointing it at Bray's left knee.

"Take it easy Boss, you know I can sweet talk my way into anywhere I want. However, in this instance, my usual charms didn't seem to work on your security team. You have some loyal people by your side, Boss. It was only when I threatened their loved ones beyond the fence did they let me in. Daddy says hello by the way," replied Bray.

She finally lowered her gun and put the safety on, but she kept a firm grasp on the grip.

"You may think you can sweet talk everyone Bray, but you'll never be able to use that tongue on me, and your father will certainly never be able to pull my strings. Or does he need reminding of that?" responded The Boss.

She left the bedroom and walked into the living room area where Bray swiftly followed behind her. When he walked in, he saw The Boss making a drink of Southern Comfort and lemonade for herself and a glass of vodka and ice for him which she left resting on the drinks cabinet. She sat down on the sofa and Bray collected his drink from the cabinet.

"You say I'll never be able to use my gift of the gab on you, well young lady..." said Bray before being interrupted by The Boss.

"Never call me young lady again, do you understand me?" ordered The Boss.

"My apologies Boss. As I was saying, today is the day I finally use my linguistic skills to seduce you. I come bearing excellent news," continued Bray.

"You have Nick?" said The Boss with a flicker of excitement in her voice, something Bray noticed which vexed him.

"No, but after some persuasive actions taken by yours truly I know where they are going."

"And how do you know that?"

"Let's just say you have one less gang to worry about, The Sick Sikh's are no more, you're welcome."

"Who?"

"Never mind," replied Bray, "We found Nick and his new friends, however, before we had a chance to detain them, we were rudely interrupted by a rival gang and they escaped. That being said, a member of the Sick Sikhs' had been following Nick prior to his escape and had overhead where Nick and his new assailants were headed. After some gentle persuading from me, he told me everything he knew."

He pulled out a blood soaked turban from his back pocket that once belonged to the recently deceased Anand, former leader of the now extinct Sick Sikhs. He threw the turban onto the table in front of The Boss.

"The group are heading further into Barnet. My guess is he doesn't think you'll jeopardise your credibility further by sending anyone into the neutral zones after him. Oh, how wrong he is."

She knew Nick better than anyone, he never hid from anything, he may have felt safe in Barnet for a while but she knew there was more to what he was doing than hiding in a place where he thought she wouldn't come after him. He had accumulated his fair share of The Boss' enemies but she knew he had some acquaintances in the city and he would be going to them for help to achieve whatever it was he was trying to achieve. She may not have known what he was up to yet, but what she did know was that if he was successful it would affect her gravely.

"So, you're telling me that your good news is that you failed to capture Nick? That you slaughtered another gang in some sort of race war? And that Nick is currently in a place where if I'm seen to have sent people to, it could create backlash against me, both from those who already hate me and potentially from those who are loyal to me? Would you please kindly let me know when the sweet talking is supposed to begin because right now I'm furious?" said The Boss.

"Who said anyone had to know you made the call to send us in after him? Me and my team can slip into Barnet, get Nick, take care of Emily and his friends, and deliver him to you on a silver and slightly bloody platter. Call off the search and the hit you've placed on them, tell the State that you've freed Nick and anyone else who has associated themselves with him. If anyone finds out or suspects that we are after them, we will tell them we have gone into business for ourselves. Everyone who matters knows how much I despise Nick, so nobody would suspect a thing. They would simply think I was out for blood," explained Bray, who helped himself to another drink.

She sat for a moment and digested what he had offered her while he finished the remainder of his second drink. She leant forward on the sofa and downed the rest of her Southern Comfort.

"This all sounds okay in theory but it also sounds like a lot of work and effort on your part, what's in it for you? Or are you still trying to worm your way back into my cabinet?" asked The Boss.

"Yes, but that's not all. I want Nick's old spot. I want to be your number two. I want to be the new Nick, a better Nick, and I want to please you like he was never able to. I want his spot and more, I want what he never had or wanted. I want you," said Bray with a serious expression on his face, one The Boss had never seen before.

She smiled at him and put her empty glass on the table. She stood up and walked over to the living room door and opened it. She looked over to Bray and with slightest of nods she signalled that it was time for him to leave. He put his glass down and walked towards the door, unsure what she was thinking or wanted from him, if anything. With his eyes locked onto her, he left the room and stood in the doorway.

"If you bring Nick back to me, unharmed and without a single soul knowing that you are working for me, I will give you everything and anything you want," said The Boss. She began to shut the door on him, when the door was almost closed, she dropped her towel to the floor, revealing the slightest glimpse of her naked body. "And I mean everything."

Bray almost snapped his own neck trying to get a look at the powerful woman he had been fawning over for years. Unfortunately for him, the door shut in his face before he could catch a glimpse of her and he was left with a semi in his pants and a mission to complete.

"Sorry Bray. I'm not that easy. Idiot," said The Boss quietly to herself as she locked the door and walked back to her bedroom in all of her naked glory.

CHAPTER 17

12th June 2016, 10:16
Swan Lane, Barnet, The Independent State of England

Emily had spent the past hour awake, after the emotional outpour from the night before mixed with hours spent slowly and quietly delving further into Barnet on very little sleep. The mental and physical toll had really affected her, and she wanted nothing more than to sleep and hide for the entire day. Doubt and uncertainty about the safety of Barnet had crept into the minds of the group, which added to their exhaustion. After the ambush in Finchley the night before, the group was no longer sure how safe the borough was. Nick had hoped that by going further into the borough they wouldn't encounter any more trouble.

When the group were finally able to stop and rest at around four in the morning, Emily opted to sleep by herself next to the lake in the Swan Lane Park; she'd figured that on a twenty-eight degree night the breeze flowing over the lake would provide her with a cool and tranquil night. What she didn't account for, however, were the dozens of mosquitos and other biting insects also hovering around the lake. Despite spending the night uncomfortable, itchy, and covered in bites she was happy to have some time by herself. Keeping so many secrets locked away in her head had drained her and being able to finally unload some of those secrets about who they really were, was a huge weight off of her mind. She wondered if Nick had thought the same. Part of her felt bad for separating herself from him after he had bore his soul, but she thought they could both use the space to get some clarity and perspective before they had to venture out once again.

Once they had reached Swan Lane after hours of travelling in silence, Will and Izzy sensed that the siblings could use some time alone. Will wanted to try his luck with one of the houses in the surrounding area, but Izzy reminded him that they were trying to draw as little attention to themselves as they could, and breaking into a house that could potentially be occupied in a neutral and governed borough was the last thing they should be doing. The pair settled for a small café on the other side of the playground. Living in a dystopian society rarely created moments of romance, and dating wasn't an easy thing to achieve, however, the couple had made a promise to each other that no matter how busy or hectic life got, they would always find time to sit down together and have a date in some capacity.

A run down and abandoned café wasn't exactly The Gong bar on the 52nd floor of The Shard, but it would have to do. The pair decided to forego sleeping that night so they could spend some time together, even if that meant dining on crushed packets of salt and vinegar crisps and warm cans of Dr Pepper. However, instead of their usual playful banter followed by some intimate love making, they spent their time discussing what they were going to do next. After hours of discussion, they had decided that for their own safety they could no longer travel with Nick and Emily. Will wanted to slip out during the night, but Izzy was able to convince him that they should show the siblings some respect and part ways with them amicably.

The pair had managed to get a couple of hours sleep, and when they woke in the morning, they walked out into the bright and sunny park together, which was now filled with a handful of people going about their day. The couple naturally felt uneasy with the amount of people walking around after they had spent the last eight months trying to find a safe haven of likeminded people to align themselves with. Seeing people with smiles on their faces was an unusual sight for the pair, but it also comforted them and confirmed that the neutral zones were indeed safe places to live. Without ever seeing the two neutral boroughs the pair were unsure if The Boss had stuck to her word by letting these communities thrive uninterrupted, now they knew she had. The pair walked down towards the lake with the intent of speaking with Emily and Nick. Emily had spotted the couple from the other side of the lake and began walking over to them.

"Hey, you sleep okay?" asked Izzy awkwardly trying to ease her way into the conversation.

"Not really, but I needed some space which was nice," replied Emily.

"Where's your brother?" asked Will.

The group scanned the small park trying to locate Nick. Emily looked over towards the small playground and saw Nick standing by the swings.

"There he is," said Emily.

He was standing in the playground pushing a small girl on the swings. The little girl's mother sat on a nearby bench smiling as she watched Nick playing with her elated child. Emily walked into the playground while Will and Izzy stood outside of the playground gate. He picked the little girl up off of the swing and helped her on to the floor. The little girl gestured to Nick who crouched down next to her; she whispered something into his ear which made him smile.

"Yes, that's my baby sister. She's okay. We like her," said Nick.

The little girl waved at Emily. "She's pretty. She looks like a princess."

Emily smiled at the little girl and then crouched down in front of her. "Me, no I'm not a princess, I'm a queen; and as the queen, I get to make other little girls princesses. Do you know anyone around here who I could turn into a princess?" asked Emily pretending to look around the playground.

The little girl looked up at Nick and then to her mother for approval. Her mum smiled at her daughter and gave her a nod.

The little girls arm shot up into the air. "Me, I could be a princess," she said ecstatically.

Emily put her hands on the little girl's shoulders, closed her eyes and gently squeezed. She opened her eyes, picked up a small daffodil and handed it to her.

"I Emily, The Queen, now pronounce you Princess of Swan Park and all of the Swans. Do you think you can accept that responsibility?"

The little girl took the flower from her and nodded her head with excitement. She hugged Emily and then ran over to her mother to show her the flower she was given by the "Queen."

Emily stood up and watched the little girl and her mother share a loving cuddle.

"Hey, let's go," said Nick, snapping Emily out of her gaze.

He noticed Will and Izzy standing outside of the playground with smiles on their faces after seeing a very different side to Nick.

"I have to tell those two something before we go."

"Who knew you had a soft side Nick," laughed Izzy.

"Here I was thinking that all you did was pout and brood like a hipster whose mum bought him a pair of straight jeans instead of super skinny," joked Will.

"I know I've been a pain in the arse and I'd like to apologise for that. As you can imagine, I've been holding onto a lot of stuff for a very long time and being able to let that all out last night has given me some perspective," said Nick humbly.

"Thank you for telling us that and for being so honest with us. We were hoping we could return the favour by..." started Izzy before being interrupted by Nick.

"Before you finish that thought, I've been thinking and I'm tired of pushing people away. I've lost a lot of people over the last few years and in the last few weeks I lost my closest friend, she chose power and loneliness over me. But I've decided I'm done feeling alone. I haven't spoken to Em about this yet, but I'm sure she won't have a problem with it. I wanted to ask you both if you would like to join me and Emily in taking down The Boss and restoring this broken country?" asked Nick bluntly.

Naturally Will and Izzy were taken aback by Nick's request. A few days ago they were hoping they could find somewhere to live that was quiet and danger free, and now they were being asked to go on a mission so grandiose and dangerous that it would either bring an end to the horrible world they lived in or bring an end to their lives.

"I know I'm asking a lot of you, all of you, but I think I've been looking at this all wrong" explained Nick. "When I decided to do this, I wanted to have as few people involved as possible; not because I thought you may slow me down, but because I couldn't bare anyone else getting hurt because of me. People like that little girl and her mother over there. Choice, option, and equality is what all of this was supposed to be about, but that got lost and taken away from us. So now I'm asking and giving you the choice to decide what you want to do with your lives. You can head further into Barnet and live out your days in peace. You can join a resistance gang and try your luck with them or you can come with me, and make a difference, a difference so that little girl and so many others can grow up in a world that isn't broken. That goes for you too Em, I helped create this world and I dragged you into it which wasn't my decision to make. So now, I'm letting you make your own decision. You all have a choice and I'll respect whatever choice you make."

Will and Izzy took a moment and whispered to each other, deciding if they were going to abandon Nick or help him. The couple stopped talking and shared a kiss.

"Damn Nick, if that's the way you used to pump up The Boss before she spoke, I can see why she got so hyped about everything she was saying," said Will.

Will jumped over the playground fence while Izzy more sensibly entered the playground through the gate.

"I think what my idiot boyfriend is saying is that we are in," said Izzy.

"Are you sure?" questioned Nick.

"Absolutely, what else are we going to do. Wait around for The Boss to get bored and randomly decide to bomb the whole city? I'd rather go out knowing we tried to stop that vindictive bitch," continued Izzy.

"Oh I do love when you talk dirty Izz," said Will before he playfully pinched her arse.

Emily, who had been silent during Nick's passionate revelation, let out a loud laugh, "You guys are nuts...but I can't think of a better bunch of weirdoes to see in the end of the world with. Of course I'm in, but you do all see the irony of what is happening right now though don't you?"

The group looked at her in bemusement.

"After all that has happened, after all the false and broken promises, the chaos and the gang warfare that has engulfed this city, we have started a gang of our own to bring an end to all of this," said Emily.

"Holy shit, you're right. Oh my god, we totally need a cool gang name, maybe we could be called The Saviours," said Will in excitement.

The group shook their heads in unison, unimpressed with the name he suggested.

"You're right, it's a little on the nose. How about The Gamers, cause, like, we are going to fight The Boss? Or maybe The Equalisers because our goal is to create equality. This is going to need some serious thought. Leave it with me guys, I'll think of something," continued Will.

Nick shook his head and laughed. "You do that mate. Okay 'gang', onwards and upwards, we have a city to save and that starts with getting to Enfield," exclaimed Nick.

The gang left the area and continued towards Enfield. The street was slightly busier than the park so the group were able to blend in unnoticed amongst the people. When they got back onto the high street, Will saw an abandoned Audi car showroom with most of the cars in the lot untouched.

"Izz, those are the kind of cars I was talking about before, an Audi TT is my car. Why don't we take one of those and drive to wherever we are going? There are a few cars up top that look like they're in pretty good condition," Will suggested.

"Sorry mate, no can do. Haven't you noticed that nobody really drives anymore? If the roads aren't blocked and you can actually find a car that hasn't been burnt to a crisp, chances are the moment you are seen driving a car someone will either try and steal it from you or trash it and inflict some sort of horrible pain on you," replied Nick.

"Hmmm, good point, I've decided I'm too good for the Audi and I'm going to walk, because of the environment and that," said Will feeling slightly saddened that he wouldn't be able to take the car of his dreams for a joy ride.

The more the group spoke between themselves, the more unaware they became with how quiet and empty the street had suddenly become. There was a lurking presence in the air which the group were oblivious to.

Nick noticed a sign pointing towards the closed Totteridge and Whetstone tube station. He walked ahead of the group slightly to make sure that they were going in the right direction, but when he turned back to call them over, he'd realised that Will, Izzy and Emily had crossed to the other side of the road. He ran across the road and caught up with them.

"Hey, where are you going?" asked Nick with concern in his voice.

"To Enfield, Will says this is the quickest way," said Emily.

"I lived near Enfield for a year when I was declared homeless a few years back. It was the only place the council could put me, even though my old place and job was in Stoke Newington. It was ridiculous," said Will.

"I know a quicker route back past the tube station. I used to get the bus that way when I'd visit old friends in Enfield" said Nick unconvincingly as he looked back towards the tube station.

"Are you sure? Will seems pretty confident that it's this way. I could go and ask someone or see if there's anywhere with Wi-Fi so we can look it up," offered Izzy.

Nick began to become visibly anxious and flustered; something Emily picked up on immediately.

"I don't think we should draw any attention to ourselves, let's go the way I know," demanded Nick.

"It's fine, nobody knows who I am. I'll go and ask someone," said Izzy walking back to the High Road with hopes of finding someone to speak to. Emily pulled Nick aside and questioned why he was acting so strange.

"What's going on? Enfield is that way and you know it. What are you up to?" asked Emily quizzically.

Izzy returned back to the gang with a look of confusion across her face.

"It's so weird, I can't see anyone. The streets are empty. It's like everyone has vanished into thin air," said Izzy.

The group looked around the streets and suddenly realised how vacant and quiet it had gotten. From the corner of his eye, Nick noticed a number of black figures had appeared from the street in front of him. For a second he felt relief at the sight of more people filling the eerily quiet street, however, that quickly changed to fear when he realised the black blurs, he could see were a group of hooded people coming towards them. The group turned away from the people in black, but were immediately met with a larger group of people also wearing black hoodies and ski masks. Nick didn't recognise any gang signs on their clothing and hadn't thought a rival gang would have made it this far into a neutral zone without being confronted by the Mayor. The group were quickly surrounded by the gang – he estimated there were at least forty people surrounding them. Out of the group came a person who Nick would describe as having a classic mum body. The person removed their hood and mask and revealed themselves as a plus sized black woman in her late 50's.

"You're Nick right?" asked the middle aged woman.

Nick looked at his sister and wondered how this stranger knew who he was; the only way she could've known who he was, was if she was aware of his alliance with The Boss, which was bad news for him and his newly formed gang.

"Yes. Who are you?" said Nick hesitantly.

"You'll find out soon enough, please come with us," said the woman politely.

Will, Emily and Izzy looked at each other trying to weigh up their options, which were either do as they were told or fight. With the clear disadvantage in numbers, they chose to walk towards the large group, unsure if they were going to be safe or not. Nick, however, defiantly stepped in front of his sister and new friends, refusing to allow them to be taken away by these hooded strangers.

"Listen lady, you obviously know who I am, so I think it's only fair that you tell us who you are before we go anywhere with you. If you don't, you and your ninja brigade are going to have to drag us to wherever it is you want us to go," said Nick brazenly.

During a moment of silence and uncertainty, Nick looked back to his group and nodded at them, as if to say, "I have your backs."

Out of nowhere, while his attention was momentarily focused on his group, a member of the gang dressed in black rushed over to Nick and jabbed him in the neck with a large hypodermic needle filled with a clear fluid.

"Ouch! What the hell did you do?" said Nick before he grasped his neck.

After about ten seconds, he began to feel weak in

the knees. His head started to feel light and he suddenly collapsed to the floor. Emily rushed over to her fallen brother and tried to wake him up by shaking him and snapping her fingers in his face.

"What did you do to him? What was in that injection?"

"I only did what The Boss' second in command asked me to do. He asked to be dragged away and I didn't want any of my people getting hurt while we did it. Count your lucky stars I didn't ask Romesh to knock him out; he is very fond of the old police baton to the back of the head technique when putting people to sleep. If your brother had continued to disobey me, I may have hit him over the head myself. Now, how would the rest of you like to travel, will you be walking or will you be dragged?" asked the woman.

Will and Izzy swiftly jogged over to the middle aged woman and her team of masked assailants, Emily, however, refused to move and stood over her brother offering him her protection. Three figures approached her and Nick's unconscious body.

"If any of you stab me with a needle or even think about touching me, you are going to seriously regret it," threatened Emily.

The middle aged woman pushed through the three people standing in front of the siblings and gestured for them to back away.

"We aren't going to hurt him sweetheart. You have my word. You also have my word that if you don't come with us you WILL be in the same state as your brother and take it from me, this stuff gives you quite the sore head once you wake up," said the woman with a hint of compassion in her voice.

The middle-aged woman offered her hand to Emily who reluctantly and cautiously took it. For some unknown reason, Emily got a warm feeling of trust from this woman; perhaps it was the wisdom and experience she exuded or the kindness she offered her, something she had never felt from an older woman before after her mother had left her at such a young age. She didn't know what it was about this woman, but she didn't feel scared going with her. The woman gestured to the three members of her group behind her to pick Nick up off of the floor, which considering how tall and heavy he was, they were able to do with relative ease.

Nick woke up several hours later in a daze feeling groggy and disorientated; however, at the same time, his body appreciated the enforced sleep the drugs had provided him. When he tried to sit up, however, he couldn't move and he quickly realised that he had been strapped down to what must have been a toddler's mattress. Before he had a second to assess where he was or what was going on, he heard a door opening and closing in the small dimly lit room he was laying in. He began to panic as the footsteps approached him while he lay defenceless on the bed. When the middle-aged woman from earlier appeared in front of him, it did nothing to ease his anxiety.

"Good evening Nick. How are you feeling? Sorry

about the straps, we didn't want you falling out of bed," said the woman who began calmly removing them. "Your sister and friends are in the church and are waiting for you whenever you're ready."

He sat up slowly, a thumping pain rushed to his head and he began to feel dizzy and uneasy again. The middle-aged women handed him a glass of orange juice.

"Go easy, here drink this. Those tranquilizers are pretty powerful aren't they? I should know. I used to pop those suckers like they were skittles... amongst other things," she said, chuckling to herself.

The woman helped him to the edge of the bed where he drank the juice. She pulled up a chair in front of him, showing her age when she let out a grumble as she sat down.

"Thank you for the drink. May I ask who you are?" said Nick.

"Oh! So, you do have manners after all. You can call me Ms Wilson," she replied.

"Where are we? Why did you bring me here?"

Ms Wilson reached over to a nearby cupboard; the door had seen better days. It had scratches all along the front and the handle had been broken off. She had to manoeuvre her fingers down the middle to pry it open. She took out a small device, no bigger than an old iPod Shuffle, and returned to her seat making another audible groan when she sat down.

"Oh god, I'm getting old," said Ms Wilson.

She put the device on a small table next to the bed

and turned it on. Nick realised it was a small recording device, something he hadn't seen since his days at university. Nowadays, he mused, most people recorded things on their phones; but he remembered when this technology had mostly been used by doctors or therapists, both of which were a rarity in today's world. The innovative plans The Boss had to revitalise the NHS had become less and less of an issue for her when trying to maintain order in her city. Fortunately, most of the boroughs had enough people in them who had at least a basic understanding of first aid.

"Be a lamb and get this thing to work. You need to hit that button and the last thing on there will start to play. I got this from one of the others and I've no idea how to use it," said Ms Wilson.

Nick picked up the audio device and clicked some buttons until it emitted a red light indicating that something was playing. There was some static and then the sound of two voices arguing about whether the device was on and if they were going to miss the radio announcement. He couldn't help but laugh when he realised that whoever was in charge of this recording had likely been holding the recording device to an old radio speaker instead of recording the audio directly onto a computer.

"OK, listen, it's coming on now, this was broadcast this morning," said Ms Wilson urging him to hold the recording device closer to his ear.

"*...nobody can really explain how they got there and why they felt that location was an ideal spot to do what* they were doing. But from the images and videos floating around on the socials, it looks like they were all having a pretty great time, until they got busted anyway. Next time you crazy kids fancy doing something like that again give ya boy 'The Eye in the Sky' a shout."

Ms Wilson shook her head, "This boy is an absolute fool, if I were his mother I'd of washed his mouth out with soap by now."

Nick continued to listen to the recording, curious as to what he was expected to hear.

"To recap, we've had some breaking news from my pigeons on the street; I've been told that the hit on Nick, Emily and his two unknown sidekicks has been called off. You hear me people of The ISOE, back off! Nick and his gang of troublemakers are free to go, and anyone caught interfering or messing with them will have to answer directly to The Boss; these are her direct orders. I'm not sure why the sudden change of heart. Perhaps her bestie Nick remains exempt from any type of punishment. Personally, that makes me hate him even more; I, for one, would've loved to see that arsehole hung for his hand in helping our fearless leader for all of these years. Ah well, long may she reign, and long may we suffer."

Ms Wilson turned off the recording while Nick sat on the bed in silence, trying to digest what he had heard. He turned to Ms Wilson who remained quiet and allowed him to sit with his thoughts uninterrupted.

"This is bad!" said Nick breaking the silence.

She slowly groaned her way up from her seat.

"Indeed. Once we heard this and we knew that you were nearby we were ordered to bring you in," said Ms Wilson

"Ordered? Ordered by who?" asked Nick with trepidation in his voice.

She extended her hand out to Nick who took it and pulled himself gently to his feet, "I think it's time that you meet The Mayor."

CHAPTER 18

12th June 2016, 19:26
Wood Street, Barnet, The Independent State of England

Nick had a brief reunion with Emily, Will, and Izzy. They were all in good spirits and were in much better condition than he was. Together they were led by Ms Wilson to the local church. It was packed full of people. Nick had suspected that some of these people were the same ones dressed in black that he had encountered earlier in the day. It was a diverse crowd – men, women and children of all colours, ages and social backgrounds, some fit and some not so fit. The majority of the church pews had been pushed to the sides of the room; with most lined with sheets and bedding. Nick could see that this church, like most in recent times, was being used as a shelter.

The vibe in the church was mostly positive, children were playing board games, some of the older people were sleeping peacefully, food was being shared, and some were even exercising and training; everyone was busy doing something. This was clearly a community and as far as Nick was aware this is how the two neutral zones in the state operated. They were peaceful and organised and had become a safe haven for people who felt trapped in the city, and as long as both the neutral zones kept their word and neither helped nor hinder an opposing side The Boss would leave them alone. Allowing these boroughs to operate independently from the rest of the state gave her a lot of brownie points with the resistance boroughs. It was seen as a good will gesture; however, she knew she had the power to shut them down whenever she wanted to.

His newly formed gang were being well looked after. They had been given food and water and seemed to mesh well with the locals. Emily read stories to some of the small children while Will and Izzy were chatting and swapping stories with members of the community. Izzy had even been able to converse in Polish with an elderly woman, something she hadn't done in years after a large majority of the Polish population in London had fled the city. When The Boss refused to tear down the fence a choice was given to the people in the city, stay or leave. Many Eastern European immigrants felt that although she had claimed to only be against illegal immigration, she had lost control and that any and all immigrants would be the first to suffer from the backlash.

After a few moments with his sister, Nick was escorted away from the group by Ms Wilson who took him to the main stage of the church. A large decorative chair was placed in between some church pews which were often used by choir singers. The chair didn't quite resemble a throne, but it certainly had the ominous look and feel about it.

"Don't tell me, The Mayor sits on his throne while passing judgement on others?" said Nick laughing to himself.

Ms Wilson stopped in her tracks and put her hand on his chest with some force.

"Listen here young man, you may have played an integral part in The Boss' rise to power, you have lived the high life and the low life, you have prospered and you have suffered, you were part of creating this world and to your credit you did it your way, from nothing to everything. Your Boss may sit on her gold throne in her ivory tower, but the people here are grounded and the man in there built this community from the bottom up. He doesn't need a chair, he doesn't even need a thank you, he just wants peace. So, before you go in there, you will leave any sass and all of your bullshit at the door. Do you understand me?" said Ms Wilson with a deadly serious visage, a look that he remembered shortly prior to being stabbed in the neck with a needle.

He felt a huge rush of guilt, shame, and embarrassment. He had to remember the chaos he had caused and to check himself before he opened his mouth and made jokes. He wasn't "the man" anymore and this wasn't his house; he was a guest in Barnet. Despite forgetting most of the values his father had taught him, he had never forgotten that you always treat your hosts with respect, especially when your host is within their rights to turn you away...or worse.

"I apologise Ms Wilson, I'm not used to this kind of hospitality and it's been a rough few years. My trust levels aren't exactly high," said Nick apologetically.

"That's OK Hun. Just remember to keep that sharp tongue of yours in your mouth. You should count yourself lucky that you even get to be here, let alone to meet The Mayor," expressed Ms Wilson who had reverted back to her calm and gentle self.

He felt nervous, in recent years there wasn't much that made him feel nervous anymore. After all he had seen and been through, he often felt like nothing more could surprise him. But the welcoming atmosphere of the church and the kind nature of those around him was something he had never thought he would have seen in this city again and it unnerved him. If the man he was about to meet was the one responsible for creating such a hospitable place to live, with all the chaos around them, he must be quite the man.

Ms Wilson pointed to a room at the back of the church behind the stage.

"He's expecting you. Knock on the door and wait to be called in. Oh, and don't knock too loudly, you don't want to disturb the animals."

"Animals?" questioned Nick.

He had only ever heard rumours about The Mayor so he had no idea what to expect. Since the city had gone all "Mad Max," a lot of eccentric people and gangs had emerged over the years and the world had become very theatrical in places. The gang emergence started off as a territorial thing, gangs like The Tottenham Mandem, The Peckham Boys, and The Westenders controlled their respective turf, but as more and more people flocked to the city the gangs became much more creative and peculiar, gangs like the Social Outcasts, the Humpty Gang and the Camp Crusaders materialized. Now there was someone who called himself 'The Mayor' who surrounded himself with animals. His mind was hypothesising all kinds of images and backstories for the man he was about to meet. He felt as if he was about to walk into the lair of a Bond villain. *"If this man has a cat on his lap, I'm not sure I'll be able to stop myself from laughing,"* thought Nick.

Ms Wilson left him to speak to The Mayor and returned back to the people. The silly thoughts running through his head had disappeared and were once again replaced with feelings of nervousness and concern the closer he got to the office. The door was slightly ajar, but he did as he was instructed and knocked gently. He heard a faint voice ushering him into the room and with that he opened the door which he instantly regretted as he was immediately struck with the wafted putrid stench of stale animal urine, soggy woodchips, and day-old cat food. The reek of animal forced him back out of the room as he tried to stop himself from throwing up. He re-entered the room, breathing only through his mouth and fighting the urge to squeeze his nose closed with his fingers. In the room was a man standing by a collection of cages. He couldn't quite make out what he was doing or what animal he was tending to, but he could see that the man was clearly busy doing something. Two children sat in the room as well, a boy and a girl, playing with some kittens.

"Take a seat Nick. I'll be with you shortly," said The Mayor.

He still had his back to Nick. All that he could make out from the back of The Mayor's head and the slight glimpse of his hands was that he was a slender, tall white man, possibly in his mid-forties with a full head of thin salt and pepper hair. He had a gravelly voice, perhaps from years of smoking. Nick often let his imagination run away with him; he blamed it on being exposed to so much television and film from a very young age.

His father was a huge movie buff and often allowed his children to watch the same films that he enjoyed, even if the movies weren't always appropriate for children. Nick cherished those moments with his father and although he didn't always understand the content of the films; like what was that glowing thing inside that black briefcase or why that man with a buzz cut kept running around the country. He knew that his exposure to cinema and television gave him an insight to a world he may never get to see in real life.

The Mayor closed the cage that he was tending to and crouched down next to the two children. Now that he had moved, Nick could see that he had been handling a large black and white cat. He smiled when he realised the cat must have recently had a litter of kittens. *"Was this man a vet in a past life?"* thought Nick as he sat down in front of The Mayor's desk. The Mayor took the kittens from the children and put them back into the cage where the mother cat began cleaning and nurturing her day old babies. The two kids were led out of the room by The Mayor; he left the door open once they had left and then went to a nearby sink to wash his hands.

"So, you're a vet then? With all the chaos around us, I didn't think anyone would still be looking after animals," said Nick.

He dried his hands and sat down at the desk in front of Nick.

"I think you'd be surprised as to how little you actually know about your state Mr King" said The Mayor abruptly.

Nick looked uncomfortable in his seat, like a child about to be told off by the Headmaster.

"Mr King, why are you in my borough? And before you answer, I want you to think twice about spinning me a yarn. I don't need any long stories about your journey or what you've been through. What I need from you is hard facts. Tell me what you are doing here and what's stopping me from delivering you back to The Boss?" said The Mayor, not taking his eyes off of Nick.

Nick stared back at The Mayor not wanting to show any fear or weakness, even though that was exactly how he felt. The abrupt, no-nonsense attitude of The Mayor made him realise that this man had fought and struggled to get where he was today. The Mayor also struck him as a man of his word, which meant he had no choice but to tell him the truth in fear of being found out and branded a liar.

"The truth...the truth is we were passing through and the only reason we were anywhere near your borough was because we had to cut through it to get to somewhere else," explained Nick.

"Where?" asked The Mayor probing further.

"Enfield," responded Nick swiftly.

"Why?"

"I'm meeting an old friend,"

"Who?"

"You wouldn't know her,"

"You don't think I'd know a high profile person in the next borough to mine? Who is she?" pushed The Mayor.

"What makes you think she's a high profile person?"

"She must be if you're risking your life to find her. Who is she?"

"Jill Sampson."

"Why would you abandon your post alongside The Boss to meet Jill? What is she helping you with?" queried The Mayor, who continued to pierce a hole through Nicks head with his cold blue eyes.

Nick knew this man would not stop questioning him until he got all the answers he required. He submitted to The Mayor's game and did as he was told;

he cut the crap and told him everything he wanted to hear.

"She's going to help me escape The Independent State of England. Me and my friends are going to get out through an escape route she created which she uses to smuggle things in and out of the state. My intention, however, isn't only to escape, I plan on bringing down The Boss and ending her reign of terror forever," blurted out Nick.

Recent events had shown him what a burden it was to carry around lies and how revitalizing it felt to tell the truth. He watched as the Mayor's piercing pupils widened at what he had told him. He had no idea if The Mayor was going to send him away, help him or kill him, he was neutral, but Nick had left him in a complicated situation.

"How? How are you going to bring her down?" asked The Mayor.

"I can't tell you."

"How?" insisted The Mayor.

"I can't tell you. I can't risk anyone knowing who my contacts on the outside are."

He took a deep breath hoping The Mayor wouldn't probe any further.

"I believe you," said The Mayor.

He stood up from his seat and extended his hand out over the desk towards Nick. Nick stood up in return and firmly shook his hand.

"Thank you for telling me the truth, unfortunately, I'm going to have to keep you and your people here until I inform The Boss of your whereabouts so she can come and collect you."

Nick's heart stopped.

"What! Why? I told you everything, I told you the truth!" exclaimed Nick.

"I know you did and I thank you for that, but I can't risk my people being hurt and you being here jeopardises their safety. If she finds out that you were here and that I let you go through with your plan, she will come down on this place and my people with an iron fist."

"This is a neutral borough; she wouldn't dare come in after you and your people. It would be a PR nightmare for her. She has a high level of trust and responsibility to her followers and attacking the neutrals would damage that," explained Nick.

"Precisely, we're neutral. We have no alliances with any group besides our own, that is until we get involved and are seen helping someone on one of the sides. In most cases, we either let people pass through our borough or we don't. You are an anomaly; as far as the rest of the world is concerned, you work for The Boss, but there are those out there that know you are trying to bring her down. No matter what I do, I'm either going to aggravate the resistance or infuriate The Boss. And to be honest with you, after seeing what she is capable of, I'll take my chances with upsetting the resistance; at least I know they can be reasoned with. I'm sorry but this is the way it has to be," said The Mayor seeming apologetic towards Nick.

"Are you happy with the world that you live in?

Living life hand to mouth? Choosing to hide when the opportunity for change comes knocking. You say you're neutral, I say you're a coward!" yelled Nick.

"Excuse me? You better watch your tone Nick. You have no idea what I've been through to get into this position and what has had to happen to ensure the safety of these people. I'm no coward."

"We've all been through hard times Mayor, and yes, some have suffered more than others, but unlike most people, you are in a position to help – to stand up and say no. But if you don't want to and you want to sit on the fence then fine, who am I to tell you or anyone else what to do. But what I can do is not allow you to stop me from righting the wrongs that I have created. I escaped from her and I will not be going back. The only way I will see that woman again is when this state is no more and she is behind bars. I know you are looking out for your people and I respect that, but I'm telling you now that my people and I will slip out of here unseen. Nobody needs to know we were here. If you trust your people like you say you do, then tell them to forget what they saw today, and we will be on our way. If you can't do that and you need to call The Boss, I don't blame you. But I warn you now, I will not be going anywhere without a fight," declared Nick with a confident desire that impressed The Mayor.

He was almost shaking after his grand speech as he stared at The Mayor with a fiery passion.

"I can see why The Boss kept you around for so

long Nick. You're quite the motivational speaker. Perhaps it was more of your own words coming out of her mouth than hers?" quizzed The Mayor who smiled for the first time since Nick walked into the room.

"Sometimes it was, at least in the beginning anyway. Now, what are we going to do? The longer we stand around with our thumbs up our arses the longer we live under The Boss' roof," said Nick candidly.

The Mayor walked towards the door and signalled for someone to come into the room. A slim blonde man appeared in the doorway. Nick couldn't quite make out what was being said between the two, the blonde man nodded at The Mayor and disappeared as quickly as he had arrived. A short while later, the slim man returned to the room, but this time he was accompanied by Emily, Will, Izzy, and Ms Wilson.

"Close the door Stewart," ordered The Mayor.

"Wow that is a powerful smell. How do you manage to sit in here for so long?" asked Will, once again not thinking before he spoke.

Izzy kicked him in the shin in hopes that he would get the hint to keep his mouth shut and keep his opinions to himself. It technically worked, as he stopped complaining about the smell in the room and instead asked why Izzy kept on kicking him.

The Mayor walked over to his desk and sat down in front of Nick and his gang. He hadn't intended to look like an overpowering authority figure, but that was the vibe he gave off. A small part of him had liked the feeling of being feared, but he had seen first-hand, like so many others had, what can happen to a person when power and fear consumes them so he had always made a point to present himself as openly and as welcoming as he could.

"Nick has told me all about what you intend to do; how you plan on escaping the state and bringing down The Boss and her regime. As I've explained to him, this puts me and subsequently my people in a sticky situation. I have worked hard, very hard to give my people another option from the two we have been presented with. There are supporters of The Boss and there are those who resist her and they all fight for what they believe in, but they also fight each other and cause bedlam. I have created a third option for the people, an option which means they don't have to fight and live in chaos. We may be forced to live here but we can choose how we live. We are proof that you don't have to fight; because of us the Greenwich borough also became a neutral zone. Personally, I hope others follow suit," explained The Mayor, "The problem we have is that we can't be seen helping you. The Boss, with all of her many flaws has been true to her word and agreed to leave us alone as long as we stay out of her way, and the resistance groups have said the same. Herein lies the problem of you being here and me knowing about your plan."

Emily looked to her brother as to gauge his reaction, but despite his calm demeanour, she could see that he too was unsure about what was going to happen next.

"So, what are you going to do with us? Turn us in?" asked Emily.

"Well you see that raises another problem; if I return you to The Boss the resistance groups will know I helped The Boss, and if I turn you into the resistance, The Boss will know I helped them. So, what I'm going to do is nothing," said The Mayor confidently.

"Nothing?" asked Izzy in confusion.

"Nothing!" responded The Mayor.

"Are you sure about this Sir?" questioned Stewart, "What if someone finds out they were here?"

"They won't. We are going to send them back to where we apprehended them and they will continue on their way. I'll talk to the people personally and tell them to forget that these four were ever here. We will wipe any footage that shows they were here and it will be like it never happened. Nobody needs to know what their plan is regarding The Boss and I will explain to the people that we felt unsafe with them being here so all parties agreed to pretend that they were never here," explained The Mayor.

"But boss...!" pressed Stewart.

"Do as I ask Stewart, and what have I told you about calling me boss!" yelled The Mayor who almost jumped out of his seat in anger.

"Yes sir, my apologies," said Stewart suddenly flush with embarrassment.

He scurried towards the door and opened it. To his

surprise, a short Tamil woman in her thirties and a small boy were standing outside. Her hand was balled up into a fist as if she was about to knock on the door.

"What are you doing here?" asked Stewart.

"I'm sorry, I- I didn't hear anything, I just came to..." stuttered the woman before she grabbed her son's hand and rushed away from the office.

"But mummy I wanted to see the new kittens, you said," pleaded the little boy.

"Sir, we have a problem," said Stewart in a panic.

The Mayor rushed out of his seat and stopped the woman outside of the office from trying to flee. He gently put his hand on her shoulder causing her to aggressively pull away from him and hold her son tightly against her.

"I'm sorry I didn't mean to startle you. Can I speak with you alone for a moment?" pleaded The Mayor.

"I didn't hear anything. I'm sorry. My son wanted to see the cats. I didn't mean to interrupt," said the woman.

"That's alright. I can take him in and show him now if you like," offered The Mayor.

"I will take him in!" snapped the woman.

It was clear to him that this woman was not only very anxious, but very protective of her son. What wasn't clear, however, was that he didn't recognise who this woman or her son was.

"What's your name? I've not seen you around here before," asked The Mayor.

"My name is Brintha. I've been in Barnet for a

while, but I've only recently started coming to the Church."

He crouched down in front of Brintha's son, "And what's your name young man?" asked The Mayor.

The boy tightened his grip on his mother's leg. The Mayor reached into his pocket and pulled out a lollipop and offered it to the little boy who quickly let go of his mother's leg and snatched the sweet from his hand with a gleeful smile.

"That's okay. You can tell me your name when you're ready. Listen, whatever you heard in there, it's all true. I'm not going to lie to you, but I'm going to ask you to do what we are all going to do which is to forget about what has happened here today. The people in there are going to disappear. It'll be like they were never here. So, please don't worry or be afraid about what you heard. Can you do that? Can you forget what I'm going to do and what I'm going to ask all of the people out there to do?" asked The Mayor softly.

She looked down at her son who was focused entirely on his lollipop. She stroked his hair and looked back up at The Mayor.

"Yes, I can forget what I heard, under one condition. That man in there, that's Nick King isn't it? I heard what you were talking about and what he plans on doing. If I could ask him something, with your permission, I promise I will forget about what I heard and I won't say a word about what him and his friends are trying to do," said Brintha knowing that The Mayor couldn't refuse her request.

"Why do you want to speak with him?" questioned The Mayor.

She looked back down at her son and was suddenly overcome with emotion. Her eyes began to fill with tears which she quickly wiped away so her son wouldn't see that she was upset.

"I need help and he is the only one who can give that to me."

CHAPTER 19

12th June 2016, 20:48
Wood Street, Barnet, The Independent State of England

Besides the strong pungent smell of cat in The Mayor's office, it was empty of everyone but Nick, Brintha, and her son. Emily had offered to look after Brintha's son while she spoke to her brother, but she had refused her offer and told her that she was the only one who looked after her son. Emily knew not to offer a second time, as it was quite evident to her and everyone else present that there were some severe attachment issues between Brintha and her son.

Once The Mayor had told Nick about Brintha's request to speak with him, he was happy to oblige, if it meant he got out of the borough safely. Emily also knew that Nick wouldn't refuse seeing her when he realised she had a young son. He had always had a soft spot for children and would automatically fill the dad role when he was amongst young kids. He had been forced into the role at a very young age after his dad died and he had to look after Emily by himself. Fortunately for him that paternal instinct came naturally to him; something he attributed to his dad being a very hands-on father, both prior to his mum running off and after. His dad refused to allow his children to notice that they only had one parent; he was there for them both, in every way they needed. He wanted them to feel like they had a hundred parents all with the different abilities and skills to support them in all the ways they needed. He was able to be a father, a mother, a brother, a sister, and a friend to his children.

Brintha was given the privacy she had requested with Nick; meanwhile, The Mayor had a job to do in informing his people of the plan and what they would be doing with Nick and his group. The Mayor had allowed the rest of the gang to take some supplies for their journey as a good will gesture, although, Stewart had made sure he voiced his opinions on the matter first. Will had once again put his foot in his mouth when he openly shared his disliking of Stewart; this time however, Izzy had not told Will to shut up because she agreed with him.

Brintha's son was happy sitting in the room playing with the brand new kittens while the grownups talked. Brintha squirmed in her chair waiting for Nick to break the ice; however, he had no idea what she wanted from him, so he found it tricky to cut the tension in the room.

"So what did you want to talk to me about?" asked Nick abruptly.

Brintha remained silent and continued to feel uncomfortable in her seat.

"Sorry, but I don't have much time to sit around, as you may have heard, I'm kind of on a tight schedule. What I'm doing needs to happen pretty quickly. Taking down a powerful regime is kind of time sensitive," joked Nick.

He looked down at Brintha's son who continued to be enamoured with the kittens.

"What's your son's name?"

"Don't you talk about him and how dare you make light of what is going on here. All of this is your fault; all of this hell, all of the lies that were promised; all of the destruction and everyone being trapped here; that is all on you; and you try and make jokes about it," snapped Brintha.

The room was silent and awkward once more, but this time a new kind of tension had been created. Brintha was now leading the conversation and Nick was the one who began to squirm in his seat. He had addressed many of the victims affected by the fallout from The Boss' administration, but he had never been in this kind of intimate and personal situation with one of them before. Droves of people yelling at him was something he could handle, but when there was someone sitting inches away from him, telling him everything that he already knew, that he was as big a part of the downfall of London as The Boss was and that if it he hadn't of been the pen that articulated her rage then maybe she would never have climbed to the heights she did.

"I wanted to talk to you because you owe me. You

owe everyone and you need to fix what you have done," ordered Brintha.

"I thought you heard what was happening here? That's what I'm trying to do," bit back Nick.

"You think I believe anything you say? You may have fooled your friends and even The Mayor, but I live in the world you created; the horrible, painful, and bleak world you and The Boss created," said Brintha trying to hold back her fury.

"I know what I have done and believe me when I say I have seen it first-hand. I have lost sleep over this, which is why I'm finally doing something about it."

"Lost? You think you've lost? You have no fucking idea what loss is!" screamed Brintha who leapt out of her chair and flipped it over making Nick jump in his seat. The loud crash of the chair had caused one of the kittens to scratch Brintha's son who suddenly burst into tears. She realised she had let her anger get the better of her and rushed to her son to console him.

"Come here JJ. Mummy's sorry. Let me see," said Brintha who kissed the small scratch on JJ's hand. "Is that better baby? It's just a little scratch, see. That didn't hurt a big strong boy like you, did it? Come on, show me your big strong muscles."

JJ smiled and let out a small laugh as he was comforted by his mother. Nick sat in shock watching a loving mother embrace her son after she had exploded at him. In that moment, he understood that this woman would do whatever it took to protect her son and that there was certainly more to her story than he knew.

"I'm sorry for getting so angry, to both of you. What I want you to do Nick is listen to my story and then you will understand exactly what I've been through and exactly what I want from you. Can you do that for me?" asked Brintha who had drastically changed her temperament from psychotic woman to the embodiment of Zen in a matter of seconds.

He nodded at Brintha who was sat holding her son on the floor.

"I met JJ's dad after I turned 17," began Brintha.

24th Aug 2002, 08:37
Handsworth Wood, Birmingham, England

She had been in that stuffy and over packed car for hours, boxes had been sliding up and down the car and bin bags filled with clothes restricted her leg room, which didn't help with the long journey from London. Brintha had already been in a bad mood and the car journey certainly wasn't helping. Her parents had decided to uproot their lives in London and move to Birmingham as there was a better job opportunity for her father. Her father was a self-made success, something he would slip into conversation whenever the opportunity arose; and after years of earning and saving, they had decided they were ready to sell up and move to a bigger place in Birmingham. Brintha had understood that this decision was best for her parents, but she didn't understand why she had to leave her friends and her life in London behind her, especially as she had planned to move back to the capital the following year once she had been accepted to one of her university choices.

She had exhausted herself and dampened the relationship between her and her parents during the months leading up to the big move. She had constantly been on their case about trying to find a way for her to stay in London instead of going with them, she had asked to stay with friends, family and even went as far as to ask if she could find a house share and work while at college to pay for the rent. Her parents had been quick to shoot that idea down as they didn't want anything distracting her from her studies, even though they were changing her college midway through her A-Levels. Eventually, she had given in and accepted her fate, but childishly decided not speak to her parents unless she needed to.

When they drove past fields and green forests, Brintha smiled, although she would never admit it, she actually preferred being closer to nature and the countryside over the polluted city of London. The only greenery and wildlife she saw when living in the city was the mixed salad on top of her lamb kebab and the rats and pigeons in the street. She had only seen pictures of her new home and she had liked how big and nice it was compared to her old house, however, she found it hard being away from everything she knew.

"We're here Brin. What do you think?" asked her Dad.

The car pulled into the driveway of a huge five-bedroom house on a small cul-de-sac. There were two garages and it looked as if the inside of the house went on forever; the pictures she had seen did not do this house justice.

"Whoa!" said Brintha in amazement.

"It's beautiful isn't it? Me and dad told you seeing the house would change your mind about moving here," said Brintha's mother.

Her parents left the car and began unloading boxes from the boot. Next door to her new house, lived a man in his late fifties and his eighteen-year-old son, Jordan. Jordan's father had been washing his car when Brintha's parents arrived at their new home. As they unloaded the car, Jordan's father stared at his new neighbours with a face like stone, he didn't say a word or offer any kind of greeting to his neighbours; he simply stood there and watched. Brintha's father noticed he was being watched, so he gave his new neighbour the slightest of nods by way of acknowledgment, a simple gesture which was rudely not returned.

Jordan's father had always been a miserable man who lived in his own bubble; however, when his wife had passed, he had become much more of a cantankerous recluse who depended heavily on his only son.

Jordan appeared from the garden and stood next to his father who continued to leer at his neighbours.

Brintha's father, who was smiling when he first arrived at his new home, was now annoyed and angry at the disrespect shown by his impolite neighbour.

"I can't believe Rich sold his house, and to a bloody Londoner as well. I bet he'll want to have work done on it. That's the last thing we need, builders taking over the cul-de-sac and making a racket all day," said Jordan's father, who had the ability to be enraged by almost anything.

Jordan watched his neighbours enter their home in an uncomfortable silence. Meanwhile, Brintha was wedged in the car trying to manoeuvre herself through the boxes and bin liners blocking her from leaving the vehicle. Eventually, the frustration of not being able to move got the better of her, so she chose to throw some of the bags and boxes out of the car door so she could finally escape from the claustrophobic tin can that was her father's Jaguar.

Jordan's father threw his sponge back into the water bucket and walked back towards his much smaller two-bedroom home. "Tell me when that lot are done unpacking and I'll finish this once they're gone," he ordered.

Jordan picked up the bucket of dirty water from the floor and began walking back towards the house behind his dad He stopped and turned back to his neighbour's car when he heard the car door slam shut. He was suddenly awe struck when he saw Brintha standing by the car. He couldn't help but stare at her, not in the same hateful way his father had been staring moments earlier, but with an overwhelming gaze. He was mesmerised by her beauty. She picked up some of the bags she had kicked out of the car and smiled at Jordan when she passed him on her way into her new home.

"Hi," said Brintha as nonchalant as she could even though inside she had been thinking, "*Holy crap, I get to live next to this gorgeous man.*"

Jordan awkwardly returned her greeting with a simple hand raise which he had fully intended to be a wave, but it resembled more of a Nazi salute.

Brintha's father walked back outside and ushered his daughter to hurry up with the boxes after he had seen her talking to Jordan. Jordan's father did the same by signalling for Jordan to come back into the house. Both Jordan and Brintha walked back towards their respective houses simultaneously while occasionally looking back at the other until they were both inside of their homes.

Suddenly, Brintha was feeling much better about moving away from her life in London to Birmingham.

Later that night, once all the boxes had been unloaded into the house, a drained Brintha was being yelled at by her father after she had let slip that she thought the boy next door was handsome. She had been desperately trying to get a word in, but her father had finally lost his cool with her, he had kept it together with her complaining about moving home and about her wanting to stay in London, but her showing a romantic interest towards a boy she had only known for five minutes was the last straw for her incredibly strict father.

Jordan had been finishing off the last of his chores for the day with his last task being to drag the bins to the pavement. His dad was always a very stringent man, but after Jordan's mother had passed away, his father had gotten much worse and was always on his case. His dad insisted that he was so hard on him because he was trying to build his character; however, Jordan didn't see it the same way, if anything, it had the opposite effect on Jordan whose confidence had been damaged ever since he lost his mother.

He rolled the bins to the street and headed back towards the house where he could finally get some peace in his bedroom and escape into his books. He had always had a passion for books. His mother would read to him every day, and after she died, he relied on his books to help him momentarily hide from the troubles he faced in life, including his father.

Upon walking back to his house, Jordan looked next door and could see everything that was happening in Brintha's home as the curtains in her house had not yet been hung up. He could tell her parents were yelling at her by the way her dad was waving his arms. He tried his best not to stare, but curiosity had gotten the better of him. Brintha had suddenly disappeared from the window and as he continued back towards his house she opened her front door and walked outside with tears rolling down her face. She'd sat down on the step by the front door and buried her head into her knees.

He froze. He was unsure if he should go back inside and ignore Brintha, or console her and ask if she was okay. The coward in him told him to run home, but in a rare moment of bravery, he ignored that voice and decided to lean over the small fence that divided their houses and speak to the sad pretty girl on the other side.

"Hi," he said timidly with a sympathetic smile on his face.

"Hi," said Brintha in return looking up at him while wiping the tears from her face.

The pair shared a laugh and with that awkward interaction, their tragic romance had begun.

Over the next few months, the pair began dating behind their parent's backs. They were the quintessential couple; they went on dates, shared stories, had sex, had fights, made up and even went on a holiday to Ibiza together. Fortunately, the pair had good friends who were willing to corroborate any lies they may have told their parents. Things between the couple were perfect until one careless drunken night in which they were seen kissing outside of their homes by Brintha's mother and Jordan's father.

They were forbidden from seeing the other again. Jordan, however, was no longer going to let his father's bias effect his life, so he told him that he would do whatever he liked and if he didn't like it, he would move out. He knew that his father wouldn't be able to survive without him, so like it or not he would have to accept that his son loved

Brintha and there was nothing he could do to stop them from being with each other.

In an act of passionate romance, Jordan climbed up to Brintha's room that night and snuck into her bedroom. He consoled her as she cried over what her parents had said and they agreed that they would continue to see each other despite their parent's views.

The next few months weren't as easy as the couple had hoped; they tried their best to ignore the resistance from their parents and when Brintha received a letter she had been waiting months to receive, her university acceptance letter, things really became complicated for the couple.

Despite the distance, the couple said they would stay together while she studied at University in London and he stayed in Birmingham to work and be with his father. No matter how badly he wanted to go with her, he had a loyalty to his father and he'd promised his mother that he would look after him when she was gone.

Jordan's father watched on as he saw his son say goodbye to his girlfriend. Before she left, Jordan handed a tearful Brintha an envelope and hugged her goodbye.

She was sat in the back seat of her father's car with tears in her eyes. She opened the envelope that Jordan had given her which felt heavier than an envelope with a letter should. She took out a piece of paper and unfolded it. It had only two words scrawled across the middle of the page in block capital letters "ALWAYS TOGETHER." She then tipped the envelope upside down and out fell a necklace with a locket attached to it. When she opened the locket, inside was a picture of the loving couple. She had been teary eyed all day, but in that moment, she could no longer stop a flood of tears from falling and her body shook from sorrow.

As her father drove away from the house, he couldn't help but feel sympathetic towards his daughter. She was starting a new chapter in her life. This was supposed to be a time of excitement and happiness for her, but all he could see was his daughter sobbing in the back of his car. He wanted to comfort her but he feared he would only make things worse; all he ever truly wanted was his daughters' happiness.

7th July 2006, 14:37
Belvedere Road, Lambeth, London

After three long years of hard work and the occasional party, Brintha had reached her graduation day. Her parents attended her graduation ceremony and rightfully showered her with praise and adoration for all of her hard work. Jordan, who had since moved to London after no longer being able to tolerate his belligerent dad's verbal abuse, had decided that he would attend her graduation separately from her parents as he didn't want there to be any tension or negativity between them on a day that was about her.

Over the years, Brintha's parents began to see their little girl develop and transform into an independent woman. They would never admit it, but a huge contributor to her growth was her strong relationship with Jordan. They had disapproved of them living together while she was at university, as they felt he would be a distraction to her, however, he supported and helped her more than they thought possible. Despite this, her parents were very protective of her and hadn't fully welcomed Jordan into their inner circle.

Jordan met up with Brintha later that evening and they sat down for a romantic dinner together to celebrate her success. Once dinner came to an end, Jordan made a not so subtle gesture to Brintha to look underneath her graduation cap which had been placed strategically on the dinner table. She lifted it up and staring her in the face was a sparkling engagement ring. She picked up the ring and before she could react Jordan had dropped to his knee and asked her to marry him.

5th November 2008, 15:20
Dulwich Rd, Lambeth, London

Jordan was standing at the altar surrounded by friends and family, most of whom were Brintha's. She had always said that her Sri Lankan family would vastly outnumber all of his family at their wedding and she was not kidding. He could barely pick out his family members amongst the mammoth crowd of Sri Lankan guests.

Notable by his absence was Jordan's father. Jordan had tried tirelessly to get his father to come to his wedding. He had even paid for his fathers' suit and a hotel room, but his father refused to be a part of something that he did not agree with. He felt betrayed by his son for picking a woman over him. No matter how many times he'd spoken to his father, he would never take responsibility or ownership for his failings and wrong doings – a jaded attitude which ultimately led to Jordan and his father parting ways on bad terms.

The thoughts of his father had swiftly left his mind when he caught sight of his soon to be wife walking down the aisle towards him. They had joked about her wearing white being somewhat of a hypocritical move, but they both agreed that it was a better option than the sari her mother had wanted her to wear. The couple compromised by agreeing to have a traditional Sri Lankan blessing after they had the wedding they wanted.

Jordan couldn't take his eyes off of his future wife as he watched her being escorted down the aisle by her father. To the surprise and delight of the couple, when her father had reached Jordan, he not only gave him his daughters hand, but he also held out his hand to Jordan and shook it for the first time ever, finally displaying a symbol of respect and acceptance towards him.

While the couple celebrated their joyous day together, Jordan's father was locked away at home by himself in Birmingham. Earlier that morning he had spent over an hour staring at the suit his son had given him to wear for his wedding; however, after hours of deliberating, he had decided that his stubbornness and distorted values were more important than his only son's wedding and he chose not to attend.

21st September 2009, 14:54
Brixton Hill, Lambeth, London

The pair had survived their first year of marriage together and they couldn't be happier. Jordan's relationship with Brintha's parents had vastly improved and he was fulfilling a three-year dream of opening a bookshop in Brixton with his new wife. Brintha's marketing degree and a small loan from her parents had been enough to help start up the business, and their passion to succeed and work together kept the business booming. The pair knew it was an ambitious dream, but they had never done things the easy way so they had decided to dive head first into it.

They had a business, a small flat on top of the shop, and they had each other. The only thing that occasionally weighed on their minds was how distant Jordan's father had become. Brintha knew Jordan missed his dad, but he refused to see him unless he could bring his wife with him, however. His father felt his pride was more important, so Jordan was forced to wash his hands with him.

1ˢᵗ October 2010, 19:28
Brixton Hill, Lambeth, London

For the first time in their lives, things for the couple had found some stability. The bookshop was doing well due to Brixton evolving from a place filled with crime and violence to a much more metropolitan area with an influx of trendy hipster types invading the town. The gentrification of the town wasn't something the pair wholeheartedly agreed with but they took an opportunity where they could and made sure their shop was affordable and accessible to all.

Unfortunately, the one thing that hadn't changed was the turbulent relationship between Jordan and his father; however, in a surprising twist of fate Brintha's father had filled the father figure role for Jordan after realising what a strong and confident man he had become.

After an extra-long day at work, where Jordan had hosted the bookshop's first book signing for a local author, he closed up shop and planned to go upstairs and do nothing but pass out for the rest of the evening in front of the TV. He had been greeted in the living room by his wife who handed him a large glass of whiskey and his favourite meal – he panicked. Although she had occasionally been prone to being overly nice to him it was very rare and it was far more likely she either wanted something major from him or was about to drop a bombshell. In this case, it was both.

She gave him a small envelope which contained a positive pregnancy test. The pair had discussed having kids a few times in the past but never in great detail so she had no idea how he would respond to the news. He fell silent and he stared at it. He downed his whiskey and continued to stare at it. She couldn't gauge a reaction from him, and she'd begun to feel anxious. It wasn't until the headlights of a passing car bounced off of his eye did she catch the slightest glimpse of a twinkle in his eyes. That twinkle grew as his eyes began to water and a huge smile appeared across his face.

"I'm going to be a daddy?" whimpered Jordan.

"Yes, you are," smiled Brintha.

"We have a baby!!" beamed Jordan.

"Yes we do."

He leapt from his seat and squeezed her in excitement, slightly harder than he should have after very recently discovering she was pregnant. Once he realised how hard he was hugging her. He apologised and loosened his grip on his wife and soon-to-be mother of his new child. The timing of their baby was a little ahead of schedule but that didn't matter, their family was growing and life for the pair had suddenly taken an unexpected yet joyful turn.

30^h Jan 2011, 11:11
Handsworth Wood, Birmingham, England

He hadn't slept a wink, partly because he knew the

near three hour journey was going to take its toll on him that early in the morning, but mostly because he didn't know what he was going to expect from his father. It had been so long since he had spoken to his father let alone seen him. He had decided to travel up alone as he didn't want to give his dad any excuses to blow him off considering he was travelling such a long way with news he had hoped would start to rebuild their broken relationship.

He took in the nostalgic feeling of his old home town when he was driving along the roads he used to drive through every day; however, the butterflies in his stomach became more and more prominent as he neared the house he grew up in.

Jordan and his father's relationship had gotten so estranged that the couple refused to visit Brintha's parents in Birmingham in case they ran into his dad. There had been some annoyance from her parents about them not visiting but they understood how bad things had become between Jordan and his father and they didn't want to add to their daughter and son in law's stress.

As soon as he pulled into the driveway of his childhood home, he didn't hesitate in getting out of the car. He knew that if he took even a second to think about going into the house, he may have reconsidered his decision and he really didn't want to drive three hours to Birmingham to have to drive three hours back without having some kind of closure, good or bad.

He walked up to the front door with the sonogram

in his hand, but before he could knock on the door it opened slowly and his dad was standing in the doorway. There was no smile, no anger, or any hint of emotion from his father. Jordan didn't know what to do, so he simply handed his father the sonogram.

"It's a boy," said Jordan, uncertain of how his father would react to finding out that he was going to be a grandfather.

His initial reaction was not unlike Jordan's, his father stared at the picture with an unreadable face. Jordan could now see where he got that vacant look from. Brintha would often express her annoyance when he made that face; no matter what was happening, be it fun, sad, happy or bad, that was the face he would pull. Half the time she didn't know if he was enjoying himself or if he was having the worst time of his life. Unlike Jordan, however, there was no glimmer or twinkle in his father's eyes, just nothingness. His father handed him back the sonogram, stepped back into his house, and closed the door on his son both literally and figuratively forever.

He didn't think his father could have crushed him anymore than he already had, but he was wrong, and all because he refused to take responsibility for his shortcomings as a father. He had become an even angrier and acrimonious old man who was stuck in his ways and would rather be alone than learn to change.

Before he left to make the long and disappointing journey back home to his pregnant wife he visited the home of his in-laws who embraced him after he had told them what had happened between him and his father. He had made his in-laws promise not to say anything to his father and he declared he would no longer make any effort with his dad. After expressing his hurt and pain to Brintha's parents, Brintha's dad pulled him aside and told him, "You may not have the father you wanted and I may never be able to fill that space, but I am going to try for you, son."

7ᵗʰ August 2011, 22:34
Brixton Hill, Lambeth, London

Jordan and a heavily pregnant Brintha were sat in their flat watching TV. Every news channel had been broadcasting coverage of the rioting; that had taken place across Tottenham the night before, after the peaceful protests against the police who had gunned down Raymond Dwyer had turned violent. More and more reports were coming in of the rioting that had continued throughout the day and had spread across the city to Enfield, Ponders End, Wood Green, Oxford Circus, and even to areas outside of the city including Hertfordshire.

Brintha almost jumped out of her skin when she heard a loud crash and the sound of shouting and screaming coming from outside of their flat. The pair rushed over to the window and saw groups of people emerging onto the main road; some looked afraid and were running away while others were marching down the streets in anger and excitement. Groups of men and women wearing hoodies and masks took over the streets of Brixton. It wasn't long before things had descended into chaos and the first wave of bricks began being thrown through shop windows on Brixton Hill. Electronics shops, jewellery shops and newsagents were immediately targeted and ransacked.

The couple had to watch on as their community burned.

Groups of people ran past the bookshop. The pair had hoped that if these people were stupid enough to attack their own city and break the law, they weren't likely to be huge bookworms. Twenty minutes had passed since the first crowd had arrived, but the carnage continued. The couple had called the police several times but the rioting continued without interruption.

A loud clatter impacted through the building and shook the floor of their flat, Jordan couldn't tell if the crash came from their building or the shop next door so he rushed to the window and to his horror he saw a group of three or four hooded people entering through the broken shop window of his bookshop.

"Shit, they're inside," he said in a panic.

"What are we going to do?" asked Brintha.

He ran over to the front door and picked up a cricket bat.

"I'm going to protect what is ours and get rid of those pricks!" said Jordan with adrenaline coursing through his veins.

"Please don't go down there, it's not safe," begged Brintha.

"I can't have them destroying what we have built. Stay here and call the police again, tell them someone is hurt and they need to get here ASAP."

Before she had a second to answer, he had already left the flat and was headed downstairs to the back entrance of the bookshop. He crept through the back office where he could hear voices and banging coming from the shop floor. He peered through the small window on the face of the door and saw three hooded figures trashing the shop. They were ripping up the books, pulling down bookcases and causing mayhem and destruction. These people weren't fighting for a cause, their only goal was to cause trouble. He had understood what it meant to fight for what you believed in and what you think is right, and it infuriated him when people took advantage of tragedy and leeched onto what others were doing in a thinly veiled attempt to get what they wanted for their own selfish needs.

He burst through the door with his cricket bat raised high and with a booming voice filled with passion and authority, only that of a person who had everything to lose could muster, he told the invaders in his shop to leave before he made them leave.

He could see the fear in the eyes of the looters in front of him, however, he soon realised that their eyes were glaring at something over his shoulder. His rage had given him the courage and dominance to confront these three rioters, but it also made him careless and lack awareness of his surroundings, when he had exploded into the room he had failed to see the fourth looter who had been behind the cash register scrounging for any money he could find.

While he had been facing the three intruders, the fourth had crept up behind him and struck him around the back of the head with a rogue brick that had made its way into the shop when the intruders broke in. He instantly fell to the floor, and when he tried to get back to his feet the group surrounded him and began beating him down. Stomp after stomp, kick after kick, punch after punch. One of the bigger men had bent down next to Jordan's lifeless body and picked up his cricket bat. He raised the bat above his head and hurled it down across Jordan's back; he raised it up again, ready to strike, but instead stood frozen when he saw Brintha standing in the doorway of the back office with a look of horror on her face as her life crumbled around her. She let out a spine chilling scream and shrieked at the four attackers to leave her husband alone. She ran towards Jordan with the intention of putting her body between his and the attackers, but as she took a few steps forward she tripped over a fallen bookcase and landed directly onto her belly.

The four hooligans looked at each other in alarm; they fled the shop and ran back into the lawlessness with the other rioters, disappearing amongst them. With a blinding pain shooting through her stomach, she slowly dragged herself to her motionless husband. She felt a warm feeling running down her legs and when she reached down to see what it was she was overcome with immense terror at the sight of blood dripping down from her underwear.

8th August 2011, 00:06
Denmark Hill, Brixton, London

Forty minutes after her fall, the pair had both been rushed to Kings College Hospital when the police had finally appeared in Brixton. Jordan had been sent to the Intensive Care Unit as he had lost a lot of blood and barely had a pulse, while Brintha was fighting for the life of her overdue child.

After a quick examination she was told that the baby was in distress and she would need an emergency C-Section. The instant they broke the news to her, she tried to get out the bed and refused any help from the doctors, she was concerned about her baby, but she was also deathly worried about the state of her baby's father - the love of her life. She had to be restrained by the nurses and was told again and again that if she didn't get the baby out now, the baby would die. Eventually, the nurses calmed her down by promising her that the second the baby was out she would be able to see her husband.

Whilst she was bringing life into the world, Jordan was losing his; the doctors had tried everything they could to keep him stable and responsive but after an hour of giving it all they could he died on a bloody surgery table. Meanwhile, Brintha had given birth to a healthy baby boy who had fortunately not suffered any physical harm after the fall. She held her new baby boy in her arms and took in the magical moment a mother has with her first born child. That moment, however, was fleeting when she saw the face of her husband in her son and demanded to know where he was and what had happened to him.

With her baby in her arms she had been wheeled to the room where her husband had passed away hours earlier. She broke down into a ball of hysteria and tears. She sat in the wheelchair crying in a crumpled heap holding a bawling baby not knowing what to do now that her husband lay dead on the bed in front of her.

She had a baby in her arms which would be with her forever but in that moment she felt truly alone. Dread ran through her head as she thought about how she would care for this baby. She wept even more when she thought about her son growing up not ever knowing who his father was. At her lowest point in her life, when she had begun to lose all hope, she heard footsteps approach from behind her and a pair of strong and rough arms reached around her shoulders and gently held her and her new baby. She turned her head expecting a doctor or a nurse to be behind her but the face she saw was a face she had not seen for many years and never thought she would see again. Jordan's father, with tears in his eyes, embraced Brintha and his new grandson. They stayed there together, hugging, sobbing and mourning over the loss of a son, a husband, a father, and a great man.

12th June 2016, 21:30
Wood Street, Barnet, The Independent State of England

It took everything Nick had to stifle back the tears trying to escape his eyes after spending the last forty-five minutes hearing Brintha's heart-breaking story. She had maintained her calm the entire time, only occasionally showing glimpses of pent up rage she had been holding onto. Her relationship with Jordan had been a huge part of her life which she remembered and clung to vividly, so much so that when she told her tale to Nick it felt almost rehearsed.

"After Jordan died and the world began to fall around us I found hope in The Boss. I even met her once at a fundraiser and I told her my story. I told her about my hardships and the financial troubles I had been facing; being a single mother with a business I could no longer support on my own after the insurance company refused to help us after the riots. She pulled me aside and we spoke privately at the fundraiser. She told me it would be okay. She held my son and told him it would be okay, and we believed her. With all of her talk about those who work hard getting fair reward, it turned out to all be crap. She turned her back on us so she could concentrate on her own agenda, exactly like the old regime did. I kick myself every day for staying and not moving back to Birmingham with my family. They begged me to come home, even Jordan's dad did, but I thought she would help, that she would be different, when the reality is that she is worse than the old government, at least with them you got a shred of help and not forgotten about and left to fend for yourself," continued Brintha.

He hadn't dared interrupt her before, but once she had stopped talking he felt he could finally speak up.

"I'm so sorry this has happened to you, this was never our intention..." said Nick before being cut off.

"I don't want an apology from you, that's not what this is about," snapped Brintha.

"Then what do you want from me?"

"You may not have caused the riots that killed my husband and you may not have been the face of this, but you had as big of a role in what happened after," said Brintha. "So, what do I want from you? I want you to start making up for what happened and I want what she promised me and countless others. You are going to save us."

"What do you think I'm trying to do here? I'm trying to get out so I can make this right."

"No, you don't understand. You are going to save us, me and my son JJ. When you escape from this place, you are going to take us with you."

CHAPTER 20

Nick stormed out of the Mayor's office followed by a furious Brintha. She was so aggravated that she forgot to bring JJ with her; fortunately, he'd known well enough to follow his mother's lead wherever she went. With so much wrath coursing through her body she launched a large church candle stick at Nick which hit him on the back of the head.

"You do not get to say no to me," yelled Brintha.

The thud of the candlestick hitting his head was so loud that it drew the attention of Emily and The Mayor who ran towards an irate Brintha and frightened Nick.

"I'm sorry for everything you've been through and I'll take the blame for it, but I can't take you or your boy with me" said Nick who continued to desperately scurry away from Brintha.

"Why not?" screeched Brintha.

"I can't be responsible for the harm of anyone else. I've got the weight of the state on my back and I can't be worrying about a kid and his mother as well. I'm sorry," said Nick making a dash to the exit of the church.

She picked up a much larger candle stick and lifted it in the air to throw at Nick but this time she was stopped by The Mayor. He struggled to restrain Brintha who had turned her anger towards him which momentarily sent a cold chill of fear through his body.

Nick sped outside to the courtyard of the church to get some much-needed fresh air after being stuck in a tiny room filled with tension and hostility. He looked up at the clear night sky and breathed out towards the stars. One positive that came from The Boss wrecking the state were the rolling blackouts in the city. The lack of florescent lighting which once eclipsed the natural lights of the night sky now allowed it to shine with its natural luminosity. The surface of the world may have been burning but the sky glowed and twinkled with a sea of stars which hadn't been seen in the city since the dark ages of Britain. For a brief time, when things began to turn sour under The Boss' command, Nick had taken to yoga and meditation under the stars, something his fiancée had instilled in him. He would focus on relaxation and positive thinking when things got too much for him. However, he had struggled to find his inner peace in recent months and it was something he had desperately yearned for in that moment.

"Rough night?" came a familiar voice from behind him.

He looked around to what he thought had been an empty church courtyard and saw Will sat on the floor smoking against the church wall. He quickly realised from the strong smell coming off of Will that it wasn't a cigarette he was smoking.

"All I've had over the last few years are rough nights, but yeah, this is a particularly bad one," said Nick sitting down next to Will.

Will took a long drag from his joint and immediately began coughing as he spluttered up the smoke from his lungs. Nick stifled his laughter at what an amateur smoker Will was and instead offered him a few pats on the back to help him catch his breath. While he composed himself Will passed the joint to Nick. The scent of the weed filled his nose and he was instantly transported back to his youth, where he would spend hours high out of his mind in in his university halls with The Boss and his friends. He breathed in the herbal goodness of the joint and blew out the smoke in a much cooler and smoother fashion than Will had done.

After spending half an hour in a purple haze with Will, he was able to find that momentary peace and tranquillity he had been searching for to take his mind away from the problems of the world. His moment of bliss had been cut short when Emily had found him after spending the last thirty minutes looking for him. She slapped him around the back of the head for disappearing to get high and yelled at him for leaving her to deal with a pissed off mother and an upset five year old.

"The Mayor wants to talk to you. He said we have to leave as soon as we can," explained Emily.

He hesitantly returned back to reality and went straight to The Mayor's office hoping for some sort of safe haven from the candle throwing assassin he'd hoped not to run into again. The Mayor had been waiting for him in his office; fortunately, Brintha was nowhere to be seen.

"Whatever happened in here between you two, I don't want to know, my concern is getting you and your friends out of here unseen and unheard. There are a few back roads we can take you through and we'll lend you some black hooded jumpers so you can disguise yourselves, but you have to go now," said The Mayor.

"About that, I know I said we were headed for Enfield, but I was actually going to make a quick pit stop first," said Nick, to the annoyance of The Mayor.

"A pit stop? This isn't a day out at the races Nick. I'm risking a lot for you so I need you and your gang gone right now," stressed The Mayor.

"And I appreciate that, but I need to collect something first, something important, in Harrow. I'll go alone, I can slip out without anyone knowing and I'll be back in a few hours. Keep my guys hidden for a few more hours and I'll meet up with them where you first picked us up," said Nick, knowing he was pushing his luck with The Mayor.

The Mayor rubbed his hands over his face and let out a deliberately loud sigh to show Nick how much of a pain in the arse he was being.

"I'm getting too old for this shit," said The Mayor. "Okay, but if you aren't back in four hours your people are gone, understood?"

Nick offered his hand to The Mayor who begrudgingly took it and the pair shook hands.

"Not that I care about you, but where are you going? I want to be able to at least tell your sister where to find your body when you're likely caught wandering around Harrow," asked The Mayor.

"I need to collect something from my old flat in Queensbury; there may not be another chance to get it before I leave."

Unbeknownst to the pair, Stewart had been standing outside of The Mayor's office listening to their conversation. Stewart scuttled behind a nearby pillar once Nick and The Mayor had left the office, once the area was clear, he took out a mobile phone and dialled a number.

"Hey, it's me. Change of plans. He's going to Harrow, alone. Yes alone. I don't know what he's doing, but he's headed to Queensbury without his little gang," explained Stewart, "No, let's not say anything to The Boss yet, I'm pretty sure calling off the hit on Nick is a bluff, but just in case it isn't, we'll keep it quiet for now. Get the word out to the Harrow gangs that he's on his way and whoever brings him in will be handsomely rewarded. This is my ticket out from under the grasp of that neutral coward. Keep mc postcd."

CHAPTER 21

12th June 2016, 23:17
Reynolds Drive, Harrow, The Independent State of England

Number 27a Reynolds Drive was a small maisonette which sat between Queensbury and Burnt Oak tube station on the edge of North West London. It was a tiny one bedroom flat that was shoddily put together and smelt of cooked onions and sausage, which had seeped in through the floorboards from the Romanian couple who once lived downstairs. It hadn't only been the horrible smell that came from the flat below, but also the constant yelling from the girlfriend of the couple who was either screaming at her boyfriend, her kids, or was banging on the ceiling. These were only a few fond memories Nick had of his old flat.

The memories of his first home weren't all bad; he also had memories of happy times spent with his fiancée, with his sister, and with his friends. He remembered the hilarious time his bigoted and misogynistic neighbour who he and his fiancée had nicknamed "Mr Hitler," was thrown out of his house and beaten up by his wife and adult children who had finally had enough of being physically and mentally abused by him. He remembered making the same joke every time he had people over about being able to see every room of his flat from the hallway because it was so small. But the thing he remembered the most was how much he and his fiancée's relationship grew when they moved into their first flat together, years before he got wrapped up in The Boss' world.

He had to constantly break into his own flat when he lived there as the door would often swell and get stuck; meaning Nick would have to climb onto his neighbours shed and pull himself through the bathroom window which was never locked. His fiancée told him not to bother fixing it because nobody was going to rob a flat that crap. To his delight the window was still broken and he was able to break into his old flat yet again. He stood in the hallway looking at every room in the flat from that one vantage point and smiled to himself as he took a sentimental trip down memory lane. Besides a few leftover curtain rails, the flat was empty. He had no idea if anyone else had resided in the flat after him but there was barely a trace of existence there now. He only gave himself a moment to reminisce. He had come to the flat for a reason, he was there to collect something meaningful. Something from his past that he needed to take with him as a reminder of how good his life was and how good it still could've been if only he had of seized the moment instead of second guessing himself, something he vowed never to do again.

Once it became clear that he and The Boss were moving onto bigger and better things, he had decided to stash the item as he felt that the time wasn't right for it to be used, unfortunately, that time never came and then it was too late. He had been up in the small loft dozens of times, the flat was so small that he had to store most of their belongings up there, especially as his fiancée was prone to hording Barbie dolls which she had deemed to be valuable and a sound investment. He knew the loft was the best place for him to hide this item as it was the only mould-free place in the flat; it had plenty of places to stash the small item and due to how difficult it was to actually get up into the loft he knew his fiancée would never attempt to go up there.

He hopped up onto the small bannister that barely had enough room to place your hand let alone two size ten feet, but he had found a way of making it work. Once he had gotten onto the bannister, he placed one foot against the wall in front of him while the other remained wobbly on it. With his front foot barely supporting him, he raised his hands above his head and undid the latch holding the loft door closed and at the last second remembered that the door didn't fall open with the grace of a ballerina, but rather with the aggressive force of a right hand from Mike Tyson. He ducked his head down, narrowly avoiding the swinging door of the loft bursting open. He held onto the sides of the open loft, pulled himself up and perched onto the side while his legs dangled in the air.

He turned on his torch and shone the light around the empty loft. To his delight, he had seen that nobody had been up in there since he had moved out. He carefully navigated his way to the far corner of the loft, balancing on the support beams of the roof. He had meant to put some floor boards down in the loft for years but it was one of those jobs that he had always said he would get around to, but never did. His fiancée would constantly be on his back about getting it done; but considering he was the only one that ever ventured up there, he never saw the point in wasting the time or money.

He lifted up a few sheets of foam insulation in the corner of the loft and to his excitement and relief he found what he was looking for. He picked up a small box and opened it. His eyes instantly began to well up as he looked down at the two wedding bands he had secretly bought for him and his fiancée. When he had proposed to her, they were both scraping through life and they had agreed that once they could afford to buy each other wedding bands they would get married. They felt that the wedding rings represented so much more than a venue or a dress, the symbolism of the rings and the eternal bond they signified meant everything to them. He had been working in a job where he was massively undervalued and was only earning enough to keep a roof over his head after the taxman had his piece.

His fiancée had been working as a freelance blogger at the time and she never knew when the next pay-cheque was coming in.

Although blogging was her dream job she had offered to get a "real" job on several occasions so she could help out with the finances, but Nick refused. He had seen what the nine-to-five grind had done to his partner's mental health so he selflessly took on the role as bread winner in the relationship so his fiancée could do what she loved.

He had worked near a second hand jewellery shop and managed to haggle with the salesman into let-ting him have the two wedding bands for a reason-able price. Shortly after he'd made the purchase of the rings, he was made redundant and lost his job. He had protested his redundancy but with minimal effort, although he needed the money and the tim-ing was awful, a big part of him was happy to be leaving a job he'd never been happy with. It did, however, make planning a wedding difficult. This was the first time that he'd decided not to tell his fiancée about the rings as he wanted the moment to be perfect. After he lost his job, there never felt like a right time to get married and that perfect moment never came, and then one day it was too late, and he had lost his fiancée forever.

He knew he had risked his life for this reckless adventure but at one time those rings were a bea-con of eternal happiness for him, now, however, they meant something else, now they acted as a re-minder to him that things can't wait until they're perfect, things need to happen as soon as they can or you risk losing everything.

Once he had gotten what he came for he needed to leave right away and get back to work. Over the years he had learnt to be overly cautious, so before he left the flat, he looked through the curtains in the living room onto the quiet street and bar a few wandering dogs outside the road was clear.

He'd decided to travel back on the same route he took to get from Barnet to the flat; he knew the area like the back of his hand, and was familiar with where most of the gangs operated, so he was able to manoeuvre around them with relative ease. The gangs in Harrow were notoriously easy to spot as they were often drunk, high, and very vocal when patrolling the streets. The heavy narcotic usage from these gangs made them incredibly dangerous and erratic; the only gangs more volatile than the Harrow gangs were the gangs which operated in the Southwark borough. Unfortunately for Nick, he was about to find out that the only reason he got from point A to point B unharmed was because the gangs in Harrow had been tipped off of his arrival.

He collected his bag and decided to use the bathroom before he left; he wasn't sure how long it would be again until he would have the simple luxury of using a real toilet after he had left the city. Out of habit, once he'd finished, he flushed the toilet. The sound of the toilet flushing followed by the trickling of the water in the tank filling up took over the bathroom. When the water from the toilet tank had stopped, Nick heard a different sound, a sound he had not heard since a traumatic day a year and a half prior.

It was the day he was tasked to accompany a division of men and women, The Boss had named "The People's Police," on an eviction mission. Before there were gangs there was The People's Police. The Boss believed that the real workers of the city should be the ones to control and govern how their boroughs operated. This quickly went to pot and the power struggles between the gangs emerged, and when the resistance gangs began to form The Boss would use The People's Police as her personal army.

One day, Nick had been asked to escort a taskforce of The People's Police into the Bexley borough to make sure all of the resistance groups in the area were evicted from the state prior to her locking down the city for good. After witnessing the brutality and horrific treatment the people of Bexley received, he vowed to never be a part of that kind of operation ever again.

The sound outside of the flat got louder and faster and when he returned back to the window and looked through the curtains he had looked through not five minutes earlier, the then empty street was now full of dozens of members of the Harrow Hounds, the number one gang that ran Harrow. The Hounds were outside banging baseball bats, cricket bats, metal poles and other weapons onto the floor in unison, a battle cry that warned whoever heard it that something bad was about to happen and there wasn't a thing they could do to stop it. The noise escalated to a rhythmic point and then it suddenly stopped. Amongst the crowd stepped out a man.

"Nicholas, come out to play!" came a voice from outside.

Nick knew who that voice belonged to and he was shocked to see that he remained the leader of the Harrow Hounds after the countless mutiny attempts made on him. Patrick Luther had been a devout disciple of The Boss, so much so that his blind loyalty to her often created friction within his gang as he would banish people from the group at the drop of a hat if they slandered her name in any way.

Patrick had been a friend to Nick and The Boss before the rioting began. They had met in a comic book shop one afternoon while they were at university. Nick had decided to write an essay on the rise of superheroes in cinema and needed some advice from a pro. Patrick was the quintessential know-it-all on superheroes and had more than one opinion on the differences between comic book and movie superheroes. Nick being a big film buff, instantly hit it off with Patrick and the two bonded over their favourite films and TV shows.

When the rioting escalated around the country, Nick and The Boss took care of Patrick after he lost his job for openly supporting The Boss and justifying the rioting on social media. Patrick and The Boss got particularly close after she became instrumental in shutting down the comic book shop that he was fired from and putting his old boss out of business. She had hired him to act as a historian for her and tasked him with documenting everything that had been happening in the city during her rise to the top. She had insisted that he captured every detail of what was happening at the time, including any mistakes or mishaps she may have incurred; however, when things started getting out of hand, he began doctoring what had really been happening in the city, something which created a huge rift between him and Nick.

Eventually Nick convinced The Boss that as a long-standing resident of Harrow, Patrick should be the one to lead The People's Police of the Harrow borough. He had been reluctant at first, but The Boss was always able to coax him into doing whatever it was she asked of him, even though he knew Nick had put her up to it. From then on, he hated Nick and swore his allegiance to The Boss and The Boss only.

"Long time no see Nicky boy. Why don't you make this easy for us all and come out here, I wouldn't want to have to go all Hulk on your arse and drag you out by your neck," threatened Patrick.

Still a massive nerd," thought Nick. However, he knew Patrick had become hardened in recent years and would do anything he could to please The Boss, including dying for her. Unsure of how he would survive this confrontation, he listened to Patrick's orders and left the flat on his own two feet.

The Hounds had formed a semicircle around the driveway of the flat. Nick looked at all of the hooded figures around him and realised there was no way out. The zero point one per cent chance he had of getting away would be if he had been able to scale the fence to his right and hope that none of The Hounds could outrun him. Even then, if he had been able to get away, there would be no way he'd get back to Barnet without passing out from exhaustion and being captured; he was trapped.

"Patrick, how are you old friend? Still leader of The Bitches I see, I'm sorry, The Hounds," said Nick trying to sound far more confident than he felt.

"I see you haven't lost that smart mouth that gets you into trouble. I'd of thought after falling so far from her ranks, you'd have the decency to keep your mouth shut. Now you've got two choices Nick…" said Patrick before being interrupted.

"Are you seriously doing the 'you have two choices' bit with me?" laughed Nick. "You may be the leader of some crackhead gang, but don't pretend like you are a big man. Don't get it twisted Pat, you'll always be that geeky little prick who used to sit on his arm until it went numb before knocking one out to cosplay porn."

Muffled laughter could be heard coming from Patrick's gang, he shot them a sharp glance, but once again Nick was able to get the better of him in a war of words.

"Funny. You know what I find really hysterical? The fact that you had the power of the world in your hands alongside The Boss and you lost it all when things got too real for you. You couldn't handle it, so you ran away with your tail between your legs like the wuss that you are," bit back Patrick. "Enough stalling Nick, we know what you are planning on doing and we know that you are alone so please, I beg you, continue to push my buttons because all I need is one excuse for me and The Hounds to send you back to The Boss a bloody fucking mess."

He looked around the street again, hoping that there was some other way out of this predicament, but it soon dawned on him that he didn't have a way out and this may actually be it for him. Months of planning about to come to an end. He put his hands up in the air hoping to look as submissive as he possibly could. He knew he was going to get roughed up regardless of what Patrick had said, but he hoped if he complied, he would only suffer minimal damage. He started walking towards Patrick and The Harrow Hounds, with feelings of despair and defeat creeping through him. He had gotten so close to completing his plan and because of one selfish and sentimental mistake, he had ruined any chance of saving the city and the country.

Suddenly, out of the darkness, a glowing ray of light hurled through the sky and erupted into an explosive ball of fire in front of Nick and Patrick. The surprising impact knocked the pair to the floor. The Hounds began to panic; they scanned the streets in hopes of seeing where the flaming bottle had come from. Before anyone could identify where the attack was coming from, more flaming bottles had landed and crashed amongst The Hounds and the tight semicircle they had created began to break apart as the gang scattered for cover to avoid being hit by the soaring Molotov Cocktails. Nick quickly jumped to his feet and booted Patrick in the face before making his escape during the havoc. He had no idea who had been throwing the flaming bottles, but he presumed due to their impeccable timing, that they must be on his side or at the very least were attacking a rival gang; either way, he figured running towards the attackers was a safer option than being trapped with The Hounds.

The streets were a blaze and half of The Harrow Hounds had fled the area, while the other half had taken cover behind walls and abandoned cars. Once he had made it to the bottom of the street, the Molotovs had stopped flying through the air; he was at a crossroads, unsure which way would be the safest route back to Barnet.

"Oi idiot, hurry up and move your arse," came a female voice Nick knew all too well.

That hadn't been the first time and certainly wouldn't be the last time that his sister had called him an idiot, and although he knew they were furious at him, a smile appeared across his face as he realised his gang had come to his rescue. He didn't have time to think about how they knew where to find him and fortunately for him, they didn't have time to chastise him for running off by himself either. Emily, Will, and Izzy had been standing by a dark path that ran behind Nick's old flat.

"I'm going to explain to you later why I'm going kill you for being so stupid, but right now, we have to get out of here. The Mayor only gave us a few of these Molotovs so we have to move now" said Emily.

The group neared the exit of the path, but before they could reach the end of it a loud metal creaking noise caught their attention.

"Hey, hey you, stop. Don't go out there. They're waiting for you on both sides. Come through here," came a male voice from a shadowy figure standing by an open gate in the alleyway.

"What shall we do?" asked Izzy.

Without a thought, Will ran towards the mysterious man. "We haven't got time to decide. We have to go," said Will disappearing through the gate.

Izzy followed after Will with Nick and Emily not far behind them. So much had happened that neither Nick nor any of the gang had time to stop and think; only act. Who was this mysterious person? Was he a Good Samaritan or was he leading Nick and his friends out of the frying pan and into the fire?

CHAPTER 22

Ricky Bhala had always been a spoilt brat, and at the age of thirty-four nothing had changed except that he was now a tall and lanky spoilt brat with a receding hairline. He was an only child from a strict Gujarati Indian family that valued men as superior to women. His parents had given him anything he wanted and he had never worked a hard day in his life because he truly believed that he was too good to work for anyone else.

His attitude of superiority prevented him from making any real friends in his life; he had felt that he should always be the decision maker and leader in any social group he was a part of. He didn't understand the value of money, friendship or love, and he always felt that nothing was ever good enough for him, which subsequently turned him into a very angry and selfish person. He was one of the many people that took part in the mindless looting and destruction during the 2011 London riots, and he continued to steal and harm for his own selfish gains in the continued rioting that followed years later.

When The Boss gave the people the choice to stay in her city or leave, Ricky opted to stay, but he ordered his parents to leave so he could keep them safe. His self-delusions led him to believe that he could run the world better than anyone else could, so he promised his parents that he would over-throw The Boss one day and when he was in charge he would welcome them back to live with him.

In his attempt to fulfil his promise, he had joined several different gangs across the state. Once he had infiltrated a gang, he would try to turn gang mem-bers against the gang leaders by spreading lies about them so he could rally support and takeover. How-ever, he could never keep track of his lies and the end result was always the same – he was found out and exiled. After he was eventually embarrassed and released from The Harrow Hounds by Patrick, he had begun to feel fed up and broken, so when the opportunity arose to not only make Patrick look like a fool, but to also gain Nick's trust at the same time, he jumped at the chance.

Despite being kicked out of a number of these gangs he was able to remain hidden in some the gang's message groups, including The Hounds, which meant he knew exactly where Nick was going to be that night. He had no idea how he was going to use Nick to achieve his dream, but he knew that he would be his best hope of dethroning The Boss and becoming the leader of The ISOE.

With his knowledge of where The Harrow Hounds operated after spending the last five months with them, he was able to help Nick and his group escape the borough and get them back en route to Barnet. Along the way, he had contrived a story about him being a resident of Queensbury who refused to move away when the gangs rolled into town. He explained that he chose to be alone as it made survival easier.

After years of witnessing his mother exploit vulnerable people in a multi-level marketing scheme and observing his father making a living by lying and deceiving people as a greedy landlord, Ricky had all the tools he needed to be a professional storyteller.

Emily, Will, and Izzy had been too wrapped up in Nick's selfish decision to abandon the group to really give Ricky the proper interrogation they should have.

Nick knew he had no right to defend himself, so he kept quiet while he received his tongue lashing and apologised to everyone when they were finished berating him. He even thanked Ricky for helping them get to Barnet. When the scolding had finally finished, the group told him that Brintha had overheard Stewart informing the Hounds of his plan, and she immediately informed them of his betrayal. He wasn't sure why she helped him, but he was grateful that she had.

Once they had returned to the church, The Mayor was waiting in his office with Stewart who was being restrained by two large guards. Tears had been streaming down his face and a large wet patch sat across his crotch and from the looks of the cuts; and bruises on both The Mayor's hands and Patrick's face, Nick knew he had been given the beating he deserved.

"Welcome back Nick. You've surprised me. I didn't think you'd survive your suicide mission," said The Mayor.

"Thanks...I guess. So, what happened here then? I thought all your guys were supposed to be neutral?" questioned Nick.

The pair turned to Stewart who continued to sob in his urine soaked trousers.

"This was an unexpected hit for us. I've known this man for many years, and believe you me, I'm more upset by his treachery than you are and twice as angry," said The Mayor.

"You've known me for years and you've done nothing but treat me like your lap dog. All you ever do is tell me what to do. I wanted to be treated with respect, the respect that you've never given to me," sobbed Stewart.

The Mayor walked over to him calmly and punched him in the stomach knocking him to the floor.

"You were saying?" said The Mayor coolly.

"What are you going to do to him?" asked Nick.

"I don't know yet, but he won't be seeing day light for a very long time. I can't have him infecting others with his poisonous mind."

They left the office and walked back into the main room which was much quieter at that time of night. The Mayor noticed Ricky sitting with Will and Izzy on a church pew.

"I see your group has grown in size since I last saw you."

"I don't really know who he is, but he helped us out back in Queensbury. He's another lost civilian; he seems harmless enough. So, where is she?" asked Nick.

He pointed to a collection of church pews at the back of the church that had been pushed together to create a makeshift bed. Nick walked over to the back of the church where he saw JJ asleep with his head resting on his mother's lap.

"Still alive I see!" said Brintha sarcastically.

"It would seem so, sorry to disappoint you, although I hear I have you to thank for that. My sister and my friends tell me that you alerted them and The Mayor of what Stewart had planned. Once Emily found out I was going to Harrow, she knew exactly where I'd be heading."

"Well, I'm glad you have such a good relationship with your sister, she obviously got all the good qualities in the family" sniped Brintha.

He smiled at the unnecessary catty dig she had made. "I wanted to thank you for saving me and I wanted to ask you why? Why did you help me after everything you blame me for?"

She started stroking her son's hair while he slept, "My son has had a bad start to life. He's never known a real home. He's grown up around terror and fear and chaos, and my job has been to protect him, to show him that good remains in this world. I want my son knowing that even in a world of disorder and destruction, doing the right thing and being good is and always will be an option. I told your sister and friends where you were, not for you, but for my son. I also really don't like that Stewart prat."

"That's as good as a reason as I need to hear," smiled Nick. "If you'll allow me, I'd like to invite you and your son to accompany us to Enfield and I promise you I will take you both out of this place and try and make up for the lives you have lost. I want to give you both the happiness you were promised."

She looked into his eyes in an attempt to measure the sincerity of his offer; one thing she couldn't deny about Nick since she'd met him was his honesty. She could see he had become a beaten man and had no reason to lie to her. She flashed him the slightest of smiles which told him that she'd accepted his offer.

"We'll leave when little man wakes up. Get some rest. We have one more hump to get over before we get out," said Nick.

The group had assembled at the exit of the church at around eight a.m.; it had been a quiet night with almost everyone but Ricky and Nick getting some much needed sleep. Nick had spent the night nervous yet excited at the prospect of his journey soon coming to an end. He had very nearly achieved his goal, and although things hadn't gone to plan and he had inherited some extra baggage along the way, he felt optimistic, a feeling he hadn't felt in years. Ricky, on the other hand, had spent the night plotting, scheming, and thinking of ways that he could sabotage Nick's mission so he could hand deliver him to The Boss. Fortunately for Nick, Ricky wasn't the best at thinking ahead so he had decided to continue on pretending to help Nick and his group until an opportune moment presented itself. It hadn't taken much convincing from Ricky to ensure that he could tag along with the others to Enfield, after helping them back in Queensbury and spending the night ranting to the group about how much he hated The Boss; Emily, Will and Izzy were convinced that an extra pair of hands wouldn't hurt in helping them achieve their mission.

Brintha, JJ, and Nick arrived to meet the group last.

"Sorry we're late, someone decided to have a lie in for the first time in a year," said Brintha who playfully poked JJ under the armpit.

"That's okay. The boy obviously needed his rest after spending all day flirting with all of his girlfriends. Bump it little dude," said Will extending his fist to JJ who bumped it back with a smile on his face.

"Hold on, why is she coming?" barked Ricky. "We can't be looking after some lady and her kid. Isn't this going to be dangerous? Who is she anyway?"

His outburst took the group by surprise as he had been relatively calm prior to this point; his real personality had started to seep through already.

"Who am I? Who the hell are you? Some skinny little boy that crawled out of the shadows. Why are you here?" said Brintha getting in his face.

He was dumbfounded at her response.

"Don't worry about me, alright? You just worry about yourself and making sure you don't trip over a crack in the street and snap in half. Get some fat on your bones for goodness sake boy; you look like an anorexic cat," continued Brintha.

Nick choked back the laughter that was desperately trying to escape his mouth. After the rocky start he had with Brintha, he had really started to like her, as had the rest of the group. Before they left the church, The Mayor appeared and made sure he personally saw Nick and his group out.

"Good luck out there," said The Mayor. "If you can pull off what you say you can, it may help me change my mind about you…maybe."

"Thank you for everything Mayor. You have my word that no matter what happens, nobody will ever know about your involvement here," said Nick shaking The Mayor's hand.

13th June 2016, 09:00
Downing Street, The City of Westminster, The Independent State of England

The Boss was sitting in her office alone drinking a glass of Southern Comfort and lemonade. She had a pile of files on her desk which contained various policies, requests, complaints and other documentation that she should be dealing with, but instead she was thinking about Nick. A knock on the door had interrupted her morning drinking; her PA burst through the door so quickly that she didn't have a chance to tell her to leave her alone.

"I'm sorry to disturb you Boss, but we've received an update on Nick's whereabouts and where he plans on going next," said her PA nervously.

She didn't say a word; she silently stared at her PA with an icy cold stare which filled her with even more nerves.

"Erm, for some reason he went to Harrow, Queensbury specifically and got in a confrontation with The Harrow Hounds. Unfortunately, Patrick was unsuccessful in apprehending him and he got away," continued the PA.

She seemed to perk up in her seat when her PA mentioned Queensbury. *"Why had he gone back to the old flat?"* she wondered to herself.

"Where is he now?" asked The Boss.

"Patrick received a call from a Stewart, I'm sorry, I didn't get a last name, but this man was working closely with The Mayor of Barnet and he claimed that The Mayor was giving refuge to Nick and his friends before granting them passage out of Barnet and into Enfield."

"Did you say Enfield?" asked The Boss in a tone that sent shivers down her PA's spine.

"Erm, Yes Boss. Any idea why he's going there?" asked the PA cautiously.

She jumped out of her seat in a rage and launched

her half full glass across the room.

"That lying piece of shit. He's going to see her!" shouted The Boss.

"Who?" asked the PA with an obvious tremble of distress in her voice.

"Jill. Fucking Jill. Get word out to Bray immediately and tell him to get his team together to capture Nick and his gang in Enfield. Tell him to stop them by any means necessary. I'm not messing around with him anymore; this is going to end now!" yelled The Boss.

"Where shall I tell Bray to go exactly Boss? Enfield is a big place," asked her PA sheepishly.

"I know exactly where they are going," said The Boss. "Get the car ready. I'm not letting him get away again, even if I have to stop him myself."

CHAPTER 23

17th August 2013, 14:17
Gosset Street, Tower Hamlets, London

Considering she had never organised an event like this before, let alone an event of this size, she had done an excellent job and it had turned out much better than she had expected. The Boss, Nick, and the rest of her team were over the moon with how many people had come out in support for the cause and to raise money for the tragedy that had affected the people of Gosset Street a few months prior.

Nick had used his minimal knowledge of event planning from his time in corporate media, as well as calling in a few favours to help with getting this fundraiser arranged. The Boss told him that people would jump at the chance to be seen helping when it came to charitable events; not because they wanted to give up their time and money for free, but because it would make them and their brand look good. She'd always been great at reading people and seeing through their crap. She knew at their core, people would be more inclined to help if they got a pat on the back and their egos stroked.

The street was full of people from all backgrounds and all classes, not everyone in attendance may have been there for the right reason, but the more people seen at the event, the better it was for the cause and the better it looked for her. She had made an effort to mingle with everyone she came into contact with that day which felt like almost every person in London. The people were either thanking her for arranging the event, asking her if she'd ever go back to doing her Vlogs on YouTube or asking her what she'd be doing next.

The fundraiser had been busy throughout the entire day, and to everyone's surprise, it had remained friendly and safe. Due to the countless and unnecessary deaths from the tragic event that led to this fundraiser, she knew that there would be a lot of animosity and anger towards the powers that be for seemingly not taking the proper precautions to prevent it. The subsequent treatment of the survivors also raised ethical and moral questions about how the lower class is viewed and treated by those in power; because of this, she had extra security readily available.

The high spirited event was filled with good food, guest speakers, celebrities, and musical acts from the local community. There were games for kids and adults, talks from politicians and government officials, and even Notting Hill carnival style parades. The only thing that hadn't gone right that day was the wrong colour bunting had been hung up, however, only The Boss seemed to care about that.

Even though he was born and raised in England, Nick never understood the obsession with British people hanging bunting everywhere.

Throughout the day The Boss' team had been spread out amongst the event; some were making sure things stayed on track, while others had injected themselves into the crowds to enjoy the merriment. Her team had grown over the years and she considered them all crucial to the movement. They had all devoted themselves entirely to her, so much so that they rarely had time to relax and enjoy the moment. She knew change was in the air, so she encouraged her team to enjoy themselves as much as they could, while they could, because after her announcement later that day, she knew that they would be working harder than they had been already. Nick hadn't seen much of The Boss during the day, but when he did catch a glimpse of her, he was happy to see that she had taken her own advice and was revelling in the festivities.

The afternoon had turned into the evening and the streets continued to get busier and livelier. The Boss had begun making her way to the main stage so she could thank the people for coming out in support and to also make an important announcement. She made her way through the crowd towards the stage, but was intercepted by Nick who had been talking to a short olive skinned woman who was wearing a 'SAVE GOSSET STREET' T-Shirt and tight skinny jeans which showed off the most incredibly toned backside she had ever seen. Her eyes were drawn to it before she even saw the woman's face, which happened to also be a thing of beauty.

"Who is this angelic looking woman and why is she talking to Nick?" thought The Boss.

"Boss, I know you're about to go on but I wanted to quickly introduce you to an old friend of mine, La... sorry, Boss, meet Jill Sampson. Jill and I were neighbours when we were kids but after my mum left and we moved away, we didn't get to see or talk to each other again. But she found me online recently and we reconnected," explained Nick.

"Well he wasn't exactly hard to find, what with him being all over my socials, usually standing next to you," said Jill extending her hand to The Boss who reached out and shook it. "It's such a huge honour to meet you. I've been following you since your YouTube days and I was really hoping we could sit down and talk through some things. You are a massive icon in the feminist circles and you've done wonders for the empowerment of women."

"Jill is a really successful women's rights activist. She presents and gives talks on feminism and equality, and I'm sorry, I feel like I'm putting you on a pedestal. What I'm saying is, she's doing a lot for women's rights and equality, just like you. I think it would be great if you two sat down and spoke about what she can do for us and what we can do for her," said Nick enthusiastically.

Despite the positive natured intent he had, he noticed that The Boss seemed more confused and annoyed at what he had said, a vibe Jill had also picked up on.

"Nick is being far too kind; for all the work I've done, I've barely scratched the surface compared to what you continue to achieve. I don't know how much you could help, but the female empowerment movement has grown and we want to change the perception of what it means to be a woman and a feminist. When most people hear the word feminist or women's rights, it's usually followed with scoffs and thoughts of short haired butch lesbians and bitter single women who have been hard done by men, when the truth is, all women want is equality and I was hoping we could use you and your brand to show the people that anyone and everyone can be a feminist. Nick has already volunteered himself to be an advocate for the cause and to speak out as "one of us." With your support, we can show the world that equal pay, equal treatment, and equal rights are available to all and not the few," declared Jill proudly.

Once again, however, Jill and Nick noticed that The Boss didn't seem interested in what was being presented to her. It seemed like all she wanted do was escape from the conversation entirely; a feeling that confused Nick, Jill and, even herself.

"I'm sorry. You'll have to forgive me. I don't feel like I can give this my full attention right now. I don't mean to be rude, but I'm needed on stage. Nick obviously has your contact information so he can arrange for us to meet properly to discuss. Nick, are you coming?" asked The Boss walking through the pair.

He had no idea why she had been acting so strange; he shrugged at Jill, gave her a kiss goodbye and followed The Boss to the stage. When she walked onto the stage, a huge roar erupted at her presence. This kind of attention had become the norm for The Boss, and she had come to really enjoy the admiration. Nick took his usual spot on stage behind her and sat with the rest of the team. Sharing the stage with them was Bray and a number of his political associates, all of whom Nick despised; however, The Boss had stressed to him that although she too despised them, they were valuable in helping her achieve what she needed to; they were a means to an end.

Nick could tell that something wasn't right with her; she had a much different look on her face than she had earlier in the day. He wasn't sure if she was feeling tense about her announcement, if it was something he had or hadn't done, or if it was something else entirely. Things between the pair had felt different leading up to her announcement; he put it down to stress and had hoped that once she had made the announcement, things would go back to how they used to be. The moment her hand touched the microphone on centre stage that look of uncertainty left her and The Boss came out, ready to go to work and take care of business.

"Hello all, let me start by thanking you all for coming out today and showing your support following the catastrophic event that hit this street a few months ago. We are here to raise money for the victims and families who were affected by the Gosset Street fire which spread across a number of flats and homes and caused the deaths of over fifty people, people who we are honouring here today. A massive thank you to all of those who rushed to Gosset Street to offer your support, be it by giving the families who had lost their homes a place to stay, providing them with food and clothing, or helping in any other way you could. The resounding support from each and every borough in this city was, and please excuse my French, fucking astonishing," beamed The Boss. "In the face of tragedy, the spirit of community was well and truly alive and kicking. People were able to put their differences aside and help for a united cause, and I for one, think that is a beautiful thing. I'd like to throw out a huge thank you to all of our celebrity friends who have come out to support us here today; all of these artists have chosen to be here willingly today and have given up their time for free."

The crowd applauded the generosity of the celebrities who came out to support the cause.

"Now I'm not going to lie. When I met some of these celebrities today, I became a bit of a fan girl. I was honestly at my most uncool around these guys," joked The Boss. "They will continue to perform for us for the rest of the evening over at the performance stage on Pollard Square. We have loads more great acts tonight including Tinie Tempah, Ocean Wisdom, and Little Mix for you all to enjoy.

All we ask in return, is a donation of whatever you can give. This fundraiser, charity event, whatever you want to call it, has been organised today by me and my team because we didn't want to just remember the dead, we wanted to honour the living, specifically those who have lost family members and friends, and those who have lost their homes and their livelihoods after the fire."

A hush came over the crowd.

"The fire and this tragedy could have been avoided and it sickens me to know that those who lost their homes have yet to be properly rehomed or fairly compensated. Because of subpar materials and resources in these buildings and homes, and after countless complaints and requests to get these materials changed, which were all ignored, what started as a small accidental fire escalated to disastrous proportions and those responsible should be taking the blame for their mistakes and making things right, not burying their heads in the sand hoping people will forget about you. The people will never forget. We will not be forgotten about anymore and I promise you all now I will never forget about you."

Another huge roar filled the street as she had the crowd in attendance eating out of the palm of her hand. The people knew she wasn't merely saying what they wanted to hear, they knew she meant every single thing she was saying. She spoke on behalf of those who couldn't be heard and the people adored her for it.

"Unlike many other political representatives in this country, when I heard about the fire and the misfortune it had created, I made sure I stopped everything I was doing and got down here as soon as I could. I got into the trenches to not only show my support, but to help, to clear the rubble and to support the people, and by coming out here today, you have shown you are willing to do the same. We are the ones who keep this country moving and I will continue to make sure that the workers, the back bone of this city, are rewarded appropriately for their hard work," continued The Boss.

The crowd continued to cheer for her, the reaction from the crowd was unlike anything the other politicians had ever seen before. All of her doubters were getting an up close and personal view of the support and the power that she had amassed. She had insisted that the politicians and the haters who had complained about her being too young to be involved in politics or discredited her because they felt that her views and ideas were too "out there" had the best seats in the house to see her at her most triumphant and were present for her announcement.

"I hope I have made it clear to you all that I am here not because I am supposed to be or because it looks good for my image, but because I want to be here," stressed The Boss. "With that being said, and I hope you don't all mind, I would like to make an announcement which I hope will have a positive effect on us all. I would never dare steal focus from this cause, but I couldn't think of a better time or a better place than with the people I love in the city that I love to officially announce that I plan to move on as an MP of Harrow and take up office in a more central location in London - as your new Prime Minister."

The sound and ovation was so raucous that it even took her by surprise, but she loved it so much that all she could think to do was stand on the stage and soak it all in. Nick and her team had joined in with the crowd and were cheering and celebrating behind her as they watched on as the woman they had been following for years continued to make waves right in front of their eyes.

"I don't run for any party, I run for myself and I run for you. I promise that I will right the wrongs the old regime have created and when I finally make it to Downing Street, I will make sure that every single one of you get what's coming to you," concluded The Boss.

Everyone was in full celebration mode as the event had taken on an extra air of positivity after the huge bombshell announcement. She looked out into the crowd and for the first time in her short political career she felt powerful, she knew she was on a path to great things and that she had the world at her feet. She waved to the crowd as she got ready to leave the stage; however, before she could go anywhere, her eyes had been drawn to some violent shuffling in the crowd, which was shortly followed by loud screaming and shouting. A fight had broken out which was the last thing she needed, due to her association with the civil unrest that had infested the city she had been desperately trying to distance herself from any further violent conflict.

She signalled to the security team hidden in the crowd to go and resolve the situation before it escalated further. However, when the team began dealing with the commotion, another fight had broken out on the other side of the crowd. The fight radius began to spread as people were either being dragged into the fights or were running away from them.

In an instant, the peaceful and elated crowd had erupted into a volcanic explosion of violence and belligerence, a full-scale riot was happening where peace stood mere moments before. The politicians, celebrities, and The Boss' team began to panic on stage when the vicious crowds began to spill from the floor onto the main stage. Bottles, bricks, chairs, and anything else that hadn't been nailed down began flying through the sky as the fighting worsened. She tried her best to spot the instigators of the chaos but all she could see was pandemonium. Suddenly, out of the crowd, as if she had been targeted directly, a glass bottle had been hurled through the sky and smashed onto the back of her head causing her to fall to the floor. Bray and Nick rushed over to her and in an act of unity they both helped her to her feet. Fortunately she hadn't been knocked out from the blow, but after seeing the blood on his hands, Nick could see that she was bleeding profusely from the back of her head.

"We have to get the hell out of here. Let's get her to the green room," yelled Nick.

The pair was practically carrying her across the stage. She ordered them to stop when she noticed the terrified MP's on-stage cowering for their lives.

"Come with us and we'll keep you safe," said The Boss feebly to the MP's. "Bray, make sure they are all safe and get them to the green room."

He signalled to his team to assist with getting the politicians to safety while Nick continued to lead her back to the admin office, which had doubled as a greenroom for the celebrities and high profile politicians. It was the most secure place at the event and had been intentionally hidden in case of emergencies.

The Boss, Nick and the rest of the VIP's were ushered into the green room to hide out in until the police had dealt with the insanity taking place on Gosset Street. Nick had taken The Boss to a private area at the back of the green room and demanded a first aid kit be brought to him right away. While he was tending to her wound, Bray and the rest of her team were making sure everyone in the green room were safe and accounted for.

She could hear the rumblings in the room, the MP's were shouting over each other, some were holding her responsible for what had happened, some were saying that they were right about her attracting violence wherever she went while others, who had previously shared those same jaded views, were now defending her and explaining that she too was a victim of these attacks and not an instigator. Despite suffering a raging headache and feeling quite dazed, she couldn't help but smile at what she was hearing.

"The cut isn't too bad but you're going to need stiches. We'll get you to the hospital as soon as things have calmed down," said Nick holding a cold compress onto the back of her head.

"I'll be fine. I've had worse blows in my time," said The Boss, still with a smile on her face.

"Why the hell are you smiling? Are you sure you're okay? Maybe that bottle did more damage than I thought," asked Nick with concern.

"Do you hear them out there?" asked The Boss.

"Who? The people fighting?"

"No, them, the MP's, since this all started those people were ready to hang me out to dry as soon as the opportunity struck. They accused me of inciting the rioting and the violence and now half of them are defending me, some of them even sound like they're concerned about my wellbeing," laughed The Boss.

"What are you talking about?"

"Do you think all of that out there happened by accident? I know there are some messed up people in this city but who in their right mind would cause a riot at a fundraiser?" said The Boss with a conniving tone in her voice.

He stared at her and tried to comprehend the magnitude of what she had revealed to him.

"Are you saying you planned this? You caused a fucking riot on purpose?" said Nick louder than she would've liked.

"Believe me, I didn't want it to have to come to this, but if I want to stand a chance in this race I need as much support as I can get from the other MP's. I put myself in harm's way for them. I was injured for them. Do you really think they're going to continue to question my involvement with the violence in this country now? They can say I attract violent support, but they can never say I orchestrated or encouraged it, not now that I have become a victim of the violence like so many others have. Once I give a heart wrenching speech about my sadness and despair over what has happened today, at an event that I funded and organised, well, it will be the cherry on top in showing the idiots who doubted me that no matter what happens I will be there fighting for the cause, even if it means getting caught in the cross-fires," explained The Boss succinctly.

He sat in front of her in astonished silence at the words coming out of her mouth.

"I...I don't know what to say. Why didn't you tell me you were going to do this? Why the fuck was I kept in the dark? Who else knew about this?" said Nick through clenched teeth.

She nodded towards Bray, who was playing the role of upstanding citizen as he made sure some of the elderly MP's and politicians were being looked after.

"Are you serious? So not only did you not tell me

what you were planning on doing but you went to that animal for help? Why didn't you tell me? Since when do we keep things from each other?" asked Nick, getting angrier with her.

"You mean like you and Jill getting back in touch? How long has it been exactly since you've been back in contact with her?" she snapped back.

"What has Jill got to do with anything? Jill and I are friends, old friends and why are you so concerned with her all of a sudden? She's one of your biggest followers and someone who could be a real asset to us. She's just like you."

"I'm sure it's her ASSets that you're really interested in, and stop saying she's like me, there's only one me, one Boss, understood," she said matching Nick's anger levels.

"Don't you dare pull 'The Boss' card on me. Remember that we both came from the same stock Mrs Lady of the People. I don't know what has come over you recently, but I don't like it. I understand that we might have to pull out some questionable moves from time to time; we may even have to hurt some people to save a whole lot more, I get that. What I don't get is you taking on that burden by yourself and deciding to keep me out of the loop."

Feeling the tears of anger and hurt fast approaching, he stood up and walked away from her; he wouldn't allow her to see him upset.

"I didn't think you could handle it," said The Boss, forcing him to stop walking and turn back to her. "You're right, the dirty tactics are unavoidable and sometimes it means having to go to a dark place within yourself to get things done and then to carry on like nothing happened. I don't think you have what it takes to do that, that's why I went to Bray and not you. You are the one who needs to keep us going when times are hard, to pick me up when I feel low, that's your job, but I also need people around me who can do the things that you can't. That's why I kept you in the dark and will continue to keep you in the dark as and when I see fit. If going to those dark places gets me my seat as Prime Minister, I will continue to do them until I get what I want."

He turned his back on her and left the green room without saying another word. He walked back outside into the disarray; he would rather face the raging mobs and rioting than deal with the hot mess that was the woman he thought he knew.

CHAPTER 24

13th June 2016, 11:30
Southbury Road, Enfield, The Independent State of England

The walk from Barnet to Enfield town centre had taken a little longer to get to than expected; having an extra person in the group who had much shorter legs than the rest of the group had caused quite a delay. After forty-five minutes of walking, Brintha had to carry JJ, fortunately for her, she hadn't had to carry the load by herself after the rest of the group were able to convince her to let them help her; everyone but Ricky, who wouldn't stop reminding the group that they shouldn't have brought a child on the road with them.

Nick had no idea where he was going to find Jill; it had been at least a year since he last had any contact with her, so he figured Enfield town centre was as good a place as any to start looking. He was prepared to scream her name until she magically appeared if he had to. His entire plan up until this point had been in his hands, but he knew that once he'd reached Enfield he was taking a huge gamble; he had no idea if she would help him or if she was still even in the borough.

Spirits in the group were high, they were in a safe borough, surrounded by people that detested The Boss and the prospect of the end being near filled the group with hope. They passed through the borough without alerting any unwanted attention, as far as anyone was concerned they were either passing through the borough or were looking to jump sides and relocate, the one thing the resistance boroughs were desperately in need of were supporters and soldiers. The further into Enfield the group got, they witnessed something none of them had seen in a long time, a bustling and happy community. Only a handful of boroughs were thriving in The Boss' new world order, and Enfield had become a place which looked like it hadn't been affected at all by The Boss and the riots. The people weren't simply surviving off of basic rations, they had become self-sufficient. There were shops, restaurants and even a school, the streets were clean and the borough looked like a place people could create a future in, after seeing how this place had evolved and developed, Nick knew who was responsible for it.

Emily and Izzy had noticed the high level of female security guards and soldiers on patrol around the borough, the rumours of an all-female gang taking over Enfield had proven to be true. The group made their way to Enfield train station and after a few minutes of scanning the streets, they were at a loss as to what to do next.

"What now? Who are we meeting here again?" asked Will.

"I'm guessing that would be me," declared a voice which Nick was thrilled to hear.

Two women holding large metal pipes appeared from the main entrance of the station, behind them followed Jill Sampson. She looked as confident and stunning as he had remembered.

"Hello Nick, you look awful," said Jill. "I've been expecting you."

"How did yo..."started Nick before being interrupted.

"The Mayor of Barnet and I have a very good relationship. We've been helping him develop his borough and build up his community over the last few months, on the hush hush of course; and out of respect, he gave me a heads up that you were on your way. I'd like to welcome you all to Enfield, follow me and we can talk. I'm presuming you're all hungry?"

After seeing Jill, Ricky was lost for words. He was completely besotted by her beauty and in an act of over confidence or sheer stupidity he took it upon himself to approach her so he could personally introduce himself.

"Hello sexy, my name's Ricky, yours was Jill right?" he said with a smarmy smile on his face.

He took her hand and kissed the top of it. She slowly pulled her hand away and smiled at him.

"Damn baby girl. I'm sorry but I have to say, you arc the finest thing I've seen in a long time," he turned to

303

Emily and Izzy who were looking on in disgust. "No offence to you girls but this chick is stupidly hot."

"Aww do you really think so?" said Jill letting out a playful giggle, "Guess what, Ricky, was it? You've just made a very silly choice."

While he tried to figure out what she meant by her comment, he had been oblivious to one of her guards who had walked towards him and proceeded to punch him straight across the face; knocking him to the floor and busting open his lip.

Jill crouched down in front of a now timid Ricky, "You see that that was her at thirty per cent, continue to disrespect me or any of the other women here and I will personally show you how hard The Femme Fatales can really hit. Understand sweetheart?" threatened Jill.

"I have to say, I'm liking this place more and more," laughed Brintha.

Jill and her two guards accompanied Nick and his gang to a nearby restaurant where they were escorted to a private dining room. A feast of meat and vegetarian dishes had been prepared for Nick and his group, along with bottles of wine and beer on the tables. A collective stomach grumbling sound came from the group who were salivating at the spread in front of them.

"Dig in everyone. There is plenty to go around," said Jill.

Will and Izzy didn't hesitate and parked up at the closest table with their knives and forks in hand; the rest of the group and a few of the Femme Fatales joined them as they sat and enjoyed a meal together.

"Grab a plate Nick and join me over there so we can catch up," said Jill pointing at a small table which had been set up separately from the rest of the group.

He was delighted to see his friends smiling and enjoying themselves. He hadn't expected any smiles during this journey, so it was a welcome surprise to see that he was able to bring them to a place where they could be happy.

"It's good to see you Nick, I wasn't sure I'd ever see you again. Sorry to be blunt, but you have tell me what you are you doing here?" Jill inquired.

"I need your help."

"I gathered that Nicholas, what do you need?"

"I'm getting out. I'm getting out and I'm taking her down once and for all and you are the only one I can trust to get me and my crew out."

"And how do you expect me to do that?" questioned Jill.

The last time she had spoken with him he had been a loyal supporter of The Boss. It had only been a short while after that had his loyalty begun to waiver, she had to be sure that he had truly abandoned his allegiance to The Boss before she could fully trust him.

"When we last spoke and you told me you would be staying here, I presumed there was a reason for you choosing Enfield. Yes, it's an anti-Boss borough, but it's also one of the many boroughs that sit on the border of London and this particular borough has a bridge directly linked to Hertfordshire and we both know what's in Hertfordshire. To be honest, part of me didn't think you'd be here. I figured you'd of found a way out as soon as you could. Have you even tried?" probed Nick.

"I forgot what a smart arse you were. Yes, I tried to escape, and I succeeded. I was outside of the fence and I could taste the freedom, but I couldn't bring myself to leave. When I arrived here, this place was like every other borough in the city. The people were suffering, and the women, the women here were broken. There had been some awful people, some awful horrible men who had been running things here, I won't go into detail about what they had done and what I had to do to get the power back, but I was able to rally these women together and we took over," explained Jill with a passionate fury, a passion Nick had always admired in her. "I gave the women who lived here the command and it has never looked better. We are doing more than getting by; we're living our best lives. The Femme Fatales are making changes and we hope to expand that change beyond this borough. I cannot and will not leave until a change has been made in this city, no matter how long it may take."

"Femme Fatales? I couldn't have picked a better name for you and your gang if I tried," laughed Nick.

"You know me Nick, I've always wanted to be Wonder Woman," said Jill impishly.

"It's great to see you Jill."

"You too Nick."

The pair raised their glasses and drank to their re-union.

"What you've created here is beyond incredible Jill. You've turned this place into what the whole city should be, what it should've been from the beginning," said Nick, feeling slightly disheartened after thinking about what the city could've been, "You said you succeeded in escaping, but you couldn't leave, that must mean you found a way out? Can you take us there?"

"Eat up Nick. Once you and your team are ready, I will take you down the yellow brick road and get you all out of here, but on one condition."

He looked at her in anticipation, wondering what she was going to ask him.

"Promise me that bitch will burn for what she has done to us," said Jill seductively as she leaned to-wards Nick.

"You have my word, and I promise you I will be the one who personally ignites the fire," replied Nick who was drawn into Jill's alluring gaze.

There had always been a mild sexual attraction between the pair which neither had ever acted on or addressed. However, in that moment, as they sat across from each other, her with the command of her borough behind her and him with the power and knowledge to bring down an empire, the sparks were flying between the two and it took all of their restraint to not kiss each other there and then. Now was not the time, the pair knew that this was a can of worms that neither of them should be opening right now.

Nick, Jill, and their respective gangs enjoyed a group meal together before the last leg of their trip to the fence. Things had been awkward and uneasy between the two gangs at first, but once the wine began to flow, conversations and stories were exchanged, drink and meat was consumed, and the afternoon felt like a night out with friends in London, which even included that sleazy guy who would inappropriately chat up anyone and everyone he could. Brintha, Izzy, and Emily had their fun with shutting Ricky up whenever he opened his mouth and laughed when he failed to flirt with every member of the Femme Fatales. It wasn't until he got a stern look from Nick and Jill that he finally relented and kept his disgusting thoughts to himself.

Accompanied by fifteen of her best, Jill led Nick and his group through Enfield Town and headed to the northern part of the borough, towards the escape route she had created almost a year before. Emily had always wanted a strong female role model to fill the void that her mother, and later The Boss, had left in her life, so it was no surprise to Nick that she took an immediate liking to Jill and had spent the duration of their short trip through the borough chewing her ear off.

"I can't believe you had the chance to escape from this and you chose to stay, that's amazing. How did you even know how to get out? Do you have a contact on the outside?" said Emily, not taking a second to breathe before asking Jill another question.

"To be honest, a lot of it was dumb luck. I knew some people in Enfield who were willing to take me in, and once I was here, I had all the time in the world to scout the fence and see if I could find a weak spot. Almost all of the borders are controlled and protected by The Boss' goons. Fortunately, we took control of the borough, including its borders, so I had all the scope I needed to find a fault in the fence."

"What did you find?"

"Unfortunately, the first thing I discovered was that The Boss wasn't lying when she said the fence around the state is electrified. Fortunately though, I only got a jolt when I touched it which was strange. I've heard countless tales of people barely grazing the fence and the shock they received was strong enough to have killed them, which makes sense considering the majority of the city's electricity is being pumped directly into the fence. After a lot of trial and error, I eventually found a weak enough spot in the fence which I could cut through and break the electrical current in that spot. For a while we used it to smuggle things in and out of the state but we lost touch with our contact on the outside a few months ago. I decided I wasn't going to cover the hole back up, I told my people about it and gave them a choice, they could stay or they could go, but none of them ever did, not a single one."

"Wow!" said Emily in astonishment at Jill's heroic story of courage and selfless leadership. "How the hell did you manage to break through the fence? The Boss has sensors placed all over it?"

She was about to answer her but before she could, she was signalled over by one of the Femme Fatales who had been scouting up ahead.

"Sorry Emily, that secret stays with me for now. If we all get out of this alive, then maybe I'll let you know," said Jill who moved towards the head of the pack to meet up with her scout.

The scout whispered something into Jill's ear and she immediately shot her hand up into the air, signalling for the group to stop walking.

"Hey, is everything Okay?" asked Nick who had made his way up next to Jill.

"Our scout says she heard a group of people near the Lee Valley Park area, the exit out of the state is beyond there, round the back of Capel Manor College," said Jill.

"So, what does that mean?" said Nick anxiously.

"It means we have a few choices – we can either carry on the way we are going, we take a slightly different, but longer way around, or we turn back and go home."

"Turning back isn't an option. How do you know that the people up ahead are trouble? We may even outnumber them," said Nick optimistically.

"Because I overheard them talking about what they would do to you when they caught you, and trust me, it wasn't to give you back rubs and blow jobs," proclaimed the scout with the elegance of a sailor.

At this point, Nick's group had stepped forward to find out what was happening. Nick looked out at his crew and offered them the respect they deserved by being open and honest with them once again.

"Listen guys, we've all made it this far together. I got you all into this and although I didn't intend on meeting any of you, especially Will," teased Nick, "You've all helped me in some way along this journey. I refuse to give up and turn back, not after getting this far. And like I said to you all when we first met, I can finish this alone. I no longer consider this my journey, this is our journey and it's up to you guys if you want to stay on it or jump off now."

There was a pause amongst the group as they collectively absorbed what Nick had said.

"Where has this guy been?" said Will, breaking the silence, "Ricky and Brintha you lucky souls, you get to see this friendly and emotive man while me and Izzy have been travelling around with this miserable prick for over a week and now, NOW that he is fun he wants to ditch us. I say fuck that. I love this new silly Nick and I for one would love to see more of him."

"Well, if he's going, you know I'm coming too. There's no telling what trouble this one will cause if I'm not there to watch him," said Izzy as she cuddled up to Will.

"You know you can't get rid of me that easy either big brother," said Emily, putting her arm around her brother's shoulder.

JJ reached out and grabbed Nick's hand. "We're

coming as well," said JJ with his tiny voice.

"You still owe me," said Brintha who flashed him a smile.

The group was standing together united, all but Ricky who was sheepishly looking at his feet and avoiding eye contact with the rest of the gang. He had spent his entire life thinking about himself while segregating and stepping over others for his own selfish needs, so the thought of a suicide mission wasn't something he would usually sign up for. Nick could see the hesitance in his demeanour.

"Hey mate, don't worry about it. You've helped me and the others so much already. If it wasn't for you, none of us would've made it out of Harrow. You've done enough. If you want to go, I completely understand. Whether you stay or go, you'll always be one of the team," said Nick, offering his hand to him.

When he shook Nick's hand he felt something that he hadn't felt in his entire life, he felt acceptance. He felt a surge of adrenaline and overwhelming happiness run through him. This bizarre feeling made him say something that even shocked him.

"Count me in too," said Ricky, feeling like the words had fallen out of his mouth without his control.

Nick laughed out loud and turned back to Jill. "It looks like me and my gang have decided to carry on with our destined path."

"Destined path? Alright Jon Snow, take it easy. We have to move quickly. If we're lucky, we can sneak past whoever is up ahead without getting into any trouble. The Femme Fatales will take the lead while I try and get you guys to the fence unseen. Let's go," ordered Jill.

She led the group past a collection of large open fields and forests', being out in the open was both a good and a bad thing; it gave the group a wider depth of field to see if any threats were approaching, but it also left them exposed and vulnerable.

After walking for another thirty-five minutes, the group had almost reached their final destination.

"We're almost there. We need to take a right at the next roundabout after the Pied Bull pub," said Jill pointing at a street sign with the words "CAPEL MANOR COLLEGE" on it.

The group quickened their pace the closer they got to the college, but when they neared the pub, the scout raised her hand up in the air again and halted the group for a second time. The scout could see a small light past the roundabout, the small light began to grow in size, and in a flash, the small light had turned into a huge blaze which engulfed a large fallen tree that was blocking the road ahead of them. Jill signalled to the group to get down and take cover. However, the scout had taken it upon herself to investigate the disruption despite Jill calling her back.

"What shall we do? Can we still get to the college?" asked Nick.

"Yes, the college is on the right, but it looks like whoever set that fire is trying to make sure we can't escape if we need to. There's no way they know about the exit. The only people that know about it are my people and they would never betray me," said Jill, uncertain of her own thoughts.

She was racking her brains trying to figure out what was going on. This was her turf and yet somehow, she had lost control. People had gotten in without her knowing, and worst of all she may have been betrayed by one of her own. A loud clatter from the pub broke her train of thought; the noise was followed by screaming and shouting and then a deathly silence. The silence was disturbed by the sound of footsteps treading over broken glass and dead leaves, the footsteps stopped, and a thud was heard. A slow round of applause followed, which in the wide open space of Lee Valley Park made it sound like it was coming from every direction.

"I have to say Nick, although I am your biggest fan and was rooting for you the whole way, I never thought in a million years that you'd make it this far, well done sir. If I had a hat I would tip it to you, instead I'll just leave this dead body here for you," called Bray who was barely visible in the dark open road.

The group had taken cover behind the front garden fence of an abandoned house. They couldn't make out who was lying underneath Bray's boot; however, Jill didn't need to see who the body belonged too to know that it was the scout. Her good friend laid dead on the street below the foot of a wicked man. She looked back at Nick with a tear in her eye and ferocity in her heart.

"I know you and your little crew are back there, so why don't you save us the embarrassment and come out here. Don't make me send in the lads to get you out. I'm sure you don't want more deaths on your conscience, or maybe you do. It's certainly something you're used to by now isn't it Nicholas, dead bodies piling up around you," said Bray, continuing to berate Nick.

Without hesitation, Nick stepped out onto the street to confront his nemesis.

"There he is, ladies and gentlemen, Prince Charming!" exclaimed Bray loudly. "Now get the fuck over here and let's end this."

He didn't stop to think and he began striding towards Bray with his fists clenched and a pure animalistic fire scorching through him, a fire that had also consumed the rest of Nick's gang and the Femme Fatales. To his astonishment, both Nick and Jill's gangs came out of hiding and marched behind Nick in an act of solidarity. Bray was bowled over by the strength and unity coming towards him. With the fight fast approaching, he continued to play the villainous role he was so good at playing. He snapped his fingers and out of the pub came twenty of The Instagrammer Nazis who positioned themselves behind him. The battle lines had been drawn and the oncoming onslaught led by Nick continued to approach with no signs of stopping.

CHAPTER 25

13th June 2016, 20:39
Bull's Cross, Enfield, The Independent State of England

Brintha, JJ and Ricky remained behind and watched from the garden fence as the battle between The Instagrammer Nazis, Nick's crew and The Femme Fatales continued with only the setting sun and the burning tree providing any light to the clash in front of them.

Brintha had wanted nothing more than to fight alongside her newly acquired comrades, but she was a mother first, and had to think about her son's wellbeing over anything else. She held her son close, but there was no sign of fear on his face. He had grown up in this world, and to her dismay, he'd become immune to this type of carnage. Ricky, on the other hand, was trembling in absolute fear. He had never been in a real fight. Any time he came close to an altercation, he would take the first opportunity he could to scurry off with his tail between his legs.

Nick, Jill, and the Femme Fatales had charged into battle with wild and erratic emotions, which made them dangerous to both themselves and the Instagrammer Nazis. Nick was driven by a determination to succeed, while Jill and The Femme Fatales were fuelled by rage and revenge for their fallen combatant. Will was helping where he could by picking his spots and going after the pawns and weaker members of the Instagrammer Nazis. He was fully aware that he was not a brawler, but he had a duty to his team. Izzy and Emily were acting as archers and lookouts for the team by throwing bottles and bricks at anyone they could see. They may not have had bows or catapults, but hurling hard objects at the enemy seemed effective.

Jill and The Femme Fatales were more than holding their own against The Instagrammar Nazis, these women were warriors and trained fighters; however, Bray's team were not adverse to using weapons and fighting dirty. For every Judo throw or well place fist thrown by the Fatales, an eye gouge or pipe to the shin was reflected back by the Instagrammer Nazis; the battle field was an array of wild swings, blood, teeth and bodies.

Nick had one target in mind, someone he had wanted to get his hands on for years, someone he blamed for causing a huge wedge between him and The Boss, and was the only other person who could seemingly whisper in her ear. In usual fashion, Bray had sent his minions ahead of him to do his fighting while he stood back and watched on, keeping his hands clean for as long as hc could. He was entirely capable of fighting his own battles, but his greatest asset was manipulating others into doing his dirty work for him; rule with an iron fist was very much his mantra. Nick was hell bent on getting to him and had no problem fighting his way through his thugs to get to him.

He made short work of the gang member standing between him and Bray, with a flurry of jabs and a left hook he sent the man to the floor *"All those years of boxing training were finally paying off,"* thought Nick. Bray hadn't moved from the roundabout, he stood in front of the flaming tree with his arms crossed. He looked like the final boss in a video game, and it was only when Nick had knocked out the two gang members blocking his path, did he begin to ready himself for the oncoming fight.

There was nothing but forty feet of empty road and air between the pair. This had been a long time coming for both men and one way or another one of them was going to get retribution. Nick knew Bray would refuse to engage in a fight until they were nose to nose, so he made the first move by taking one slow step after another towards him. Bray remained calm and motionless the closer he got to him, refusing to budge, refusing to flinch. He'd almost reached him, but when he began to pick up speed in anticipation for the bout, one of Bray's gang members blindsided him out of nowhere and tackled him to the floor. He was temporarily vulnerable and defenceless. Bray had found his opportunity. He finally rushed over to Nick and began attacking him while he was on the floor wrestling with one of his disciples.

Nick managed to push the gang member off of him, but before he could properly recover he was kicked across the face with furious force. He collapsed to the floor, which allowed Bray to take full advantage by delivering a barrage of kicks and punches together with his devoted squaddie.

Emily, Will, and Izzy were preoccupied with the rest of the Instagrammer Nazis and were unaware of what was happening to Nick. Jill had caught a glimpse of Nick being beaten down but she was hit in the stomach with a baseball bat before she could get to him. His only hope had been Brintha and Ricky who had seen the entire violent altercation go down.

"Oh my god, they're going to kill him. Ricky, we have to do something!" yelled Brintha.

Ricky continued to cower behind the fence. The thought of going anywhere near the frenzy left him unable to move.

"I'm sorry, I can't, I'm too scared to move," quivered Ricky.

"Well snap out of it. You don't have time to be afraid. These are our people and they need our help, so come with me or I'm going to drag you over there," ordered Brintha.

She took JJ's hand and hurried him to the front porch of the house behind them.

"I need you to be a brave boy, okay Jordan. Can you do that for me while mummy goes and helps our new friends?" asked Brintha gently.

He squeezed his mother's hand and nodded in agreement. "Yes mummy, I can be brave."

"Brave like Hulk?"

"Brave like Hulk!"

"Nothing will happen to mummy, but if it does, I need you to find Nick and go with him okay. He will keep you safe. Understand?"

He nodded at his mother again. He hugged her and sat down on the porch of the house like she told him to. She ran over to Ricky and tenderly pulled him up to his feet.

"That kid over there has grown up in this horrible world and even he knows that sometimes you have to fight to survive. I know you're scared, but if you don't do something to help you'll be scared forever - now get it together and come with me," said Brintha sympathetically.

She delicately took him by the hand and pulled him towards the scuffle. They passed through a trail of unresponsive bodies and crouched down in front of the Pied Bull pub, which was as close as they could get to Nick without being spotted.

"Wh-wh-what do we now?" asked Ricky with a tremble of fear in his voice.

She scanned the street, desperately trying to find a weapon or vantage point the pair could use to get the upper hand, but she had no luck.

Meanwhile, with the help of her loyal army, Jill had managed to get back to her feet and they were able to fight off the remainder of their attackers by using some less than dignified tactics when she remembered that men had a unique weakness between their legs. She wasted no time in trying to get to Nick; with a steel bar in her hand, she ran towards him and struck the gang member attacking him over the back of the head, incapacitating him. The sound of metal hitting skull caused Bray to drop his guard and turn his attention to Jill, Nick took advantage of this momentary distraction and tripped him to the ground. A stunned Bray was quickly mounted by Nick who repeatedly punched him in the face.

Once Will, Izzy, Emily, and the Femme Fatales had managed to scare off the remaining Instagrammer Nazis, Emily rushed over to her brother who had become blinded with rage and continued to repeatedly pound on Bray's face.

"That's enough Nick," shouted Emily.

She tried to pull him off of Bray, but he shoved his sister away. After seeing Emily getting knocked down by her brother, Will raced over to Nick and tackled him to the cold ground.

"Stop mate, he's had enough. You're better than this. You aren't like him," yelled Will.

He looked over to his sister who was being helped to her feet by Jill which snapped him out of his frenzied trance. Will helped him to his feet and walked him over to his shaken sister.

"I'm so sorry Emily, I couldn't stop. I'm so sorry," said Nick, hugging his sister tightly.

"It's over, okay. You got him. We still have a job to do remember?" pleaded Emily.

"What are we going to do with him Nick?" asked Jill.

"We're going to take him with us. He's too dangerous to be left here and I want to personally deliver him to the powers that be on the other side," said Nick.

He walked over to Bray who was slumped on his knees facing away from Nick. When he heard Nick's footsteps approaching, he unexpectedly swung around and pointed a gun at him.

"Actually Nicholas, I won't be going anywhere and neither will you," said Bray who had that sick sadistic smile on his face once again. "I was hoping I could've ended you with my bare hands during our little game of one-upmanship, but it seems like playtime is over."

While the majority of the group was being held at gun point by Bray, Ricky and Brintha had remained in hiding by the pub, yet to be seen by anyone.

"What are we going to do? He has a gun," whispered Ricky in terror.

"I think if we cut through the beer garden we can get around behind that man and take his gun or at least distract him long enough so Nick can get the gun away from him," said Brintha, ignoring Ricky's panicky state.

"Are you crazy? Are you trying to get yourself shot? Where did he get a gun from anyway? You do what you want, but I'm getting out of here. I can't be here," said Ricky, working himself up into further hysteria.

Before he could make a run for it, she grabbed his arm.

"Get off me. I'm not even supposed to be here. This wasn't the plan. This was never the plan," cried Ricky.

"What are you talking about? What plan?" asked Brintha in confusion.

"It doesn't matter. He's going to take my glory anyway!"

"What glory? What's going on Ricky?"

"I only helped Nick and the others so I could take him to The Boss myself. I don't deserve to be here. I'm better than this. I'm better than all of you. I deserve to be praised, not him," said Ricky, revealing his true self in a moment of folly.

He pulled his arm away from Brintha who continued to grapple with him so he couldn't escape after his revelation. In a panic, he used all the strength he could muster and pushed her off of him and onto the road. He ran through the back of the pub and disappeared into the dark forest. Bray was briefly distracted by the sight of Brintha falling onto the street. Nick dived towards him in an act of bravery and the two fell backwards to the floor, with the gun in his hand, Bray began aimlessly firing the gun into the night sky before landing on the floor with a thud. As the gun blasts echoed through the air, Bray had managed to get to his feet before Nick and vanished back into Lee Valley Park, fleeing from the unruly carnage he had caused.

Nick jumped to his feet and was poised to run after

him, but before he could his attention was brought back to the group when he heard the blood curdling shriek of his sister. It was only then had he realised that although he hadn't been shot it didn't mean anybody else hadn't.

"Oh my god, Nick, please, help us," screamed Jill.

The gang were huddled around Brintha when he returned back to them. She was lying on the floor gasping for air while blood was pouring out of her stomach. Will and Izzy had their hands on her stomach and were doing all they could to keep the pressure on the bullet wound.

"What do we do? Nick, what the hell do we do?" asked Will frantically.

His face was flushed and his eyes had sunk into his head. The truth was he didn't know what to do.

"Has anyone got something for the wound? Will, go to the pub and see if you can find something," ordered Emily.

Before he could run to the pub, Brintha feebly raised her hand up in the air.

"Wait. Please," whispered Brintha, struggling to speak.

She looked over at Nick and with the slightest hand gesture she ushered him to come over to her. He crouched down next to her and took her blood stained hand.

"I need you to keep your promise. You hear me? You get my boy to safety. You save him and then you save us all," said Brintha weakly.

He squeezed her hand and with tears in his eyes

nodded to let her know that he would take care of her boy. She continued to gasp for air, each time finding it harder and harder to breathe, the gasps had become far and few between, and all of a sudden she took that final breath she was unable to catch.

A sombre mood had enveloped the atmosphere on what had turned from a day of hope and closure to a day of mourning and dismay. Stillness took over the group and they remained silent for what felt like an eternity, unfortunately, this meant that nobody had realised that JJ had come out of hiding and was staring into the empty eyes of his dead mother.

"Oh my god!" said Izzy, realising JJ was amongst them.

She rushed over to him and tried to shield him from the sight of his deceased mother. He squirmed away from her and calmly walked over to Nick who was holding his mother's hand and took it away from him.

"We have to go. You promised," said JJ, looking at a tearful Nick.

He kissed his mother's hand and lay it lovingly across her chest, "Bye mummy, I love you."

He took Nick by the hand, who remained frozen in shock and began walking him up the road towards Capel Manor College.

Before anyone could take a second to grieve or mourn over the loss of their friend, JJ and Nick had already disappeared out of sight.

"We'll give her a proper burial. There's a cemetery not far from here," said Jill, as his gang walked away to help Nick fulfil his promise to save JJ and the country.

CHAPTER 26

13th June 2016, 21:44
Bullsmoor Ln, Enfield, The Independent State of England

During the short walk it took Nick, JJ, and the rest of the gang to pass through Capel Manor College towards the escape route out of the city, Nick hadn't said a word. He held onto JJ's hand as tightly as he could and followed the directions Jill had given him through the college campus. He was exhausted and fed up and the death of Brintha had him in a catatonic state. Emily, Will and Izzy could see he wasn't himself and tried on a number of occasions to communicate with him, but with no luck. Instead, they decided to be there for him by making sure the mission was completed without any more disruptions. They had escaped the battle with Bray by the skin of their teeth, however, with him still at large they had no idea where he was, so they had to remain on high alert.

"I hate this place. It's freaking me out," expressed Will, who did his best to speed through the dreary campus.

There was something about an abandoned college that he'd found eerily unnerving, all those empty desks and chairs pointing towards the front of the class with nobody there spooked him. JJ's robotic like behaviour since his mother died was only adding to the unsettling feeling he felt.

"I don't think it's much further. What you should be freaked out about is how weirdly calm JJ is being about his mum. Do you think we should say something Em?" said Izzy.

"I don't know, to be honest with you. I'm more concerned about my brother. Once we get out of here, I think we are going to have a different problem on our hands. This journey has taken its toll on him and it's going to be tough trying to get his head back in the game."

"He's been through a lot, we all have. But as long as we stick together, we'll be okay," Izzy said, trying her best to reassure Emily.

The gang continued towards the edge of the college grounds where they squeezed through a gap in a broken brick wall which surrounded the college campus and led onto an over grown and narrow path. The path sat next to a small river which was surrounded by overgrown bushes, nettles, and other greenery forcing the group to have to walk in single file along the path towards the river's end.

"I think I can see it," said JJ, who had become so overwhelmed with excitement at the site of the grand fence that he pulled his hand away from Nick and ran towards it, disappearing behind a large shipping container that sat in front of the fence at the end of the river. His sudden escape was the jolt Nick needed to reboot himself from his state of shell shock.

"Shit, JJ, get back here!" yelled Nick.

He ran after him, but when he passed the shipping container and stood in front of the imposing fence he became immobilised when he saw Bray holding onto JJ with a gun pointed at his head. Emily, Will and Izzy caught up to him and stood stunned at the sight of a battered and crazed Bray holding a gun to a child's head while blocking their only way out of the city.

"Bray, what the fu..." roared Nick before being interrupted.

"Shut your fucking mouth Nick. Just shut the fuck up. You're going to listen to me now!" exclaimed Bray. "You think you're hot shit, don't you? The truth is you're nothing. You had everything, but you didn't have the balls to do what needed to be done. But do you know who can get things done? Me, and The Boss has always known that too. Speaking of which, she has something she wants to say to you."

With his gun pointed at a crying and distraught child, he bent down and took a tablet computer out of his bag and held it up towards Nick. On the tablet a video call had been made and on the other end of the call was The Boss looking back at him. He was flooded with an array of emotions at the sight of her face, feelings of wrath being the most prominent. He had hoped that the next time he saw her she would be locked up.

"Hello Nick," said The Boss.

He was unresponsive and stood staring at the screen completely overcome with emotion.

"Are you pretending to be frozen so I think there's a connection issue or something?" mocked The Boss.

He continued to stare at the tablet in silence, bubbling with anger.

"I can tell you didn't expect to see me again so soon and you clearly aren't coping very well with that, so I'm going to talk and for your sake, I hope you listen. I'm not going to bring up the fact that you've betrayed me, which you have, but instead I'm going to tell you straight. If anyone from your little gang leaves my city I will make you suffer. Not suffer like you think you have already. I mean, REALLY suffer," threatened The Boss. "Now, I know you may be thinking how could I possibly hurt you anymore? Well, this is how..."

The Boss momentarily moved out of shot, revealing that she was standing in an office Nick had been in very recently. In that office was the physically assaulted and barely conscious body of The Mayor of Barnet who had been tied to a chair in the middle of the room. She walked over to him and yanked his head up so he was facing the camera.

"I will hurt you by destroying all of those who helped you get to where you are now and that includes this neutral bitch. We will finish what is left of his followers, whether they knew if you were here or not, and then I will come for that cunt Jill and her little gaggle of Amazonian wannabes," promised The Boss.

She let go of The Mayor's head which flopped backed down onto his chest and she returned back to the tablet.

"Now, if I were you Nick, I would not test me or even dare to think that I'm bluffing. You know more than anyone how serious I am. This can all be avoided if you do what I say and come back to me. I want you back by my side where you belong."

"Belong?" said Nick, finally breaking his silence.

"If you come back to me and stop doing whatever it is you are trying to do, I will forgive you. You'll have a lot of making up to do for what you have done and I will need a great deal of convincing if you want me to keep your sister and your gang alive. But we both know you can be quite the persuasive speaker, so I'm sure you'll find a way," said The Boss hoping he would obey her.

"You said I belong with you. I don't belong anywhere near you and you definitely don't belong where you are," said Nick, venting his frustration. "You've never belonged in this world and I can see that now, all you've ever done is try to mould this world into what you want it to be, which is something you can control, just like you tried to control me."

3rd June 2016, 18:51
Downing Street, The City of Westminster, The In-

dependent State of England

Nick and The Boss were in her office. She was sat calmly behind her desk while he was standing on the other side of the room, breathing heavily. The office had been trashed after he had thrown furniture all over the room and smashed glasses onto the floor. Once he had finished with the glasses, he stomped over to her desk and pushed everything off of it onto the floor.

"Are you quite finished Nick?" asked The Boss, maintaining a cool head.

"You've gone too fucking far this time, she's my sister. You can't lock her away and punish her like she's one of your supporters you are trying to make an example of. You will release her and you will do it right now!" demanded Nick.

"THIS is too far for you? This is where you draw the line? Take a look around you Nick. Do you see the world we are living in? Have you forgotten all of the terrible and messed up things you've seen and done? Or have I all of a sudden gone too far because she's your sister? She broke the rules Nick, again, and she needed to be taught a lesson. Trust me, she's getting off lightly and yes that is because she is your sister. If anyone else in my team started consorting with someone from the resistance, well, you've seen what I do with those people haven't you?"

"Yeah, I've seen you murder them and make them 'disappear'. Actually, you don't do anything. You have someone else take care of your dirty work for you!"

She stood up from her seat and leant over the desk to face him, her cool demeanour had begun to falter and she gritted her teeth in annoyance over his erratic display and cutting words.

"Your sister has been pushing my buttons for far too long now Nick, and after I personally sentenced her, she had the audacity to step to me. You need to have a word with that little girl. She must be starting to lose her bloody mind if she's trying to come at me like that."

"She's losing HER mind? Her? You've got to be joking," laughed Nick. "I see the world we live in. I see what we created. We started a revolution. But when things got a little too crazy, I begged you to step away from it, to leave it where it was and to hand it to someone else before it got worse. But you couldn't do that. We could've had our lives back, together."

"Don't forget that it was you that decided to end things, not me," sniped back The Boss.

"And why do you think I did that? Why do you think I asked you to keep our relationship a secret from the public? It wasn't only to protect your political image. It was because deep down I was ashamed of the person you were turning into. Do you know what I say to people when they ask about us and if we are an item? I tell them that nothing has ever happened between us and that the love of my life died when The Boss came into this world. I tell them that I loved a woman named Lauren Milton, an intelligent and driven woman who wanted to help this city and make it a better and equal place for all. I tell them that I planned to marry that woman, but instead she was taken away from me during The Boss' rebellion. That's why I ended things with you Lauren, because you were no longer the woman I recognised. You were no longer the woman I wanted to marry and grow old with, and you certainly aren't the woman I'm in love with anymore," professed Nick before he walked towards the door.

"Where are you going?" asked The Boss with a tear in her eye, which she quickly wiped away before he could see.

"Far away from you," said Nick, leaving the room and The Boss behind him.

13th June 2016, 22:27
Bullsmoor Ln, Enfield, The Independent State of England

"I loved you Lauren, but your lust for power ruined everything. We could've been far away from this, as husband and wife, but I wasn't enough for you, was I?" asked Nick.

She refused to answer and instead chose to keep her poker face on and stared expressionlessly at him.

"Look at you Nick, you blew it with her. You are a loser and you don't deserve anyone like her," sniggered Bray.

He had momentarily forgotten about Bray until he goaded him. He took a step towards Bray, who in return squeezed JJ closer to him and hovered his finger over the trigger of the gun.

"Careful Nick, unlike you, you know I won't hesitate to do what needs to be done," threatened Bray.

"Is this what you've been reduced to Lauren, shooting kids? Hurting everyone around you? What ever happened to your no guns policy, huh?" pressed Nick.

"Do you think it's only food and supplies that get imported in from outside of the state, sometimes fire power is a necessity," interjected Bray.

"Guns were essential in ensuring my reign. You couldn't understand that, so I kept it from you. Until there is order, I will do what I need to do to survive and keep this city in line," replied The Boss.

"I know you will, but I will no longer be a part of that. I have enough blood on my hands already. I would rather die knowing that I saved at least one person from living under your rule than ever be by your side again," said Nick defiantly.

He took another step forward causing Bray to turn his gun from JJ to him, he smiled at Nick, as if to say, *thank you for giving me an excuse*. He pulled down the hammer of the gun and gently pressed his finger on the trigger.

At that moment a loud metallic banging coming from the bushes drew his attention away. A large rock hurled towards him which narrowly missed his head, however, while evading the rock, JJ took advantage of the distraction and quickly bit down onto his hand as hard as he could. Bray dropped the tablet onto the floor and with his other hand, he smacked JJ across the face with his gun. Nick ran towards him and forced him to the floor for the second time that night. His gun fell out of his hand and landed next to him.

As the pair fought for position on the cold concrete floor, Emily picked up the gun and pointed it at Bray. He stopped squirming on the floor and put his hands out in front of him. Nick got off of him and took the gun from Emily and held it towards his head. Another rustle came from the bushes and Ricky stumbled out into the clearing holding a rock in each hand. Once Nick had realised that he had been saved by Ricky again, he gave him a nod of appreciation.

Bray slowly got to his knees and put his hands over his head in submission, meanwhile Will and Izzy checked to see if JJ was okay. He was awake and responsive, and with the help of Will, he was able to get to his feet. He had a large gash across his head which Izzy cleaned and bandaged with an old bandana she had. Ricky picked up the tablet and handed it to Nick after he had re-joined the group. The Boss had been on the video call throughout the commotion; she had heard but not seen everything that had happened. The power balance between Bray and Nick had drastically shifted, now Nick was the one with the tablet and more importantly he was the one with the gun.

"Don't do anything else stupid Nick. You've already done enough damage. Please don't force my hand," said The Boss.

"He isn't going to do anything. He's a coward and a punk," said Bray viciously. "We've all seen what he's capable of and that's absolutely nothing. That's why whenever you needed your dirty work done, you came to me and not this chicken shit. He was too afraid to get his hands filthy and even you knew he wasn't able to do what needed to be done. That's why you had me incite so many of the riots. That's why you had me round up all of your traitors and your enemies and have them exiled or killed. You never deserved Lauren and you certainly never deserved The Boss. You couldn't even seal the deal with her when you had the chance. But don't worry Nick, I know without a shadow of a doubt that she would've turned you down and told you that she could never marry someone like you, because she is a Boss and you are a spineless pawn."

He looked Nick dead in his eyes and smiled a toothy white grin at him. With the gun in his hand, Nick looked back into Bray's cold and soulless blue eyes and smiled right back.

The recoil of the gun had been much stronger than he had thought it would've been. Having never fired a gun before, he now understood why people wore those big earmuffs at a shooting range. Everyone present had their hands over their ears, everyone except for Nick and Bray. He was fuelled by madness and retribution and the ringing from the blast of the gun, although prominent in his ears, hadn't fazed him, and if Bray had still been alive he would have likely been less concerned with the dull ringing radiating through his ears and more worried about the bullet sized hole that had pierced through his skull. He collapsed on the floor in front of Nick, immobile and lifeless. Nick dropped the gun and turned the tablet around to face Bray's body so The Boss could see it.

"This is what I'm capable of Lauren. This is what you have turned me into. This is what you have forced me to do and I will not stop until you join him," declared Nick turning the tablet back around to face him. "I'm coming for you and I'm going to bring you and your entire regime crumbling down."

She looked deep into his bloodshot and glassy eyes and realised that he would never stop on his quest to defeat her, not until one of them was dead. She took a deep breath and closed her eyes; she took a moment to think about how bad things had gotten between them. Where love had once united them, only blood, war, and retribution now drew them together.

"So be it," said The Boss, opening her eyes and looking at Nick.

She turned away from the camera, pulled out a gun, took aim at The Mayor of Barnet and shot him dead between the eyes with a single clean shot. When she turned back to the camera she had a look of intensity that Nick had never seen before.

"You think you know me Nick? You think you can

beat me? You're right, Lauren Milton is dead, and in her place stands The Mother Fucking Boss, and this bitch is going to rain down a shit storm of blood and fire on everyone. Everyone who has ever opposed me, everyone who has ever smiled at you or said hello to you or has shown you a shred of compassion. I'm coming for them. I'm coming for your sister, for your friends, and for anyone else you've ever come into contact with. Whether you leave or stay, you will never succeed in bringing me down because there will be nothing left of this place once I'm done with it; just me, standing on the ashes of those who have ever doubted me. You better bring everything you have Nick because I will be waiting," vowed The Boss.

She ended the video call and disappeared from the screen, leaving Nick to stare at his own reflection on the tablet. He flung the tablet into the river and the gang regrouped unsure what they were going to do next. When Emily approached him with JJ in tow, he took JJ by the hand and began walking towards the fence without saying a word to his sister.

"Hey, where the hell are you going?" shouted Will.

He continued to walk away with JJ being dragged behind him. Will looked to the others for help and reassurance, but not even Emily knew what her brother was doing. He ran after Nick who had reached the secret exit out of the city.

"Oi, I'm talking to you. Where the fuck are you going? Didn't you hear what she said? She's going to kill everyone!" bellowed Will.

He ignored him again and focused his attention on removing the shrubbery that was hiding his exit to freedom. Once the shrubs had been moved, he pulled apart the cut hole in the fence which led to the bridge out of the city. JJ watched on as Will become increasingly incensed with Nick. After no longer being able to stand being ignored, he pulled Nick to the ground in frustration. With no will left to fight, he stood up and faced his friend.

"She's about to start another civil war and you're going to leave?" said Will, "We can't leave. We have to stay here and fight. We have to stop her on the battlefield and not through some shot in the dark out there,"

"He's right Nick, we can't go now, not when we know what she's capable of, and especially not after what she has sworn she will do. We need to unite as many people as we can and fight back," said Izzy who had been reenergised with a sense of duty.

He looked to his sister and without saying a word, she knew what he was asking her.

"We have to stay Nick. I have to stay. This isn't just your fight anymore. Like you said before, it's all of ours and if we leave now, we are turning our backs on everyone in there who is suffering at her hands. As long as we all stick together, nobody can break us. I know you think the answer is out there, but we are here, and we can do something about what is happening right now," pleaded Emily.

He put his hand on her face and gently stroked her cheek.

"I promised that I would get JJ and everyone else to safety and that's a promise I cannot break."

She began to sob knowing that her brother's mind had already been made up.

"Please Nick, we need you, don't do thi..." said Emily, before being interrupted by a loud uproar coming from the college.

Jill and the remaining Femme Fatales had come out from the woods behind the college and began running over to the group; they were flushed with sweat and gasping for air like they had just run a marathon.

"What are you all still doing here? We need to get out of here now, she's sent her army after us. They appeared out of nowhere and they've taken over our borough. I don't know how she knew you were here, but we have to go now!" yelled Jill with a frantic urgency.

Jill and The Femme Fatales ran to the other side of the river and sped down it using the overgrown trees as cover. Will and Izzy watched as Jill and her gang disappeared amongst the trees, Ricky quickly followed suit and ran behind her. Will turned back to where Nick had been standing with JJ, but in his place was nothing but an empty hole in the fence and a distraught sister who was clinging onto the fence as she watched her brother fulfil a promise he made to a dying mother.

An irate Will couldn't believe what he was seeing; he was able to catch the faintest glimpse of Nick who was running away into the dark abyss with JJ.

He nodded to Izzy who calmly guided Emily away from the fence and held her hand as the remainder of what was once Nick's gang hurried after Ricky, Jill and The Femme Fatales. The group fled the area, desperately trying to avoid a battle in which they were vastly outnumbered. They needed to get to safety, regroup and figure out how they were going to unite the city against The Boss for the impending war she was bringing to the ISOE.

As Nick's sister and the first real friends he had in years, ran further towards the heart of darkness, he was running away from it. With a new companion by his side, he was determined to achieve what many had deemed to be unachievable. His journey had only begun and from here on in his plan would rely heavily on those beyond the fence. He never thought that he would get this far into his mission to topple The Boss, but now he was truly venturing into the unknown. What he did know was that he wouldn't break, he wouldn't falter, and he would not look back until his mission was complete.

CHAPTER 27

He hesitantly shuffled back into his bedroom where Lauren was fast asleep. He put the toast and coffee that he had made for her on the bedside table and kissed her gently on the cheek repeatedly until she woke up.

"Morning pisshead," said Nick lovingly.

"Morning. Aren't you cute, making me breakfast in bed. A girl could get used to this kind of treatment."

"Well don't, because it won't be happening very often," teased Nick.

She smiled and began eating her toast. He avoided looking at her and started fiddling with his shorts, a tell-tale sign that he was anxious about something, a sign that she had seen a million times before whenever he needed to apologise to her for something he'd done wrong

"What's the matter? You're pulling at your clothes. Did you do something bad last night?" asked Lauren.

"Me? I wasn't the one putting them away last night with your lethal mix of Southern Comfort and Malibu. If you knew who your mother was, I'm sure she'd have taught you to never mix your spirits," said Nick, desperately trying to change the subject.

"Stop stalling," said Lauren, taking a sip of her coffee, "What's the matter?"

He took out his phone, pushed some buttons and handed the phone to her.

"Holy crap! How did we not hear about this last night?" gasped Lauren, scrolling through the phone.

"Malibu and Southern Comfort, that's why," laughed Nick apprehensively.

"I can't believe a peaceful protest turned to rioting and violence so quickly. I can see this getting worse before it gets better," exclaimed Lauren, who jumped out of bed and hastily put on her jeans. "I need to get a video out about this as soon as possible. Can you get the camera ready for me babe?"

He took her gently by the hand and tenderly brought her back to bed.

"What if you didn't?"

"What do you mean?" replied Lauren.

"This is big. We both know it is, and it's exactly the kind of thing you've been posting about. What happened last night, the violence, the unjust treatment of a minority, it all backs up everything you've been talking about in terms of equality. Do we really want to get wrapped up in this? It could really blow up and not necessarily in a good way. Maybe we need to take a minute and think about how involved you actually get, in case it takes us over," implored Nick.

She looked at him and lovingly squeezed his hand.

"I have to say something Nick, you know I do. There are people out there who count on me to speak for them and that's what these YouTube videos do. They allow me to express the thoughts of the people that are getting caught up in the violence on the street, the Raymond Dwyer's of the world who are being harassed daily, those who work two jobs to support their families, while the super-rich get handed tax breaks as the rest of us struggle to stay afloat. I'm not surprised a riot kicked off over yet another act of unnecessary violence and murder. Bloody hell. How else are people supposed to react when another person is gunned down without sufficient cause. I don't like the way it was handled and I think a riot is a pretty extreme way to display your frustration, but I get it. There are amazing people in this country, but we are run by people who have no idea what valuable resources they have in their own country, tell me this, how does some sixty year old dickhead of a politician who has grown up in a life of wealth and power, think they can relate to a person like me or you? They don't know what we go through on a daily basis, they don't know our frustration, and they never will. So, why are they running the country?"

He smiled to himself after her impassioned speech.

"What's so funny?" asked Lauren smiling back at him.

"You. You've come along way Ms Milton. That was one hell of a passionate speech. Are you sure you need my writing expertise to help you with all of this?" asked Nick light-heartedly.

She kissed him and looked into his round hazel eyes.

"I will always need you Nick King, and that passion I have inside of me has always been inspired by you. You opened my eyes and you helped me find my voice. I promise you now, if things ever get too much for us, we'll walk away. We'll walk away from it all, hand in hand, together."

Printed by Amazon Italia Logistica S.r.l.
Torrazza Piemonte (TO), Italy

11490914R00203